WASHOE COUNTY LIBRARY
3 1235 00574 136
P9-DVY-490

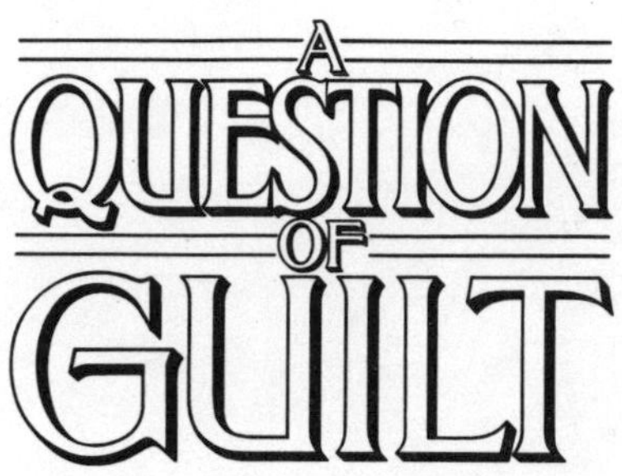
A
QUESTION
OF
GUILT

A QUESTION OF GUILT

FRANCES FYFIELD

POCKET BOOKS
New York London Toronto Sydney Tokyo

This book is a work of fiction. Names, characters, places and incidents are either the product of the author's imagination or are used fictitiously. Any resemblance to actual events or locales or persons, living or dead, is entirely coincidental.

Originally published in Great Britain by William Heinemann Ltd.

POCKET BOOKS, a division of Simon & Schuster Inc.
1230 Avenue of the Americas, New York, NY 10020

For information address Pocket Books, 1230 Avenue of the Americas, New York, NY 10020

ISBN: 0-671-67664-4

First Pocket Books trade hardcover printing August 1989

10 9 8 7 6 5 4 3 2 1

POCKET and colophon are trademarks of Simon & Schuster Inc.

Printed in the U.S.A.

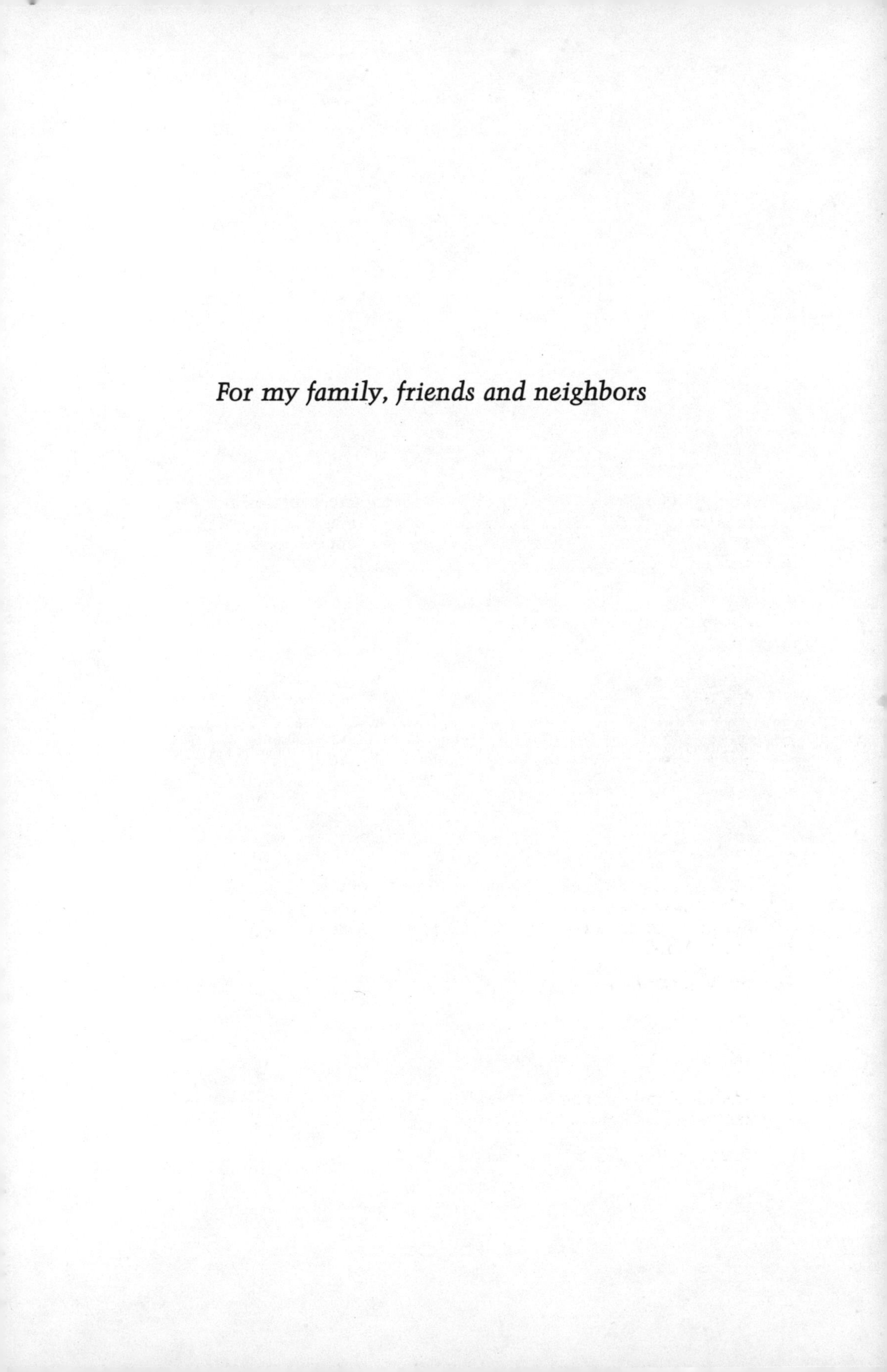

For my family, friends and neighbors

PROLOGUE

Sylvia Bernard slept beside her husband, sharing his deep, untroubled sleep. They never argued; they were comfortable together in a small and luxurious house like two curled cats in a tasteful basket. Michael Bernard turned over once per night, pushing aside the clutch of the duvet and the heat of his wife's body, then slept again, happy.

Flitting lightly, breathing heavily, Stanislaus Jaskowski failed to admire the quality of the designer curtains as he moved across the garden, but he coveted the car in the driveway, pausing to stroke it as if it were alive, stung by its coldness. Sweat froze on his forehead, and his tongue moved constantly, licking the moisture from his upper lip. When he had planned a little more, this would be the real thing, perfect, shocking, but not today: some other more courageous day than this. And in daylight, even if he had not been so afraid of the dark, he would have craved the innocence of daylight. After that there would be no more nagging, and he would have been a hero once at least, providing for them all. A hunter, happier than he had been ever since a child, and not often then.

A Georgian front door elegantly screened from the road by the evergreens made it easier. Stanislaus shivered, remembered the whiskey left in the car and crept away. The tinted glasses he wore intensified the darkness, giving him the appearance of a sinister clown, a description which would have hurt, even enraged him as he strode away, relief increasing in proportion to his distance from the house.

As he walked, he observed. Such a beautiful street, but the sight of those dignified buildings, fine windows and impenetrable doors filled him with horror. What a noise he made: next time he would wear soft shoes, the kind he had worn for dancing, and after the next time, or the time after that, he would be as happy as he had been then. Perfectly happy.

Footsteps at one in the morning were not rare in a street so near the city, and Helen West heard Jaskowski's without noticing as he passed her lighted basement window and hauled himself into his car. Applying the last piece of tape to the boxes containing the last debris of a marriage, she decided the occasion called for another drink, rather than tears. Of course it was easier without him, without the tension of his presence, easier without anyone at all. After two years' absence and the formality of divorce, they could even talk to one another, not that he had ever wanted to stop, and any kind of improvement in life was worth celebrating. The last of his possessions: how long they had remained with her, indicative of his belief in the good life, her dislike of the way he earned it, and how much he had hated her for finding out. Now she supposed he had happiness in kind. Ah well, like gold and tweed in the same garment, glitter and homespun do not match.

Helen went into her bright kitchen where ferns and plates hid the age and lack of equipment. She surveyed the gin bottle with distaste. Wine? None. She boiled the kettle. Coffee? None. Cocoa? Who would have believed it, thirty-six, and resigned to cocoa. Cocoa and brandy, needs must in the middle of the night. Sipping this brew, which even one as careless as herself could recognize as faintly poisonous, she wondered, with an interest which was merely academic, what it was like to be happy.

* * *

A QUESTION OF GUILT

Detective Superintendent Bailey, yawning in the gloom of the interview room, had ceased to contemplate the nature of happiness, or even trouble his mind with a prospect so unrealistic. Such an abstraction was not his concern and he had ceased to desire a state so unattainable, preferring survival with dignity. The youth on the opposite side of the table, staring at the yellow wall, stiff with fear and contrived insolence, his hands trembling even as he sneered into space, believed he had no options at all, least of all happiness. Happiness would have been not to have carried the knife, or used it on flesh. Happiness might have been a belief that he was not about to confess, was stronger than the silent man opposite, or the same man might give him bail. Fat chance of happiness.

Mrs. Eileen Cartwright, widow, forty-six years old, black-haired, sallow, least naturally blessed with physical favors than any of those who were awake to their own conditions, and with nothing more in common with any of them than the same square mile, stared at her empty television screen, smoking her fortieth cigarette of the day. Her room was cluttered, possessions gathered within touching distance, her mind as clear as her best crystal. At that moment in time, Eileen did believe in happiness. She believed complete and utter happiness would be hers some day soon, to hold and wonder at like an object of priceless and simple beauty. There was no belief in any God as free from doubt. She would fulfill her right to perfect happiness; pay and wait for the gift to be hers.

CHAPTER ONE

Monday morning. Arrested by the pile of papers. A quick first look at the report like a runner measuring the distance of the work. Helen read with her coat on, grumbling into a cheese roll.

Court date: Jaskowski: remanded in custody until 24 March, 10 A.M.
Court Clerk: J. Kehoe.
Solicitors: Daintrey and Partners, Dalston. Good, not a bent firm. Or at least not known for it.
Defendant: Stanislaus Jaskowski, age forty-four. Married, four children. Polish origin, born UK. Occupation: hospital porter. Part-time occupation: private investigator. Address: 31, Hackington Estate East, London N5.
Antecedents: Previous convictions: Two, spent, both theft employer (see CRO). Previous employment: antique dealer; business failed. Domestic circumstances poor, but clean council flat. In arrears with rent, all children under age of five. Take-home pay, £150 per week. Large HP debts.
Charge: For that you, on 18 November 1986, did murder Sylvia

Bernard at Cannonbury House, Cannonbury Street, *contrary to common law.*

But not, thank God, so common. Helen settled further, resigned to the next few pages.

Brief Summary of Facts: The deceased, Mrs. Sylvia Bernard, was found in the hallway of her home address at Cannonbury Street at about six-thirty in the evening of Monday 18 November by her husband. She had been dead for some eight hours, the result of numerous blows inflicted largely on the head and neck with both sharp and blunt instruments, most likely a hammer and a knife. It appeared at first a frenzied attack without apparent motive, Mrs. Bernard being a well-respected woman, married to a solicitor, (Michael Bernard of Messrs. Bernard, Miles and Haddock, EC1), for eighteen years. No suspicion attached to the husband, but it was only through lengthy questioning that he revealed reluctantly that his wife had complained to him of being followed, both with him or alone, on several occasions. Bernard stated he had dismissed this as fantasy on her part, although believing there was some truth in it. After some hesitation, he stated to the investigating officer that he believed that both he and his wife may have been the subject of some irrational attention from a female client of his, Mrs. Cartwright, who appears to have maintained an unhealthy affection for Mr. Bernard ever since he had acted for her in the disposal of her husband's estate several years ago. Bernard stated that this affection was not reciprocated in any way by himself, but he had been aware that her presence in restaurants, theaters, sporting events, coincided with his own far beyond chance. Mrs. Cartwright is a businesswoman, and Bernard frequently acted for her. It is respectfully considered by the investigating officer that Mr. Bernard willfully or naïvely underestimated the nature of Mrs. Cartwright's affection for him. He presents himself as an unemotional man, and describes his marriage as contented. There are no children.

He was of the opinion that Mrs. Cartwright either followed him, or had him followed. Enquiries among local private investigators revealed that one of their number, a retired Detective Constable of this force, had been engaged between 1980 and 1983 to follow both Mr. and Mrs. Bernard and report on their movements to Mrs. Cartwright, especially the movements of the former. This task had been done with great circumspection, until it was resigned in favor of a more lucrative overseas contract in 1983. The private detective describes his client as obsessed with Mr. Bernard and his welfare, and was of the view that she would have immediately sought a replacement for his services in furtherance of that obsession.

[The phone rang. Helen ignored it. Too early for concentration on the spoken word. These written words were bad enough.]

In brief, after considerable enquiries Mr. Tysall, brother-in-law of the defendant was spoken to by police. He admitted to helping Jaskowski, during 1985 only, to follow a man answering to Bernard's description. This was done at various times. Both men work shifts. Jaskowski was questioned. Initially uncooperative, when faced with certain evidence from his building society accounts, he finally admitted to being hired by Mrs. Cartwright, first to follow Mrs. Bernard, then to injure her, which he refused to do, and then to kill her, to which he agreed. He was paid five thousand pounds for this task with a further sum of five thousand to follow six months later. His client was Mrs. Cartwright throughout, he knowing her only as Eileen. There is ample corroboration for his receipt of the initial sum.

However there is little corroboration of his knowing Mrs. Cartwright. They were never seen together. Aside from Jaskowski's lengthy confession, virtually no independent or circumstantial evidence against her exists. There is evidence of devotion to Mr. Bernard, but nothing concrete to link her to the murder. She has been arrested, interviewed at great length, to no avail. She denies any contact whatever with Jaskowski; her bank balance does not reflect the payment by a single withdrawal. There is nothing but his admissions, which explain the incidents with disturbing completeness. However these are the admissions of a co-defendant, and not sufficient to secure conviction as long as he is a co-defendant.

Mrs. Cartwright was therefore released and is still at large, pending your advice. It is the view of the investigating officer that she should be rearrested, again pending your advice. She is guilty of murder, and should be indicted for such.

Coat off, out of the Ladies' Room into her own. Late, but not very: time for a little grouting and making good of a tired face, six hallos in the corridor and two more chapters of life history from staff. She would never be late if she did not know them all, and she would be early if she did not listen so much.

Then Helen returned to the huge file with acute distaste. It complemented her hangover in its pale, already battered state. When would they issue new files less flimsy than these? By the time this one was completed, the cover would be in tatters, held together with Sellotape in celebration of the technical age. She yawned. Well—a contract killing, not normally detected, not a middle-class pastime, since successful North Londoners of the professional classes did not possess this kind of single-mindedness, to say nothing of the cashflow or the contacts. She pulled herself from the seat, cracking her ankle against the desk as she did so and tripping over the telephone cable, two daily hazards she rarely survived without swearing or bruises on her way to the large metal filing cabinet, standard issue, civil servant grade 6 for the use of. The design and contents of her room owed nothing to research unless studies had been undertaken expressly in the alienation and discomfort of the human species. She retreated to her chair carefully as the telephone rang, its tinny sound accentuated by its cracked casing, the result of her hourly tussle with the trip wire.

"Hello? Helen? Hang on a minute; what was it I wanted to say?"

"I don't know. You're the boss. You tell me."

"It's Monday, Helen, and I'm due in court—don't be funny. I remember now. That file . . . the murder, Mrs. Whatshername."

"Yes. I've just read the report."

"Good, good." He coughed. Helen would have liked him less if he neither smoked nor panicked with such regularity. "Good," he repeated. "I'm dreadfully sorry about it."

"So am I. It's the normal human reaction when someone's killed. Anything else?"

"Shut up. I mean I'm sorry you've got it. You weren't supposed to have it, but Brian's sick. Wouldn't have sent it to you in the normal run of events. Bit close to home for you, isn't it, geographically, I mean? Bit difficult prosecuting a murder so near your own patch. Do you think you should do it?"

"I really don't see why not. If you knew my little corner of London, you'd see there was a vast difference between the site of this murder and the street containing my pit. More your social status than mine, if you see what I mean. I'm hardly likely to meet the merry widower in the pub, and I'm not about to call on the murderous lady. Besides, there's some advantage in knowing the area."

"Do you think so?" The voice of the Crown Prosecutor swelled with relief. He had long since lost interest in cases themselves once the trauma of allocating them was over and his own schedule could continue. "Well, if you're sure . . ."

"David, get off the line, and find something else to growl over. I'm busy."

He giggled, his deceptive response to a rising panic. Helen was his favorite solicitor and she never made a fuss: there was no one else he could have trusted with a case of this importance. No one else in an office full of misfits, young idealists, displaced barristers, incompetents, worthies and other underpaid legal refugees from the commercial world who formed this odd little minority of lawyers who were willing, if not always able, to survive conditions of work which could hardly be described as comfortable. Helen would sort it out: her office might be a tip, she might spend half her time on other peoples' work, and all their problems, but she was clever and quick, and what was more, she was well aware of the futility of screaming for help. A committed prosecutor—that was Helen.

Committed. Helen Catherine West had been once, committed to an unfashionable belief in the law. Maybe that uncertain time of life, or the consistency with which she somehow failed to impress promotion boards by her distressing habit of confessing ignorance wherever she found it, but her allegiance had shifted from the committed fraternity into the one which realized how a primary purpose of work was to do it well and pay the mortgage. There was little enough to be gained from the professional prosecution of criminals and the small rewards had not included popularity, status, frequent enjoyment, satisfaction, or gratitude. Self respect, maybe, but not much of that.

She combed her hair, rearranged her papers for a long session of reading, looked at her face in the mirror, which she did too many times a day with something between resignation and puzzlement, noting the laughter creases, the bags beneath the eyes, that irritating frown line on the forehead which seemed to grow by the hour. She smiled at the reflection and pulled a hopeless face in an effort to charm herself which always failed. Get to work.

Emptiness was easy to hide. Perhaps she disguised the cracks with laughter more effectively than she imagined. She saw too much, and in all her accidental knowledge, found too small a quantity of anger alongside far too much dangerous compassion. Bad habit in a prosecutor, noticing desperation in passing faces, struggles slyly revealed in a method of walking and talking, all those symphonies in failure however poorly played. Pity was a cancer incapable of research. Also the failure to be surprised. Worse still, so little genuine evil despite newspaper verdicts which encouraged the public to hunt this animal or that, and moral indignation became a luxury she had ceased to be able to afford. It had moved into memory along with hatred or even acute dislike. She missed its passing, like a religious belief.

Prosecuting people was only the same as protecting them, the inevitable suppression of some individuals in order that others might stay alive in relative freedom, a sort of dramatic wheel-clamping exercise, something which had to be done even by one who drew a short enough straw to be damaged in the doing, as she had been: each year eclipsed by that insiduous lack of hope, enlivened by jokes. Stuck with it, bound until death by weary, cynical, all embracing love of the human race, never eclipsed by more than grim pity.

The light in the office was poor. Too many hours in the working day, and this only the first. Helen sighed, squinted beneath the neon, wondered if she needed glasses, suspecting she did, reminding herself to shop for food at lunchtime, but unable to remember what it was she needed. Reluctant to begin reading the remainder of two feet of paper while duty and habit dictated she would.

Confessions first. Attack the document unwittingly designed to consign Stanislaus to a lifetime inside. Why a hammer and a knife, for God's sake? Wouldn't one of them have done?

". . . I, Stanislaus Jaskowski, made this statement of my own free will . . . [Oh, Stanislaus, I hope you did.] I used to be in antiques [for which, read house clearance, Helen thought cynically] but that didn't work out. I work as a hospital porter now, and a couple of years ago I had the idea of doing part-time work as a private investigator, because I thought I would be good at that, and I needed the money. I didn't advertise or anything, just did bits and pieces for other firms when they were busy. Mostly following husbands and wives. You get known, and sometimes I would be phoned up out of the blue, especially after I put an advert in the Hackney Gazette for a couple of months, giving my home number.

"Sometime in January 1985, I was phoned up at home by this

woman. On reflection, it must have been January. She had an odd voice, and she asked me if I was a private investigator, how much I charged, and things like that. As far as I can remember, this person said the work would be in and around Islington, which suited me, being so close to home, and because I know it. I told her that would make it cheaper. The person asked me where I would like to meet, and I suggested a pub outside the area in Hackney, close to where I work. I suggested The Cock in Hackney Broadway. I told her she wouldn't be known there. Most of the customers are black. I could tell she wasn't.

"We met the next day at about twelve o'clock. I turned up on time, and the bar was empty, apart from a woman sat in the corner. She was drinking bitter lemon, which was all I ever saw her drink. I went up to her and said, 'Are you waiting for anybody and is your name Eileen?' She had told me her name on the phone. She never gave me another name at any time, but she is the woman you pointed out to me at the police station, Eileen Cartwright. She said, yes she was Eileen, and I got a drink of whiskey and sat next to her.

"She took a fifty pound note from her purse and gave it to me as a retainer. She said, 'I would like you to follow a chap who is a solicitor with an office in Fleet Street.' She gave me a description, and either then, or later in the conversation told me his name, Michael Bernard, and where he worked. She also told me that he drove a gray BMW. She said he was a dear friend of hers and that he was in trouble, but would not tell me what. I wasn't particularly interested. She told me she wanted him watched from the time he left work at about five-thirty until he got home, on Monday, Tuesday and Thursday of the following week. It was a Monday when we met, and I was to report to her the following Monday. She would phone me to arrange it.

"I think the first week I did the three runs on my own. I spoke to Eileen on the phone and she asked me to repeat it. I think the next week I took my brother-in-law with me because it was so boring. Mr. Bernard didn't do anything much, sometimes stopped for a drink or went into another office, but he was generally home by seven-thirty. I used my car, which is an 'S' registration Escort, white, a bit rusty.

"The following week, I met Eileen in the same place as before, and she asked me to do another week's work in my own time. She didn't even seem too interested in the result. I can't be exactly clear about the next point, but during the meeting after that, Eileen told me someone was trying to drive Mr. Bernard mad, that someone being his wife, and if it didn't stop he was going to have a nervous breakdown. She asked me if I could do anything about it, suggesting the wife could be harmed. I said I would think, and see if I knew anyone who could help.

"The next time I met Eileen was as a result of a phone call from her. This time we met in a car-park in Hackney, in her car. It was a new car and I sat in it with her. This was many weeks after the first meeting, months even, and she had been getting me to follow Bernard at least once a week. A nice little earner, but I still couldn't pay my bills. I gamble a bit, sometimes. The subject of harming Bernard's wife hadn't come up again after I had told her that I did not know anyone who would help her, and she had said it didn't matter. I got the impression that she had been thinking about that all the time, and so had I. I was always waiting for her to say something more. On this occasion she told me she wanted to discuss what was going to happen next. I did not know fully what she meant, but because of what she said at that earlier meeting I was prepared for it somehow.

"I asked Eileen for her name and address, and what exactly do you want done. She knew that I had thought about it. I'd thought about how much I could ask. We were in trouble at home.

"She replied, 'Let me start at the beginning.' Then she told me her address, which is 51 St. George's Street, above a shop, she said. We had a long conversation. She told me that she wanted Mrs. Sylvia Bernard killed. She said I would have seen this woman when I had followed Mr. Bernard home, and that she had a metallic green Golf car. I had always suspected that Eileen had wanted more than the woman just beaten up and this confirmed it. I said, 'It will cost you a lot of money.' I think she said five thousand, and I said, 'Double that.' She said it seemed an awful lot and she could not give it to me all at once. She could give me five thousand pounds in a few weeks, the rest afterwards, probably two or three months. I agreed. She just said she wanted the woman killed, and kept saying she was a very bad woman. In the end she said she would leave it for now, but in a few weeks she would phone me to say she had the money and I was to go to her house in Islington and collect it. She would expect the job done by the end of November, because Mr. Bernard always went away abroad for Christmas, and after that it would be too late. I said I would go to her house either on the day she telephoned me or the day after. All that was in September. She still had me follow Mr. B, sometimes both of them."

[Pause. An irritating knock on the door. Junior prosecutor in search of advice. Come back later if it isn't urgent . . . You're sure it isn't urgent, not for today? See you later, ten minutes, okay?] "I drove from my house in Hackington East to several streets away from hers the day she rang me, which was on 29 October, the day before my wife's birthday. I parked my Ford Escort where I showed you, and I rang Eileen from the telephone box, which I also showed you. She had given me the number. It was about eight-thirty. I said, 'This is Mr. Jaskowski, will you let me in? I will be about five minutes.' I walked from the car to her house, which is where I showed you. Her car was outside her house, and a door at the side was open. I went upstairs to her part of the building where you go straight into a living room on the left of the front door. She had told me previously she would be there.

"The lights in the room were off, apart from a small lamp, which did not give very much light at all. The rest of the light was from a street light outside. As I walked into the living room, there was a large cabinet to my left piled with material. The room was full of furniture, all of it old as far as I could see, and there were curtains and bits and pieces of things on all the chairs, not much space to sit down. In front of me was a big armchair with one leg broken. Too much put on it. A coffee table in the middle of the room was clear, and there was a fireplace which looked as if it had been used, because of the ash in it, but I could not say how long since it had been used. The room was not warm, and, as I said, it was dark. I also recollect a number of silver items which shone in the light from the street lamp. The whole atmosphere was very strange and she had two pairs of gloves on the coffee table in the middle of the room. Eileen said to me to put on one of the pairs of gloves, because she did not want my fingerprints in the room. She apologized for the mess, said it was stuff from her shops. I put on a pair of brown, thin leather gloves, and she did the same. They were new, and they fitted me, which I thought was odd. I sat down on the settee, which is one of those chaise longue things and she offered me a drink. The whole atmosphere was very strange and I said I would like a whiskey, but she brought me some gin instead, I don't know why, I don't like it.

"She pointed towards the sideboard, and I saw a big envelope on top of the material. She said, 'I have the money all there. I have been up all night cleaning it with methylated spirits to get rid of any fingerprints, but we should discuss some details before I give it to you. I don't want you to write anything down.' I noticed she had a notebook, which she looked at. Then she asked me some questions. First, could I trust the person who was doing the work to keep quiet? I said yes, and that I might do it myself. I think she knew that. She said she was able to keep quiet, herself, I mean, but if she were ever double-crossed, someone would pay. It was a warning to me. Then she said that if the work was not done inside three weeks, she would want her money back. She asked me if I had anything which would connect me to her, and that if I had, like my note of her phone number, I should destroy it: she would do the same. She then repeated that if the job was not done before Mr. Bernard went on holiday she would expect her money back.

"Then she gave me the envelope. The money had a very strong smell, which worried me when I came to change it and put some in the Building Society. The other five thousand pounds, she said would be paid later, in March of this year. March the twentieth, to be exact, when I was to meet her in the same car-park we had used before. If either of us could not make it, we were to return one week after at the same time. I was not to telephone her. She warned me again about destroying her telephone number, so I tore it up in front of her. She then left the room, telling me to leave after she had gone and close the side door behind me. Holding the envelope, I went, and drove home to my wife.

"I cannot tell you how happy I was as I went home, because I knew I had the money in my hands to pay off my debts. At that stage, I never intended to harm Mrs. Bernard. That might sound a strange thing to say now, but that is exactly how I felt at the time. When I got home I hid the money in an old fridge, all of it except some, and told my wife that one of my mates had paid something he owed me. I brought six hundred pounds into the house and over the next few days paid all the rent, insurance, arrears to the HP companies for the things we have in the house. I put some of it in the Building Society, and the girl asked me what I had done with it to make it smell like paint. I told her I was a painter, and she joked, told me not to keep it in a tin. I was worried by that.

"After a week, I had spent not all of the money but most of it. I was terrified Eileen would get her revenge on me if I did not carry out the job. As time went on, I could not think of anything else. I had told her all about my family, and I was afraid for them too. Don't ask me why I did not think about that earlier, but I didn't. By 10 November, I was going out of my mind, drinking far more than usual, which is a lot.

"I decided to make some attempt to make it look as if I had tried to kill Mrs. Bernard. I was working late turn at the hospital, that is two in the afternoon until ten at night. I telephoned Mr. Bernard's office from a phone box and made an appointment to see him at nine-thirty on a Wednesday morning in case he decided to go into work late that day. On the Tuesday after work, I went out drinking, bought some whiskey for my car. I slept in the car for a few hours in the hospital car-park, got up about half past seven. With me, I had a saw which I had wrapped in gift paper and a bunch of flowers from outside a station, Highbury I think. I still didn't believe I was going to do anything to Mrs. Bernard, but I drank some of my whiskey before I drove from Hackney to Islington. The traffic was very heavy; I thought I was never going to get there, but I did. I put the car in one of those streets which doesn't need parking permits. Something in my mind was telling me not to go, but it seemed like I was too far to stop, so I sat in the car for a long time, wondering how I could get out of this situation. Drinking all the time, nerves and guilt I suppose. I then decided to go and at least make an attempt to do it, though as I have said before, I still didn't intend to kill her."

Helen felt her mouth begin to dry, and cradled her empty coffee cup closer.

"When I got out of the car, I had the gift-wrapped saw and the flowers in my hand. I forgot to say I had been one night, more than one night, looked closely round the house where she lived and I knew what it was like. I walked around for a bit first before I actually went into the street, put an empty bottle into a waste-paper basket. When I got to their house, I stood outside and looked up at it for a few minutes. I saw Mrs. Bernard at a window upstairs, talking on the phone, and then I thought, I've got to do something now. Didn't mean hurt her badly, just something to make it look as if I'd tried. I couldn't just stand there. She looked nice at the window. At this stage, I didn't know what I was going to do.

"The front door was slightly open; she opened it wider. I asked her, 'Can you sign for this parcel, please?' She said, 'It's a bit soon for Christmas, isn't it?', but she went back inside for a pencil, then came back with a pen in her hand. I don't know what it was, but she looked at me as if I was dirt, just like dirt when she first opened the door. I thought, 'If she smiles at me nicely, I'll have to just go away,' but she didn't smile. When she came back with the pen, she didn't smile either, and when she held out her hands for the parcels, she sort of jumped. It was as if she suddenly knew that I hadn't come about those. I grabbed hold of her, and she started struggling and screaming, and I panicked and we both fell onto the floor inside the door. I tried to calm her down, shouted at her I hadn't come to kill her, but she kept on screaming and fighting. She ripped all the buttons off my shirt and I think I tore her blouse. I kept saying, 'Don't worry,' but she wouldn't stop. Then I hit her; I hit her with the claw-hammer I had in my coat pocket. I had the hammer and a knife in my coat pocket, so she would see them and think I had come there to kill her. Then she would have reported someone had been there to kill her, and Eileen would know that I had tried even if I had not done the job. Even after I hit her, she struggled. She didn't scream, just made noises, still grabbed me, even after I hit at her hands.

"I lost my head and I can't remember how many times I hit her with the hammer. I stood up, then knelt down, and thought she was still alive, still moving a bit, so I panicked again, and stabbed her in the throat with the knife. I don't know how often. Then I picked up the parcels which had been dropped and ran out the door. Took the knife and hammer with me, and my coat off outside. Ran back to my car.

"In the boot I had some overalls which I use for working, changed into them and took all the clothes I had on to a launderette in Upper Street. It wasn't busy so nobody noticed me in there. I went to my brother's and told him I had been out all night after a row with my wife. We often have rows, and my brother wasn't surprised and let me stay with him all morning until we went for a drink at lunchtime and I went back to work.

"I burnt my coat and my overalls in the hospital incinerator. Also the knife. I put the saw and the hammer in there as well. I finally put the shirt in there because it was ripped, and I borrowed one from one of my mates who has left now.

"I am deeply sorry for what I have done, and I find it hard to say how I feel. I never intended to kill her, but that doesn't make that much difference now. I wish she had smiled at me, and then I would have just frightened her. I might have told her what Eileen wanted done to her. I don't know why I did it, except I was frightened. I thought that Eileen would kill me, or my wife. If she could get me to kill someone else, why shouldn't she get someone to kill me, or one of my children? I have not been so good to my children but I love them. I have brought such misery to them and many people, and I am prepared to face up to my punishment. I have told you everything: I will help you get Eileen now. She is a bad woman and I am still afraid of her. Without her, I would never have got involved. It is not easy to explain. I have never done anything as violent as this before in my life. Having the money was nice, very nice. She knew how much I wanted it, and she waited for me like I waited for her. I could have made something with the money.

"I owe you an explanation of why I have told you so many lies since you arrested me last week. Couldn't say it at first. Every time I think of what I've done, I feel like being sick. Sometimes I am sick. That's why I lied. I will give evidence against Eileen. She is the one I saw in here last week. There is no one like her, no one as strong as that. She made me feel like a little boy with her. She will get away, find someone else as weak as I turned out to be, and do it again. She has done this to me, and she will do it again."

Automatically, Helen checked the subscription.

"I have read this statement, and I have been told that I can correct, alter, or add anything I wish. This statement is true. I have made it of my own free will."

Written in the defendant's backhanded, not illiterate scrawl. No alterations or additions, making it difficult for him to claim after such a lengthy autograph that the admissions were penned under threat of violence or withdrawal of bail. This one would have known in any event that liberty was no more than an academic issue. This one had an articulate hand and voice, may even have enjoyed the attention.

Rapt attention, to everything he spoke or wrote. Stanislaus had lied for three days before falling on the neck of the investigating officer in an agony of tearful remorse, and the story which unfolded would have had them all ears with all its incredible feasibility. Helen suddenly saw a different slant to wise David's warning that this case, this hideous document of confession, was too close for comfort. Not nearly as easy in this to distance herself from the average man defined as a criminal by his actions, one outside the normal buffer zone which separated him from lawyers, captors and judges as well as his average victims. An unusual perspective, one rank amateur persuading another to kill a solid middle-class citizen not three streets from her own door: the kind of victim she might have been if some nasty trick of fate kept her married and idle with a richer solicitor than the ones she knew now. It was not so much the eccentricity which stunned her, but the nuances, the little fingers of fate which had so assisted the plan. If only Mrs. Bernard had smiled at Jaskowski, avoiding the activation of all that fear, he might not have struck her after all—might have accepted instead a pat on the head, retired like the whipping boy he was into the more familiar realms of failure. Did she know? Did she pay for the risk? Helen could not begin to tell.

She turned to the interview of Eileen Cartwright. Hours of futile questions, delivered by Detective Superintendent Bailey, interviewer par excellence, questions to a mask of a face with few replies, none of them helpful or incriminating. Helen's eyes were held by a passage toward the end of the notes, a kind of finale.

"Madam, I have questioned you for several hours. Although you concede a great fondness for her husband, you deny any knowledge of the deceased, or of Mr. Jaskowski. I do not believe you. Let me give you the details of what happened to Mrs. Bernard. She died of thirty injuries, inflicted with hammer and knife . . . Her clothes were torn, her fingers broken in warding off the blows. She fought back, with all her strength. Can you imagine those few minutes, Mrs. Cartwright? Can you imagine what she must have felt?

"Answer: No Reply. (Note: Interviewee did not speak. But smiled. Asked for cigarette.)"

A smile. The only response to long and grueling pressure. The kind of love which could inspire such hatred in a Mrs. Cartwright was beyond Helen West, so far beyond her as to inspire fear and revulsion, an uneasy restlessness far removed from the usual sad acceptance of yet another tragedy. Vague, uncomfortable awakening of curiosity and anger and a need for air. Pushing aside the gray net curtain, least aesthetic or effectual of security precautions, she opened the grimy window. Looking down into a grimier basement, she felt a soft rain, and noticed for the first time the beginnings of spring.

* * *

"Give us a break, sir. I haven't had time to get all the stuff out yet. And I don't want help."

Bailey smiled. It was worrying when he smiled. "All right. I'll go away for a few minutes. You might move faster if I'm not watching."

"That's right, sir. Go and get a cup of tea. Do the crossword. I won't be long."

Geoffrey Bailey, known as Geoff by his colleagues, most of whom seemed to bear the same shortened names, was indistinguishable from most of comparable rank in his dress, deportment and manners. Like them, but quite unlike them, he had moved through the phases of Detective Constable and Sergeant as a walking tribute to Messrs. John Burton, tailors, embellished with street-market leather, and like them, now owed his sartorial elegance to Marks and Spencer. The few who espoused sober silk ties, as opposed to those bearing the pictorial legend of some previous crime squad, owed these to the same source. They were beyond corruption in the main; spoke within the parameters of rank, about their children, gardens, homes, cars and work, frequently in that order, careful, if occasionally wildly indiscreet, in the giving of confidences. A reserve born of the knowledge that secrets are never secret in the course of a police career, which had always involved a kind of clumsy dance. Two steps forward, three sideways, to protect one's back—from one's friends.

Here the similarities ended. Geoffrey Bailey had not waltzed in this, or any other fashion for some time. While it was a reasonable bet that a man obtained his recommendation for promotion in this organization through the ability to take and execute orders in a fashion which obliged but never outshone his immediate superior, Bailey's upward rise had been more circuitous. He had been nudged onwards in the last ten years through his sheer indifference to the prospect, coupled with the acute discomfort he caused in any man unlucky enough to be his supervisor. An alternative route to higher places, this unnerving presence of his, certainly never calculated to achieve what it had. He was liked, well enough: respected, certainly, but rarely loved, never greeted with more than the hollow hail-fellow-well-met enthusiasm, and a kind of flattening against the wall. In return, he gave respect where it was due, courtesy whether due or not, and kindness whenever he could make it anonymous. Enigmatic, unglamorous, dry-witted, careless with protocol, good to other ranks, suspiciously bookish, but not a theorist, not at home in this or any other army.

Ryan he respected as the invaluable legworker, door-to-door questioner in the Bernard case, and Ryan wished he could emulate such an apparently easy rise in rank, putting it down to Bailey being long, thin, and therefore suitable for the uniform of a suit.

"You know," he had said, explaining Bailey's enigma to general disinterest in the canteen. "It's the lean and hungry look. Thinking too much. Makes a man dangerous. Also gets him promoted. People don't want him around. Too good to push down, so he has to go up. Not that he cares. Not about anything really."

"Go on . . ." More polite than curious over the chips.

"Nothing I can think of. Not a car, nor nothing, except books. No kids, or none around. No woman. Not one that phones him at any rate."

"He had one once, you know. They reckon she went mad." Guffaws. "Mine's mad already . . . Wish I didn't have one. That he should be so lucky."

Conversation turned, with the easy inevitability of a tide, the way it did whenever Bailey was discussed. He had overheard such snippets before and knew they entirely misunderstood the nature of the subtle aversion he aroused by his unconventional life and his less predictable reserve. A little hurt was inflicted by the isolation: something more in the nature of actual bodily harm rather than grievous. Bailey knew that his was a mild form of leprosy, unlikely to get worse.

Today was a bright spring morning, but his mood, normally as reactive as a barometer, remained low. "See Ms. West, her office 10 A.M.," was the terse note in his diary. Ryan, bag-carrier, was finally ready: they collected the neat box files for the appointment, both slightly apprehensive. Geoffrey never knew what to expect, while Ryan always expected the worst and voiced his thoughts.

"Trouble with solicitors," he announced, steering his new car through the Upper Street traffic with more than his normal care, "is that some of them are good news, and some of them are bad. I mean, some you can get on with, some you can't."

"I couldn't have put it better."

Encouraged by this response, Ryan drove faster, and added more. "I've heard this one's all right, though. Quite sharp. Nice."

Bailey nodded again. He had heard nothing of the kind, in fact nothing at all concerning the solicitor on whom they were obliged to impose their large presence, his height, Ryan's bulk, and he was in any event quite resigned to having to take whoever or whatever was imposed on him. Ryan's wisdom was perfectly sound: some were good, some were bad, but they couldn't help the fact that they were all lawyers. In Bailey's eyes, criminal law was a good deal more adversarial than it seemed. War games were played for real between police and criminal: played again in as deadly, if more leisurely fashion between defense and prosecution, but law enforcers and law breakers would always be at war with lawyers, and the first two categories would always have more in common with one another than they could ever have with their legal allies. Not that the bonds tying them were unaffectionate, or even disrespectful: simply bonds which exist between differences of kind who need each other, like a parent to a disappointing stepson. Bailey had realized a long time since when he had first brushed his only suit and presented his case papers to his brief, why such an occasion did not involve a meeting of minds, however common the objective may have been. Despite all he had gained since then in rank and experience, he still saw his policeman's arena as the street, the raw material of life, while the lawyer's was the courtroom and the preparation for it. Shuffling and evading, joking and pretending, protecting the professional man from too much truth, Bailey had eased his way enjoyably through many a conference with solicitor or barrister, always aware of the difference, always hating his necessary abdication to their forensic skills. They were the ones who would carry the street into the courtroom and revive it there like a play. They never picked up the pieces. They could hardly know better.

He hated it less now because, like everything else, it mattered less, but he still loathed the first interview with the new lawyer, always feeling he was buying their time without paying. They rendered him helpless, these interpreters, until he knew them well enough to judge what level of reserve he should maintain, and he disliked wondering what kind of sympathy, what kind of service he was going to get. The days were long gone when a police officer could complain that he had spent his life looking up life's back passage without being able to afford the mortgage on a solicitor's garage, but the divisions were the same. Even with his own law degree, and his self-imposed education, Bailey knew it. Lawyers breathed a different kind of air.

"Could do with a wet," Ryan grumbled, closer to earth as usual. "Sat with two of them wallies up here for more than four hours once, going through this and that. Never put the kettle on once."

A diplomatic error Miss West was unlikely to commit. She was in the kitchen room, removing the fungus from inside her battered coffee mugs when Bailey and Ryan, larger than life, discreet as nuns, made their way into her office.

To Ryan's surprise, Bailey sighed slowly, an outward breath of relief, scenting in the stuffy room a whiff of familiarity, a mildly rebellious, non-institutional air, a comforting untidy anonymity.

"God, what a mess," said Ryan, casting around to find a few inches of floor space for his boxes of paper, incredulous at all the other paper, instantly suspicious, but it was precisely the mess Bailey liked, a kind of organized chaos close to home, reminiscent of his own cramped office quarters, but worse, badly lit, badly furnished. Files lay everywhere in drunken heaps on the desk, on the floor, on the cabinet, allowing only a narrow path from the entrance to the room. Clearly the phone had been used as a football. There was a brown plant decked with the plastic ribbon it had worn on presentation, still unaware of impending death by neglect, a couple of equally dead milk cartons, a tray full of correspondence, an out-tray similarly full, and a crammed waste-paper basket. Cleaning ladies and others appeared to have given up on Miss West, who was ignorant or careless of the fact, indifferent to the décor and any impression it might create, struggling a little to stay abreast. So far, Bailey thoroughly approved. The tasteful prints, tidy offices with greenery peculiar to lady solicitors and estate agents had never appealed to him. Besides, the view he received from the door of the room told him she was not pretending overwork, and he had always known that the best means of ensuring that a task was done was to give it to the busiest person he could find. The factory room was all the better since he could sense the order which Ryan could not, the same order which existed in his own stable, hidden to all but his own eyes, a kind of secret efficiency which discouraged close scrutiny and prevented interference.

They waited, standing politely. Bailey still finding impressions in the place of a person who did not wish another to be able to inhabit it, who had several methods of working, not just one, and who wished to remain unknown. Miss West, should she choose to appear at all, was not important enough for Bailey to have formed a picture of her beforehand. She was merely a cog in a process. He had only hoped she would be something other than pompous in offering a minimal level of usefulness. Nothing more. It was the room itself which had mellowed him, so that when she appeared, bearing coffee in chipped crockery, slightly overflowing and sugared not to his taste, he, like Ryan, found the introduction a pleasant surprise. Ryan almost showed her to her own seat, and being a tidy man, watched fascinated as she removed a pile of documents from beneath it and transferred more to the window-sill to make room for their own. Bailey did not offer to assist in this resettling process, but admired the way she achieved it.

"Well," she said finally, lighting and offering a cigarette simultaneously, producing an ashtray from a drawer. "This is a fine piece of investigation, if I may say so, raising quite a few problems." Not original, but true. "Before we go any further, I take it we all accept the truth of Jaskowski's story, at least in all its essentials?" There were vigorous nods of assent. "That being so, you want to know how soon you can arrest Mrs. Cartwright, the real murderer. If I can put it like that."

"Yeah," said Ryan.

"And you probably know the answer to that, although you may wish it was different."

Bailey did, and certainly wished it was otherwise. Ryan, the eternal, if selective, optimist, even in his pessimism, had hoped vaguely that legal advice might wave some magic wand, produce some unknown avenue which would allow incarceration of Mrs. C, that horrible woman, the same afternoon. Galling for him to arrest her once only to deliver her home again. Sensing his frustration, Helen spoke to him rather than to Bailey, whose better understanding she could take for granted.

"Well, in case you doubted it, we can't charge Mrs. Cartwright until we have evidence capable of convicting her. As things stand now, there's not quite enough to commit her for trial, or at least not enough without Jaskowski's contribution. He's a co-defendant until convicted himself, and the evidence of a co-defendant can't convict without substantial corroboration. You know that. Nor can he be asked at this stage to open his mouth, because he can't be presented as a witness of truth until he has nothing to gain. Until he's convicted, he has plenty to gain—by lying. The evidence of an accomplice can be destroyed so easily: you can imagine defense counsel's line, 'Oh yes, Mr. Jaskowski, were you hoping for privileges in prison by telling us all this?' But even that's not the main problem: the main problem is the fact that we can't introduce the corroboration for his evidence without introducing the evidence itself."

"You mean we can't produce those statements about the smelly pound notes?" Ryan demanded belligerently. "Can't we point out that the only way he would have been able to describe her house so well was by having been there? Can't we tell the jury about the gloves we found in there? With respect, miss, what the hell's all that if it isn't corroboration?"

"It's corroboration, good corroboration, but none of it will make any sense without him giving evidence first, because it all hinges on what he has to say. He's got to give the evidence before it can begin to be supported by all these other facts, and he hasn't any status to give it at the moment. He's the lynchpin. I only hope he doesn't know how important he is. Without him being a competent witness, in the legal sense I mean, what have we got?"

Ryan shuffled. No magic tricks, and he did not understand it, not at all, although he was old enough to know that law, morality and common sense meet at few crossroads. All he knew was that there was a wicked old woman sitting at her own fireside, five thousand pounds poorer maybe, but still free. Murder as the result of middle-aged passion was beyond him. Himself, he did not expect to have that kind of energy at that kind of age, and could scarcely have raised it now as he cruised dangerously close to his first divorce in the knowledge that if he followed the regular CID pattern, he would not be in a position to pay anyone such a sum for the disposal of a girlfriend or anything else in his geriatric years. All gone in maintenance payments to former wives. His coffee cup was empty. Gloom hung over him like a cloud of insects, rising slowly as Helen went on speaking gently, still addressing her remarks to him, which was more than a little flattering.

"It doesn't mean we'll lose her, you know. Your report, Mr. Ryan, shows that she has no intention of moving anywhere. She's sitting calm as a cucumber. As soon as Jaskowski pleads guilty at the Crown Court, and his solicitor says he wants to get it over with as soon as possible, he becomes a competent witness. Mrs. Cartwright can be arrested immediately, charged and battle commences. Correct me if I'm wrong, Mr. Bailey, but I don't see this woman giving an inch. She'll fight from every ditch, and Jaskowski will be easy to discredit. She'll also spend rather more than the other five grand she didn't have to pay Stanislaus on hiring the best legal talent she can find."

Bailey nodded agreement. "Good. I like a fight."

To his surprise, she grinned, transforming her serious face into that of a girl. A mischievous grin, full of disrespect, crumpled, likeable, acutely intelligent. In the same moment, he decided he could trust her more than average and politely dismissed Ryan to collect the photographs which he had deliberately left in the car.

"There's just one matter," he began, as Ryan's steps retreated away down the corridor, "and you might know full well what concerns me."

"I think I might, but go on."

He hesitated, wary as ever of trust, however minimal. "I know we can't arrest her. We'd only have to release her again, having shown our hand, and, as you've guessed, I don't really think she'll fly. She may think we don't take Jaskowski seriously; she has such utter contempt for him herself, you see. If she knows what she faces, she chooses not to believe it. Yet. She's being watched, of course, but we have no legal right to prevent her skipping, just supposing she should try. What on earth do I do if she does? She can afford it."

This time her gaze fastened itself firmly to a point on the wall beyond his shoulder.

"Officially, Mr. Bailey, you should inform me immediately. Officially, I shall then bang on the closed doors of my ever-cautious superiors, who will tell you with more clout than I can muster to let her go, because the law is the law even for Mrs. Cartwright. That much you knew very well before you asked. Unofficially, you must do as you think fit, but please give me some kind of notice. Then I can arrange to be out of the office for as long as necessary. What you do with her, Mr. Bailey, if she tries to slip the net, depends on the risks you are prepared to take. Personally, I hope these are many, and I shall help as much as possible, but you have to remember, my back is only slightly broader than yours."

"I understand." He smiled back. "I hope it won't come to that. I don't think it will."

She relaxed. A slim hand with short, unpolished nails, took the cigarette he offered before she continued.

"Now, I should like you to tell me what I want to understand for myself, but don't strictly need to know, which is, what the hell's she like, this woman? In detail if you can. Is it madness, sadness, or what? I don't know why, but I have the feeling she's already justified this, won't regret any of it: she has this sinister kind of confidence. Tell me about her. What do you really think of her?"

The wall clock ticked as he paused, hand trembling slightly around the cigarette as its smoke curled toward the ceiling.

"It doesn't signify what I think. Whatever I may think is irrelevant."

"Of course it signifies, and it's entirely relevant to me." She was quick and certain.

"Very well. Where do I start?"

"That depends on you. You could begin with the fact that she frightens you."

A pair of tired eyes met her own, brown eyes, too blank to register the alarm he felt at such baldly stated discovery, while hers showed him not prurient curiosity, but a genuine need to understand. He noticed the vivid intelligence of the face, resented and liked at the same time the uncanny sensation of being understood, and felt a brief shame at his surliness. That, and a desire to confess. He wondered briefly if she had also understood his quiet passion for talking, the articulacy so rarely exercised for lack of a listener he could respect, an equal in understanding. Too old at forty-six, too skeptical, too reserved through his dislike of wasting time, Geoffrey Bailey could not have fallen in love so summarily, but he did fall into liking, and he did, as far as he was able at the time, speak a little of his own mind.

"She's the kind of prisoner," he began, "you can't joke about. Oh, you can imagine how it was tried. Everyone tries to raise a laugh. But the custody officer and the men who brought her in tried to make jokes about her, you know the kind of thing—hell hath no fury . . . get a load of that . . . who would fall for a battleaxe like this one . . . why choose that for a bit on the side?—but all the funnies fell flat; you walk her from the cells, through the charge room toward the interview room, and everything falls silent. People just stop and stare at her, even the drunks arguing the toss at the counter. She has a certain something. Charisma?"

"Maybe she should have gone on the stage."

Bailey smiled. "Films, perhaps. *Omen 3: The Devil's Aunt.* All I can say is that she strikes a chill. Not the chill you feel from a psychopath, someone beyond reason, who does things you couldn't contemplate for reasons you can't contemplate either, someone beyond the touching of any hand or heart; she's not mad in that sense, but she's so utterly single-minded she becomes terrifying. I can believe that she had that woman killed by an effort of will, didn't need the agency of Stanislaus, and we might have found the victim in as many pieces as we did simply because Mrs. Cartwright had turned long-distance gamma rays in her direction and simply wished her dead."

He paused, fished for a cigarette. Ryan returned, familiar enough not to knock, and Bailey continued as if he were absent. "It's that which is so frightening. The will of her. The non-mad will of her. The belief in herself and whatever she did, whether minding the shop or organizing a death, made no difference. And there's a contrast for you—her shops. Antique lace, exquisite stuff if you like that kind of thing, couldn't be more delicate, sold gracefully in Camden Passage and Bermondsey, sold so well that Mrs. Cartwright had no financial problems. Odd stock in trade for a woman so obsessed. Delicacy and brutality." He was embarrassed by Ryan, "I'm sorry. I'm rambling more than a bit."

"No you aren't."

Again the feeling that she understood him before she spoke. Again the prickly feeling of resentful relief.

"She has two or three friends who adore her. Pale women, whose lives she's mended, like her lace, and who rely on her. So gentle, they say, 'What would we do without her? Couldn't harm a fly.' But I can't find it in me to believe that there's any good in her at all. I think she blackmailed Stanislaus, not that he'd done anything disgraceful, just emotional blackmail. She used the whip hand of shame. I think she does the same with her friends, her customers, and she tried to do it with Bernard. Used kindness and devotion as a weapon, which he dodged. Half of me thinks she might have killed the wife because she really believed he would fall into her arms; the other half reckons it might have been to punish him for not coming to heel, for resisting her at all. The rest, if that makes sense, thinks she did it for fun. I don't know. What I do know is that it's all entirely straightened up in her mind, as you guessed. I simply wonder who else she's destroyed, or plans to destroy. I think she's gone through life like that. Manipulating, destroying, throwing away, without anyone realizing." His long hands fluttered. Bailey was not a man of gesture, and now he had almost run out of words.

"You asked me to describe her: I can't. All I can say is that she's a woman of extraordinary strength. Not entirely unattractive in a way, like a lizard or a fat snake. Obsessive. Evil, I think, rather than bad. Bad rather than sad, because I can't think of her as sad. Rare to find anyone evil. Thoughtless, malicious maybe, but evil, no. I doubt if any of this helps at all."

"You're wrong. It helps a lot. Will she mesmerize a jury?"

Bailey laughed. "Even she'll have a problem with twelve men at a time. Her influence is best when she's dealing with an individual. Like Stanislaus."

"Was he so easy?"

"It can't have been easy to persuade someone to commit murder for you. Even for ten thousand pounds he wanted so much. Not easy, but obviously not impossible. Stan's not without a brain, but he's a superstitious dreamer. That helped him to do it, and helped him confess."

"Not evil? On your terms?"

"Not in that league at all, whatever he did, however horrible. In fact," Bailey paused, wondering how far to trust her with his eccentricity, knowing he would suffer from Ryan's incredulity, "he's really quite likeable."

"Oh come off it, sir. How can you like someone who did what he done? Man's a bastard. Like him? I'd as soon sell my mother."

"I don't see why an assassin shouldn't be likeable," Helen interrupted quietly. "I don't see why not. He could even be trustworthy, lovable, kind to animals and children, like someone in the Mafia: but is he telling the truth? I mean the whole truth?"

Geoffrey looked at Ryan. Ryan looked at Geoffrey. Mutual incomprehension.

"Yes," said Ryan. Geoffrey was silent.

"Enough of the truth?" Helen insisted.

"Enough," said Bailey. "I mean by that that it contains no lies, his truth. I believe that that statement under caution is absolutely true, although, God knows, I've thought that before and been wrong. It's just that there's something missing. Perhaps nothing vital. Don't ask me why I think it, but I do. It's only complete as far as it goes, which is more than adequate."

"Something missing? Or someone?"

Ryan was puzzled. Bailey's head shot up in surprise, nearly anger. Damn her for being so astute.

"Yes," he said slowly. "Someone. He had help, our Stanislaus. Someone, apart from her, who didn't stop him. Stanislaus couldn't keep a secret if he tried. I can't believe he did all this without any help but whiskey. And I'm ashamed of myself. He told me everything else, and I couldn't risk asking him who it was. That's where I've failed."

Helen did not call it failure, but she did not reply. She was looking at the face, wondering how one pale, uncertain assassin had ever resisted its power, its weary compassion. Shook herself; carried on. Spring had sprung. In the form of another articulate intelligence, and a case which had already cast a spell.

CHAPTER TWO

Mr. Stanislaus Jaskowski of Hackington Estate was committed for trial today by the magistrate sitting at Highbury, charged with the murder of Mrs. Sylvia Bernard. Mrs. Bernard had been found dead at her home address in Cannonbury Street. Jaskowski, who is forty-four, married with four children, said nothing. There was no application for bail. Another suspect connected with the murder is believed still at large . . ."

That was all. The second formality of murder. Helen saw the *Evening Standard* report, and others identical. Frustrating for them to be allowed to say so little even though they had heard better snippets from the public galleries where they gathered daily in dozens of court peripheries like flies around sealed carrion, buzzing and whizzing in frustration. Such a promising murder story from the first.

"Blond solicitor's wife brutally beaten to death in own £400,000 home: no clues whatever. Husband questioned but released. 'I'm broken-hearted,' he said to our reporter." Shocking stuff, even in North London terms, where the Turks shot the competition for drugs, the Irish broke skulls as often as they broke bread, and the indigenous population had a fashion in mugging babies. The draw of a solicitor's wife as victim dragged three of the Fleet Street weasels to court in the hope of hearing details worth printing later when the trial was in progress, and they could scribble as they pleased to fill a page or two, but not now. Nothing to be published which could possibly interfere with a fair trial. Nothing for today but three lines and an hour's gossip with one another. They could have added the details of the defendant's dress without their editors risking a summons for contempt, but frankly it wasn't worth it, even though his suit, and the completely ordinary, even respectable look of him surprised them all, in so far as surprise was ever a feature of a crime reporter's life.

It was not inefficient of them to miss what little drama there had been in the seedy anonymity of the busy court. When Helen had arrived early enough to check that each original statement was signed and witnessed, before the eagle eye of the magistrate's clerk could see otherwise, the building had been empty and clean, even the graffiti in the lavatory scrubbed. By ten-fifteen, all those answering bail had crowded into the foyer, fingermarking the lists outside each court to find their names before retiring to plastic seats to drink coffee from plastic cups, filling the air with nervous smoke, the floor with debris, the atmosphere with coughs and conversations, half muttered, half rowdy, the court corridors as cluttered as a station cafeteria, food and drink only ever half consumed, all eyes on the clock. Resignation and pretended indifference on old young faces. Most had traveled this road before; simply wondered how sharp would be this bend in it, how steep the fine. Anything you say, your Worship: don't let me go to prison. Little enough wickedness, plenty despair.

Twisting his way through the crowd, papers in hands, Helen on his left with her eyes skimming the crowd for Jaskowski's solicitor, Bailey saw her, Mrs. Eileen Cartwright, clutching a large handbag like a shield, sitting upright in a seat immediately facing the entrance to Court One, eyes fixed on the door as if willing it to open. A harmless member of the public outside the room into which Jaskowski, crucial witness against her, would be brought from his underground cell by means of two jailers and one set of handcuffs, while she waited and watched unrestrained, dressed in black, as if for a funeral.

"Hang on, Miss West," Bailey touched her arm and guided her back a few steps.

"What's the matter?"

"She's here: bloody woman." His face was white with anger. "Mrs. Cartwright. Sitting outside Court One like an ever-patient relative. Jaskowski's wife's here as well. He'll go mad if he sees them both: he's frightened enough already. What the hell does she think she's doing?"

Helen shook her head slowly, guessing. "God alone knows. She's probably come to upset him. Remind him she's still on the same side of the fence as his wife and kids, whereas he isn't. Something like that perhaps? Curiosity? Bad taste, watching the man you hired for murder being shuffled along for trial? Let's ask her."

"Should we?"

"Why not? Forewarned, forearmed. She shouldn't be here. It's obscene. We should ask her. Not that she has to tell us; she knows the virtues of saying nothing."

Bailey hesitated, struggling with a sense of propriety. "She's not under arrest," he ventured, far too aware for once of strict legality.

"I'll do it," said Helen. "Lawyer's privilege."

The strange quality of fear, as varied as love in all its manifestations, touched Helen with a shade of itself as she approached Mrs. Cartwright who remained unnaturally still, only raising her head without the slightest adjustment of her body when she heard herself addressed. There was an insolence in it, a bravado in the stillness, as if the presence of the other standing above her was insufficient reason to alter her position by as much as a fraction or make any other gesture indicating attention. A subtle, humiliating rudeness, seen by Helen for what it was.

"Mrs. Cartwright?"

"Yes. Why?"

"I'm Miss West. Prosecuting Mr. Jaskowski, who should be committed for trial this morning. Which you realize, I expect. I know you've been questioned about the same matter. Do you mind if I ask why you're here?"

"I do mind in fact. I'm not in prison. I can attend any court I want as a spectator, any time I want, can't I? I don't have to give reasons."

"No you don't, but it would make my life easier if you would." Helen smiled pleasantly, aware at the same time of an itch in her skin, uncomfortable under the intensity of the woman's sudden myopic glare. She could feel a rush of blood to her eyes, perspiration beneath her arms, and her hands damp on the cover of the file.

"I should hate to make anyone's life more difficult." The reply was politely ironic. "I've nothing to hide. I came to watch because I'm curious. That man is telling lies about me, and I want to see him. I want him to see me, since he says he knows me. I have come for him to see me," she repeated.

"Oh," Helen was at a loss for words. She paused, felt the second rush of blood carrying the swift anger she needed.

"Why do you want him to see you? To intimidate him?"

The returning stare was blank, deliberately blank.

"What do you think? Leave me alone. I've done nothing."

The anger was cold now, cold and closed like Mrs. Cartwright's face, as clearly hidden in mild, blunt words.

"Mrs. Cartwright, you do have the right; but if you sit in that court and try to make Jaskowski look at you, I'll ask the magistrate to have you removed, and I'll tell him why. I know you won't listen to me, and that might not shift you, but hear this: there are three journalists here, and once I say my little piece, they'll chase you out of the building, hound you for photographs and comments. Have you met them before? They're extremely determined. They'll follow you home and camp outside your door, life will become very uncomfortable, and I doubt if police protection will be forthcoming."

The expression did not alter. Helen ignored the face, and went on. "Now, there are several things you can do. Sit right at the back of court and out of view if you insist on watching the circus, which will only last five minutes, not much opportunity for staring him out, is there? Or leave now. I suggest the latter. Your visit is pointless. You won't be allowed to upset the defendant for your own reasons, whatever they are, and if you stay, you won't be seen by him. He may be on trial, but not by fire. Or by you. Do you understand me?"

Bailey listened. For a moment, Mrs. Cartwright did not move. The black, expressionless eyes scanned Helen's blue ones before she rose in a single movement, brisk for her broad size, and left the foyer with a solid, dignified tread. A woman who had completed an errand and had others listed for the day. A useful, worthy, efficient middle-aged lady, model citizen, passing through the crowd politely as they parted for her. Helen watched, relieved.

"You have to admire her," she muttered, palms damp and cooling.

"Admiration? For nerve? Coming here, or to any court, before she needs? Yes, I agree. Admiration, not respect. Do you know, she's wearing the same skirt and blouse she did when I arrested her, and all the other times I've seen her? Always the same clothes. Do you think it's a gesture of contempt for the world at large, cheap, but effective gesture? How do you like her?"

An attempt to lighten the tone, rewarded with an uncertain smile.

"Not much. Of all the people to meet in a black alley at night, I'd rather Jaskowski. But it gives me a taste, though, of what you must have seen when you interviewed her. She inspires fear. She makes me think," Helen paused, pushed at her hair with one hand, clutching at words, "of always being in the dark."

"Oh no." Bailey laughed. "Don't let her touch you so, Miss West. You," he added with an awkward and mocking gallantry, "are more suited to light. That's where you belong. In the daylight."

Eileen had conquered the dark, turning the fear of it into an addiction. She had come to like the dark, although it had been such a challenge to conquer and make it tolerable. The oblivion of real sleep was never possible now except in a darkness as total as blackout, and only in her father's armchair in the treacherous half-light of the living room did she suffer the half-sleep which prodded her into life with the old familiar terror. Only when the sleep had come unbidden did she dream at all. She dozed like this after leaving the court, plodding her measured retreat to the deeper colors of her house, hiding her fury in footsteps deliberately slow.

There had been so little sleep of late; so many septic dreams like these.

A blurring of three male figures into the screen of the television set as her eyes closed. All of the figures ageless, but none of them young. There had never been a young man in Eileen's life, nor a child. Not even herself: however she tried, she had never been a child, not a real child, could not recall infancy or innocence, or anything invoking the supposed happiness of either.

"Tell me a story, Father."

"No, child."

"Please . . . I'll tell you one then."

"No."

"Please . . . ?"

"Go away, child."

"Yes, Father."

Far longer than years competing for his love, strong dull father. What else could she do, she without a mother, with such a face to guide her elegance? Only the brash, brown, northern cousins, visited reluctantly once a year and never invited to return, until at last they too, ceased issuing invitations.

"Poor child," said Aunt Sally, scolding her own sons. "Cooped up with that dry man. Ian, Simon, you must both be nice to her, you hear? Doesn't she have any friends?" The two boys choked on toast, helpless with mirth at the very idea. Friends? Ridiculous. How could she have friends? Fat, solid Eileen, with the pebbly glasses, the black hair like wire and the pasty, sallow skin. "And legs like tree trunks," Simon smirked, "and spots," Ian added, "And fat fingers; she doesn't want friends. She doesn't know how to play." "She's like a slug," said Simon. "No, a fat frog." "More like a toad," finished Ian, choking again as Eileen, hated cousin Eileen, emerged from behind the door which had failed to block this crescendo of insults. Smiling as if she had not heard. Each boy looked at the other, collapsed in the face of that silly smile. They had forgotten to mention the brace.

If father spoke, it was a lecture or an order, and she welcomed both even as her teenage spots disappeared and she settled into a broad, squat twenty-year-old of spectacular plainness, who dreamed vainly of assisting in the creation of the obscure books which provided his merely sufficient means. "Hilary's wife," said the same aunt, "must have died in an accident of boredom," but that fate was not imminent for Eileen, the only child of a surviving parent who thought her stupid, clumsy, infinitely tedious and repulsive to look at, imagining quite rightly that she never guessed his opinion. Keeping it hidden was his single concession to fatherly duty, part of a breathtaking selfishness, but at least he could say he never once told her. He could not have done worse. Eileen believed, because of her father's silent lies, that love was always reciprocated in the end as long as one persisted, believed fervently that if you gave it, worked for it unceasingly, the devotion would be returned. I love you: therefore you will love me. There could not be a simpler formula than this imperfect equation, believed with utter conviction.

There had been a mama, of course, whom father had loved once, but it had been like the passionate interest inspired by a fascinating book, and once he had read it, he put it away. There was no one else for unloveable Eileen to love, and being both shy and inept in a world which did not like her, she started to collect. She collected bits and pieces, first indiscriminate rubbish, then not. Old fabrics, early Liberty scarves, ancient ribbons, buckles and bows, lace. She collected small items: tiny silver jugs, thimbles, sewing cases miniaturized beyond usefulness, hand coolers in marble and wood, purses in needlepoint which had blinded eyes, lawn handkerchiefs, small samplers, egg spoons and fruit knives, hand mirrors, brushes and combs, cruets, and furniture for dollhouses. It was as if her interest became confined to things which could be held comfortably in one hand, tactile, controllable things, easily assembled together, easily hidden. Next, cameos and miniatures; then coins, icons, beads, broaches, lockets containing twists of hair and stern portraits, tiny figures in jade, and rings. Nothing flashed or shone with more than a subdued gleam: no trash, no glitter in her rich collection, begun with childish pence, continued with modest pounds, flourishing in all the years when plastic was more convenient than oak, glass more fashionable than jet, and a junk-shop a treasure trove.

A mountain of lace had adorned her room, and still often did. Little pieces in the beginning, bits removed from jumble sale blouses, then yards, edgings from torn sheets and silk petticoats found in the 2/6d boxes of the East End. She was astute, bargained for halfpennies in the way she still bargained for half-pence, with the same powerful persuasion she could employ when she became a seller, which was rarely before her father died, since he despised commerce and declared it vulgar.

But the best of it was the way the collection gave her grace, dignity, and interest. All Father's friends, dry sticks, considered her odd, but found her collections charming, and it was these which gave her status in their eyes. Eileen had collected as a child for no reason but the desire to have pretty things which she could call her own: as an adult she knew the collection was her lifeline to the rest of the world and the only means whereby the human race would notice her at all. An odd young girl became an ugly woman sharing a starved heart between an unresponsive old man and beautiful things. Equal passions, only one of them disappointing.

Until the first death, that was.

Eileen slept. Outside in the street, a bulky figure strained to see the light in her window, decided she was out and he would return later. Eileen would have preferred his visit to this orgy of nostalgia, would have opened her window in the cold to call him back if she had known. "Come back," she would have shrieked. "Come back! Don't leave me now."

Papa, dead in bed one careless morning. A little flushed and twisted, natural, if puzzling, causes. Armed with all the natural dignity of the sepulchre, Francis Cartwright, his onetime colleague, officiated at the soulless cremation Father had ordered for himself. Eileen wrapped the best of her treasures and had them burned with him, a dramatic gesture she failed to understand, even as she made it. Francis had squeezed her hand: she thought she had seen him weep, but she might have been wrong—her eyesight had always been poor. "Poor girl," said Francis, "alone in the world." He looked at Eileen, and looked at her exquisite possessions while Eileen looked back. "I'm not alone," she protested, "I'm not even lonely," and if she had been able to ignore the reactions of the world she might have believed it.

Eileen clutched at railings for support before finally clutching Francis. She did not understand: she was so good, so generous, so respectable, and no one wanted her. She would have to try harder, make changes, get rich. Twitching in her sleep on the afternoon of Jaskowski's committal, Eileen remembered that resolution. Money would bring love: keeping it was a question of will, so she would be rich. She leased the damp ground floor of the house, began to trade in bric-a-brac down Portobello, leased a shop for the same purpose, then another in Camden Passage. Possessor of house, shops, and the beginnings of solid income, she was as eligible as she would ever be, and no more ungainly than before. To complete the two-year revolution, she married Francis Cartwright, believing that she liked him, and that he loved her.

Harmless Francis Cartwright, impecunious academic, forty going on seventy, needed a wife and didn't mind who; anyone who would encourage him to finish his book on medieval English. His motives were simple, not even dishonorable: he wanted a house of books and someone to keep him in it, while her motives were simpler still. She wanted to be loved. Unbeautiful Eileen, with her heavy bosom and heavier thighs the memorable feature of a woman with an equally solid face, believed this was part of the bargain. To be fair to Francis, he was not a bad man, and in some measure at least, he did his duty and battled with Eileen's virginity until he had relieved her of it, filling her with infertile seed and himself with disgust in the process. Eileen in nightgown was not a pretty sight, and over a few hopeless years, it became worse than the vacuum which had existed before it, with headaches for Francis and leaden despair for his spouse.

Eileen rallied again, knew that effort was its own reward. Cook better, provide better, heat his study and titillate his bed, will him to love her with the sweat of her brow until he responded, and all this provoked was irritation. There was one halcyon period after four years of marriage, when Francis had his first heart attack and relished the care he received, but after that, dislike settled on his forehead like a cloud of summer insects, and still she persisted, Eileen against the Matterhorn of indifference until his slow fuse burned away.

"Why don't you talk to me, Francis? You never talk to me these days."

"Yes I do, Eileen, I'm preoccupied, that's all. The book's almost finished."

"You don't talk to me, Francis. You don't listen either. Do you love me at all, Francis?"

Under the beam of her spectacled eyes, and the light of their garish kitchen, he had hesitated. Eileen had no eye for interior color, only for objects and fabrics, so that the room mirrored her ugliness just as the whole house reflected her stark lack of appeal.

"Of course I love you, Eileen. I've told you so. You know I love you."

"No I don't. I should like to know. Do you love me, Francis? What have I done wrong?"

Francis was suddenly more afraid of the lie than he was of its opposite. He should have suppressed the whole of the truth, he owed her that, but he was too worn for caution.

"All right. You asked. I do not, could not, and never have loved you. How could I? How could anyone love the lump you are, or even like it? You're an ugly cow, Eileen. An ugly, insensitive cow, who behaves like a prima donna with a dishcloth. Stop thinking about being loved. It's indecent."

The gray shock of his words sank like a stone as a slight perspiration appeared on her forehead.

"My father loved me."

"Your father despised you."

"No." The voice rose and fell into a whispered plea. "No, Francis: he loved me."

"Then he lied to one of us. Not to me, I think."

He could not recall how long was the silence which followed, how deep his own regret. But to his amazement, the apologies and denials given later were accepted. Francis chose not to question why, but life between them stumbled on without being dramatically worse. She smiled as often, spoke less, nagged never, worked hard, and Francis decided he had been forgiven.

Eileen stirred, half opened her eyes. Why had none of them loved her? Why did it matter so little in comparison to the triumph she had felt in Sylvia Bernard's death? She had performed a service in putting such an abomination out of sight. Hating her had been more rewarding than loving Bernard. Hatred made her alive. Of Stanislaus, Eileen did not think at all as she woke from her doze. A mere agent, who had broken his word, who dared to cross her: not enough of him to hate. Then she thought of that girl, arrogant and bossy, how dare she speak like that? Sylvia and that lawyer girl, so alike, so bloody perfect, so righteous in all they did, and so stupid. Smiling while she burned, with their good figures, good clothes, males on arms like silver bracelets, protected by all the men who had so ignored her own progress, all of them hideously bland and ungrateful.

Eileen was awake. Hatred always dispelled dreams and the thought of the girl was a new toy for her mind. What was there now but hatred? Love persuaded no one, but hatred worked. She stirred, heart beating, mouth hungry. So many duties, and she had always been a creature of duty. Slowly she dialed a familiar telephone number. Fate was about to be unkind to her, but she was not imprisoned yet. And there was her friend, her only friend, in times all ripe for revenge. Somebody, she told herself, loves me only, and will earn my spurs for me.

CHAPTER THREE

I'm sick of the stories of the psychic detective," said Bailey. "You know the man. Feels the blood of the victim on his coat and then on his brain, and goes off panting like a sniffer dog after drugs, making the odd mistake, but thinking deeply, half killing himself with guilt at his own inadequacies: missing three more murders before he reconstructs the whole unlikely scenario in his mind, without anything as vulgar as a clue or a piece of forensic evidence. And then homes in on his target. If only I knew him. I might catch some of his talent, some of his charm. To say nothing of his appearance."

"But he doesn't exist?" Helen asked.

"I'm sure he does. He couldn't be such a convincing character if he didn't exist somewhere, but wherever it is, it isn't in my shape or my size, and it certainly isn't in the form of anyone I know." Bailey laughed. "Can't understand why I let myself read about him so often. A hard day at work on the gruesome facts, back home to the pit and out with the Maigret novels, to read myself into an inferiority complex. He'd define my nature as masochistic."

"Does that make you more of an expert on murder?" He laughed again, a deep chuckle at odds with the narrow frame.

"No one's an expert on murder. Some of us are experts on one particular aspect of murder and even then only after a while. You do so many different things from the cradle to the grave of a police career, I mean, no one does nothing but murder: squads are formed when they're needed and not until. I suppose I've seen a couple of dozen as investigating officer, dozens more in a supporting role, but I don't feel an expert. Murder has a different impact on coppers, money for one, overtime for as long as the investigation lasts. I don't believe anyone would spin them out deliberately, but I've heard howls of protest when the killer's caught within twenty-four hours. I'm digressing: I'm no more an expert in murders like this one than I am in any other kind of crime, not beyond knowing exactly what to do when they occur, who to telephone, what instructions to give, what kind of precautions, that kind of thing. After that, I can spot the gaps in the jigsaw puzzle, but I can't pretend to do much more than that, can't fathom why, or predict. I'm not fooled as easily as I was twenty years ago, but I'm still fooled. No psychic skills whatever."

"But you don't need them with the average murders," Helen said. "Aren't the luckiest detectives people like Ryan, all skill and energy without much insight, and aren't the usual explanations written on someone's wall in capital letters? Isn't it mostly messy without being complicated? What we call the domestics, husband and wife, father and son, tragic without being difficult?"

"Messy, but not complicated? Sounds like a comment on married life before murder."

"You know what I mean. There's nothing mysterious about killing, not most of the time. Murderer and victim know one another, lover against lover, family stresses, jealousies, all those make up the majority. Then there's murder for rape or robbery, blameless victims. Or murder for gain, professional murder, gang-land politics, but the motives are usually clear, and after a lot of fancy forensic footwork, so is the culprit, whether you arrest him or not. Perhaps you just don't have much opportunity for magic detection: would have it to use if you did. Not part of the scientific age."

"You're being kind to me, Helen."

"You're asking me to be kind."

With inconspicuous ease they had slipped away from the formality of the first two meetings into comfortable first names. Impossible to sit stiffly in a pub at seven in the evening after two hours of counsel's intelligent pomposity and not relax the professional acquaintance when they had both privately considered themselves the only element of sanity in the whole case. Carey QC was eminent, able and sharp, also a bore, aware of his own abilities, regarding solicitors as a lesser breed of human animal and policemen as something strange on the periphery of existence. Although he was irritatingly suitable for this case, his heavy humor was only apparent in the courtroom, lacking in chambers where they had been squashed against the green walls and tolerated without much concession.

Ryan had taken home his awe and his bad temper to his wife. He had scarcely listened to what had been said, Helen noticed; looked like a man who was distracted. Ryan had not wanted to listen to pompous claptrap: he had other fish to fry and the law was an ass by comparison. Helen and Geoffrey, of one accord, slumped into the nearest public house, not the wine bar favored by barristers, the pub with orange walls favored by lesser mortals. This was the second drink, and Bailey's normal terse reluctance with words was melting fast. Like two animals who had sniffed the air around one another, he and Helen had tacitly agreed on mutual liking, and the silence which followed her last remark was companionable.

"You're right, in the main," he continued. "More often than not the explanation for the death is far from obscure. It isn't the hunt for the culprit which makes it glow, it's the hunt for the victim's life, the rights it gives to forage for information as impertinently as we do in so many people's lives. No, not the motives: there are few enough like this, respectable body smashed to pieces in its own hallway, with no killer on the horizon, no obvious reason. More often, he's round the corner, or someone says within the first hours, 'I bet it was Johnny done it,' and you know where to start and why. Far more human ingenuity in robbery, while murder is likely to be nothing more than the longest short cut anyone can take. I mean, why does a son murder his mother, or a husband his wife? Why don't they just leave home? Almost anyone can commit murder, you, me, the girl next door, there's no skill involved, but what sets it apart is being able to take the lid off the can of worms, ask the sort of questions which would normally have me shot: the only time they'll let you. Makes murder an education. When else would you ever get the intimate history of a marriage, what the partners really thought of one another, and what the neighbors thought of them? It shocks me still, paralyzes me with surprise, what people will notice, store away, and never say until after a murder. Then they say so much, often unprintable."

"What did the neighbors think of Mrs. Bernard?"

"Ah, they weren't particularly rewarding. Ryan did the neighbors. Ryan loves talking to people, especially females. I never knew a man with such a knack for women. Wherever they are he'll find them; he only ever produces female witnesses, three or four this time. Quite excited he was. Anyway, not a neighborly road, more fun when they are. Most of them work by day, and the Bernards hadn't been there longer than six months. They seemed to move house every other year, more fashionable all the time. I gather Mrs. B. was known as a lucrative pain in the neck to all the local estate agents. She never stopped looking for the perfect house."

"And had she found it?"

"I don't know. Shouldn't think so. Another drink?"

"Let me get it. You got the last."

"Wouldn't hear of it. You might be emancipated, but I'm not. Same again?"

Bailey's concentration was not deflected by the interruption. "No help from Mrs. Bernard's neighbors. Pleasant, polite lady, they said. Obviously never needed to borrow a cup of sugar, and if she had, they wouldn't have been in. Not many housewives in that neck of the woods where it usually takes two to pay the mortgage. She found enough to occupy her time. Her diary was like a history, cataloguing everything she'd done for the last few weeks. One ironic thing: she was expecting a delivery of flowers when Jaskowski arrived. No wonder she opened the door, poor woman. Plenty of friends in Hampstead and Highgate, where there seem to be more wives like her. She always turned up on time, and was always pretty. Same age as Mrs. Cartwright, although you wouldn't guess it."

"Gentlemen friends?"

"Well, no, not any you'd notice."

"Shame. The perfect wife in the almost perfect house."

"Not your type, Helen, the unliberated woman, washing successful husband's socks, and receiving the large allowance?"

Helen sighed. "Oh, I don't know. Most cold mornings, when I lie in bed thinking up ridiculous excuses not to get out of it, that kind of life seems a wonderful idea. I wouldn't even wash the socks. But what about him? Sylvia's husband, I mean. The provider."

"Suffering from guilt, and so he should. On a reading from my unchauvinistic mind, you understand, I think he led Mrs. Cartwright up a garden path. Just a bit. Not the first time he's had a profound effect on female clients: a few legacies from the older and more affectionate; he seems to have a way with them. Oh, I believe him when he says he never went to bed with Eileen, or wanted to, though I've come across stranger tastes and even uglier mistresses. Sorry, that is a chauvinistic remark, but I don't believe him when he says he never gave her any encouragement either. She isn't that mad, that directionless. Apart from that minor dishonesty, he's an unexceptionable man, handsome and charming, wonderful manners. You'll probably fall for him. I gather most women do."

"Now that really is chauvinistic," Helen laughed, "or just prejudiced. But I'll overlook it. Go on."

"I think Michael Bernard loved his wife after his fashion, but if it wasn't for the manner of her dying, he'd recover pretty quickly. As it is, it'll take longer."

"You're rather hard on him. When you say encouragement, I take it you don't mean encouragement to kill his spouse?"

"No, no, I'm sure not. I don't mean that at all. I just mean . . . encouragement. Bernard was like a man with a pet he didn't understand: he let himself touch her, flatter her vanity and she him, that's what I mean. He encouraged the hopes, but not the consequences, poor bastard."

They were silent for a minute.

"Perhaps that's what real love is," said Helen, suddenly depressed, trying to dismiss it. "Willingness to go to any lengths, a belief in being right about it. No room for doubt."

"God save me from it then," said Bailey, sensing the downward mood, and smiling her away from it. "And on that note, preferring as I do to live happily, is there time for a last drink?"

"My round, I insist."

"With respect, no. My pleasure."

An animal being stroked, but lightly. Nothing personal in the conversation: no more than a chatting in the warmth of sympathetic company, but Helen relaxed like a cat, full of the mild sensation of being placed in a corner, looked after carefully, a temporary peace, a small relinquishing of the daily battle to survive. There was no particular need for the alcohol, but she liked to drink it: no sad craving for acceptable male company, but she liked that even better; at least two desires momentarily satisfied. Rare to sit at ease with a man as distinctive as Bailey, even to speak of a cast of characters, victims and criminals, as if gossiping of old acquaintances. When she thought of it, the conversation was almost as satisfying, and not dissimilar. Bailey returned to see her handsome face pleasantly vacant, her whole stance nicely slouched. He had stopped in his path from the bar, suddenly struck and pleased by this view he had of her as a stranger unconscious of his observation. A woman seen in this revised glance as youthful without being young, girlish without being a girl, elegant without fuss, self-possessed without self-consciousness, open but hidden. He saw what he had merely noticed before: long, thick hair falling from expert pins, a small muscular body with more of the strength of an athlete than the grace of a dancer, graceful nevertheless; a face of resignation, slim, practical hands. An unassuming beauty in the features with the wide, slightly lined forehead, crow's-feet visibly cornering large, dark eyes, a crooked nose, firm chin and chiseled mouth. To his discerning eye, the clothes were good, stylish without being obtrusive, like Helen herself. The cosmetics on the face had been applied with a confident and knowledgeable hand, and despite such help, she was as natural as air, better like this, when the day's stresses had unraveled the air of command. He liked all the colors of her: was absurdly flattered that she seemed as comfortable with him in this nondescript place as he was with her. Pity time was so limited. Pity she was a lawyer and he a policeman. On another day, he thought, we could be enemies.

"You know," she said, a follow up to nothing, "I feel better."

Better than what? He did not ask, but his answering smile was a blessing of acknowledgment. It extended from his chin to his hair, the way Geoffrey's smile did, lifting the shutter of his face and exposing hallmarks. A creased face, with one magnificent frown line lending it gravity, other lines hatched in like shadows in a drawing, until the smile adjusted them all into the complexion of another man, less English, far less severe. It was the smile which betrayed him to Helen, just as her leaning unselfconsciousness revealed that portion of herself he had seen. A mutual interest, perhaps: a little affection to mull the mutual respect. The last drink consumed to inconsequential talk, in peace.

"I'll drive you home."

"No, please. No need. You go the opposite way."

"It's no trouble."

"I don't believe you, and it's no trouble to get a taxi, really."

"If you're sure," both slightly withdrawing from the touch of a smile and the mellowing of wine, pleased to retreat a little. Nothing personal. Going home separately, no trouble, only slightly the wiser to one another, both pleasantly warmed. Bailey waved briefly and strode away, while she took her businesslike step over the road, pausing once on the crossing to look back at him, just as he paused to look at her. One more slight wave, embarrassed, both caught in an act of open curiosity handled with ease. An uncertain pair, blessed with social graces, almost ungracious in the reserve of their parting. Far from romance, such a limited acquaintance, but yes, she liked him, the look of his bony figure as it moved away from her, liked his observation, his intellectual ease, his lack of typicality. As for the man, he had just remembered the pleasure of simply liking a woman without wanting, and a kind sensation it was, one he could not remove from his mind.

The house of the Detective Superintendent was as different from those of his colleagues as was the man himself. He was childless for a start, parentless to boot, but it had not always been so. Halcyon wedded days, years in the modern Chelmsford house with the unmodern wife, mowing the lawn with the best of them, had brought him finally to this. Not everyone's taste, not even his own some of the time, not a suitable place for a child. There had been the one and only child, whose tenure of life had been brief enough to break the heart of the father, the spirit of the mother and with it, six years' optimistic marriage. Happy years, despite so much pulling and twisting, testing and probing, unblocking of tubes in the long trial of his wife's progress toward pregnancy. Bailey had thought that if she did not have the child she so desired, she would reach the insanity she merely touched with the finger of her intense longing, while he had only loved his daughter when she became recognizable in all her gorgeous, puckered features, twisting his heart in her tiny fingers. Cot death, as they watched television, relieved at her unusual quietness. And while some named disease might have made acceptance possible before guilt and loss made ravenous inroads into their lives, this nebulous cause gave scope for both, a grief of awful bitterness. I love you, he had told her. I love you: hold on to me. There is an end to this . . . , and she seemed to believe him, seemed to stop herself from standing in the child's room, shaking and weeping months after, so that Bailey ceased to hold his breath, began to hope they would survive, until the day when he failed to remove her from the upstairs room where she had locked herself to scream at the world, howling for his benefit an endless stream of hideous invective. Bailey lived as he lived to lose the vision of his struggling wife in the hands of brown-coated officials looking like removal men, with her scratched and dirty mouth wide open, screaming toward him the obscenities she could not normally have known, let alone understood in her usual, gentle life. So much so young, they said: grief, they said, crazy with hatred.

Not the end, could not have been the end even if Geoffrey had possessed less will and understanding, but it was the beginning of the end. Sophie left their house on more heart-stopping occasions than he could count, flying to be pursued and persuaded home, only to fly again within the month. "I am not fit to be a wife," she would say. "Look at what I have done." "You have done nothing," he would say. "You are my beautiful wife, fit to be a queen, come home, my love," pampering her without giving way to crying himself, until, soothed by his belief, she stayed between flights like a caged bird hating its master, looking for the space between the bars.

Until his power for reassurance failed: she fled again, and his energy with her. Not anymore. He no longer knew if he pursued her for her sake or for his own and this time, let her go, smoothed the path of her release, still caring. Ceasing to bang his skull and heart against the brickwork of disaster was a doubtful relief: when it stopped, there was peace, but copious bleeding, and in those agonized years of his wife's breakdown, when the daily tragedies of work only mirrored his private hell, Geoffrey Bailey had acquired his frightening patience. It was then that he became so intimately acquainted with the several kinds of madness, skeptical of success, bland in his approach, secretly helpless day in day out, awash with pity, even while he knew the futility of it.

"Who needs it?" he had laughed away the hesitant queries of those who wondered how he lived so far outside family life. He never wasted time on explanations which would explain nothing. There was never a shortage of women, just a shortfall in the desire to try, although he had borrowed bodies and affections out of the available pool, handled with care, only to replace them in what he hoped was undamaged condition. Good enough life for all that; not worth risking for more heartbreak of loving. He wondered if Helen West's independence was as complete as it seemed or as final as his own, since instinct told him she lived alone. Probably: such women were strong, so much more complete as creatures and so skilled in compromise.

So how would the same Helen react to his present home? Top floors of a converted warehouse in an unfashionable part of the East End neglected with good reason. Spacious and uncluttered, furniture scarcely uniform, yards of open shelving constructed by himself; no sign of pretty chintzes. Bailey had hounded the auction rooms for the huge settee, four-seater freak of diminished glory, bliss to the behind and a place where he often slept. The walls were decorated with the books on the shelves, prints he had framed himself and hung on the white painted bricks. The floor was sanded wood, polished at irregular intervals in a fury of frustration, adorned with a selection of rugs exotic and otherwise. An oak table, complete with matching oak chairs, a mahogany school clock, two faded armchairs, and an open fire completed it. Equipment gleamed in the kitchen annex, no fun to buy compared with the happy scavenging and bargaining he preferred. That was all. One colossal room, a bathroom, a spartan bedroom, lamp for reading, another odd chair and desk: tailored for ease, Bailey remembered as he switched on the lights and watched his home spring to life. Nothing new or valuable in the whole mixed bag of his possessions, but as they presented themselves to him, all in their own places, he knew he was home. Pointless to cook, bread and cheese would do when he could use the same time for reading or pottering with the clocks he repaired, radio for company, glass of red in hand. What would Helen think of such profound ordinariness, such unadventurous pastimes among the shelves of books which fed his imagination with everything from history to drama and all the endless detective fiction he consumed with such scornful fascination? The eclectic collection of a late self-educated man. Would she like the adopted cat which scratched inelegantly on the balcony? Why worry: she would never see. Hands clumsily restless, he ignored the wine when two glasses failed to please, and went to bed with a book. Nicolas Freeling's Van der Valk: endearing character, irritating style, a story of *crime passionnel.* Very apt. He must tell Helen: she might enjoy it. Then again, she might not. In any event, she had no business in his mind, none at all, and it irritated him like an unaccountable rhythmic sound, this repetitive thought of her. He was better off with fiction on the page, being kind to cats and polite to those he despised. Leave me alone, Helen. And as the thought formed he imagined he knew the likely response from abrasive Miss West: she would say she had not asked to be in his head and he should not blame her.

If Geoffrey Bailey had half hoped that Helen West was vexed with the same irritating, reciprocal thoughts as his own, he would have been disappointed. Not that Helen would have been immune from that glimmer of satisfying, safe attraction if there had been time to dwell on it, just as she might have sighed with the enormous satisfaction of reaching home without the phone shrilling as she placed her key in the lock, as if the two mechanisms were connected. She always answered, could not fail to answer in case it was a cry for help, in case it changed her life, although she knew, kicking her bag aside in the rush toward the ringing, it would be neither.

They had queued for her attention, the telephoners, like planes banked above an airport. First widowed father, mercifully short, a two-whiskey complaint rather than a five-whiskey babble. Time she went home. Then there was brother: could she lend money? Then friend Kelly, "Helen? Thank God you're in . . . ," a strained and tearful voice choking at the other end of the line, broken-hearted. "He's done it again, the bastard. What am I going to do?" Poor Kelly, believer of false promises painted on tissue, dumping problems as unselfconsciously as she might have dumped litter: so did Father, ex-husband, and half her acquaintances. Helen admired it, felt old, cold and defective for hiding herself so much, envied such public confession, wished she could copy that and help the rest, and slipped slowly from chair to floor, legs against the wall, head by the door, acutely uncomfortable for the hour it took to make Kelly laugh.

In open defiance of her silent plea, Helen's phone rang again as she made coffee.

"Hello, darling."

"Hugo? Where are you? Hello?"

Hello, ex-husband—keep it light and cheerful, "You sound close."

"In Paris. On business." Hugo was never anywhere ordinary doing anything without purpose. "On my way home, I think. Hope you don't mind my calling. What time is it?"

"Ten-thirty, here."

"Not late then. Have you got a minute?"

"Of course."

"Simply for words of advice from the store of your wisdom." At least Hugo was polite. He hid all demands, large and small, in that cloud of courtesy she remembered so well for its irresistibility. A mild anxiety at what would follow glued her hand to the receiver.

"What advice? More to the point, what wisdom? Didn't know I had any of that." Again she reminded herself to keep this light as pastry. There was a tiny hesitation.

"I may as well tell you . . . I'm thinking of marrying again, but I'm not sure. That's why I want your opinion. First hand."

"Well. What do I say but congratulations? Many of them."

"No, not yet, please. Thinking of it, I said. You're sure you don't mind my asking you? You're wise, Helen, and I need the help. I was sure you wouldn't mind. You're so sensible, darling . . ."

You're being evasive, Helen thought. You didn't tell me you wanted to chat to your ex-wife about a future one, since you've certainly made up your mind already. I find this distasteful, just a little humiliating.

"Of course I don't mind," she said, swallowing the line. "But I don't quite see how I can help."

"But you can. I'd like you to meet her."

"Meet her? Just the two of us? A friendly lunch? Mulling over your tastes in food and other pleasures?"

"Don't joke, Helen. It's too serious. No, I mean the three of us, in London, next week. We'll pick you up about eight. For dinner. I suppose you're still in the same little basement?"

Her garden flat was immediately eclipsed into a thinly disguised cellar, and her life, reflected through his eyes, was petty and dull.

"Hugo, it's rather a strange suggestion. If I were her, I might just resent it."

"Oh no, she doesn't mind. I just want your opinion, but all I've told her is that we're still great friends and I'd like her to meet you."

"And she agreed?"

"Of course."

Hugo's impatience was sharpening his tone. "Wednesday, then?"

It defeated her why she agreed, and then she despised herself for agreeing the moment the phone was down, all her lines of resistance collapsing a moment too soon. Not quite allowed, one more call to go.

"Helen? Darling, where have you been?"

So many darlings in one evening. How wonderful to be so loved, so finely cherished.

"I'm sorry, Adrian. I've been so busy . . ."

Adrian, romantic Edwardian, eighty-three if a day, grandfather to none, alone in his room, praying for visitors and playing one indulgent friend against another in ten minutes' diatribe each. No visitors, he said. Helen knew it was a lie. An old man's lie, and thus a forgivable one, like her father's sometimes, Kelly's sometimes, and Hugo's none of the time. Visit the day after tomorrow with the chocolates he liked. He had forgotten the visit of the day before.

"I should think so. I may forgive you if you do come, but I don't see why I should. I long to see you, darling. You're so selfish, so young. Don't be so busy."

No, don't. Stop being busy, stop listening. Stop having days trying to be cheerful and capable followed by quiet evenings entirely devoted to bombardment by phone. An ordeal to be renowned for kindness, or even worse, for sanity. What a joke; what a big joke, for any of them to imagine her as sane, wise or strong. How little they knew. It's as well, she thought, that I really love you all, or I'd be madder by now. Take the phone off the hook? Like to, but can't.

A slow crawl to bed, to sleep in that pretty salvage of divorce, threatened island of a woman who, obliged to live alone, actually enjoyed it most of the time. Not in the cold light of dawn, or when the nightmare woke her and she could have breathed again at the mere touching of his back. Not when the Hoover broke, the lights fused and the bookshelf disintegrated. Always the little things which carried such premonitions of defeat into her life. Tragedies were easier somehow, less irritating, fewer choices, and even these did not stand in the way of the frequent calm pleasure of living alone in a home she enjoyed as much as this.

Some suppressed intuition was telling her Geoffrey Bailey would find this space cluttered and dark, another instinct asking her why she should think any such thing. No more than a fear that he would not see it for what it was. Insecure but private, secluded from view by a garden which was Helen's pride, if not always her joy; hidden behind a huge wall which separated it from the school playground beyond. She loved the garden, battled with it ineptly, and if ever home by day even loved the midday screaming of playtime, repeated on the two evenings a week when other children used the same ground for football practice beneath floodlights which cast a flattering glow against her windows while muffled whistles and shouts broke the silence of the garden. No wonder the place had been the cheapest thing in a posh road, but Helen had known she would enjoy all those comforting untroublesome sounds of human life so safely removed from her own privacy by the wall, cheerful in the close distance. The rooms at the back were avenues of light from the south-facing garden; bright kitchen, bathroom, tiny study and bedroom beaming sunshine whenever sunshine appeared. On the street side were the two large rooms which were so dark by comparison she gave up the effort of pretending they were light, painted them in definite colors, strong fabrics at the windows, dark patterned cushions on a plump settee, pieces of old polished mahogany to catch the light of a winter fire. Hotch-potch rooms in the end, real fire, full of bits and pieces, too many patterns, dozens of pictures: a bit like a junk shop without the crowding, as full of detail as Geoffrey's was empty but as tidy as her office was not. Hundreds of books, but not as many as there would have been if she had not lent them out and forgotten who had them. She liked possessions as temporary friends: not like Hugo who adored them, carried them with him like an Indian prince with his rubies, always terrified of loss.

Loved Hugo, yes. She saw herself in the bathroom mirror, wondered briefly if he had ever missed her face, even once. Would not have missed him for worlds of worthier men, but wished she had not learned betrayal as thoroughly, or been left as empty. Recovery had worked a slow but sure passage over two long years.

Bed. Blissful friendship of the duvet and a tattered Maigret novel. Monsieur Maigret, psychic detective, would have understood Mrs. Cartwright, the bad, sad, Jaskowski, and the silly vanities of Bernard. Geoffrey Bailey would like this book if he had not liked it already: she would give it to him and he would say if he had read it already. No, he might fail to appreciate that. There was an intimacy in lending books which was open to misinterpretation. Better not. Policemen and lawyers should be allowed to breathe their different air, each uninfected by the other.

In a different home in a different street, Eileen Cartwright felt the liberty to examine her own reflection in the mirror after she had polished the bathroom. One day soon they would take her away, and they would not find her in a dirty house.

Even the bathroom was full of memories. A very ordinary bathroom, fitting scene for the demise of such an ordinary man, following in the wake of a sleepless night for Francis, sleepless only because she had been so wakeful, and, watchful as he was those days, he ignored the hints of pain. Intense pain as he stood poised before the mirror, razor in hand, understanding the taut band compressing his chest, only sufficient time to reach for the pills in the cabinet before his knees buckled and he began to slip methodically to the floor. Curled like a fetus, he scrabbled at the top of the small brown bottle which would not respond to the weak grip of his fingers, would not turn or lift. The voice he had used to call for his wife sounded deafening in his ears as he used the rest of his strength to smash the bottle against the side of the bath, watching the presence of blood with surprise, his smeared and slippy fingers refusing to grasp one sugar-coated pill of the dozen scattered on the floor. Surely he saw her bulky figure through the glass of the door, and saw her hand, more efficient than his own and free of blood, turning the handle.

"Eileen . . . help me. Please. Pills . . ."

Fingers as well as his limbs had lost control. The hand beckoning hers flapped in a feeble effeminate gesture. Dimly he watched her stoop, saw her rise again in the bathroom mirror, expanding to a height which seemed enormous before she bent toward him. Delirium, perhaps, but she seemed to be smiling, offering him a shard of glass. The glass of her spectacles was clean and shimmering: the glass of the shard was unmistakably brown from the bottle. The final memory was dimmer still. He had shaken his head, watched her rise larger than ever, receding away from his open mouth. Then there was her shadow again, growing distant on the far side of the glass door, closing it gently behind her as she retreated from his soundless scream.

Eileen gave the mirror one last wipe. He had been writing his book: that was where the love had gone. Then he had died. Not her fault. She had spent the day after the funeral cleaning her wares with untroubled conscience, just as she had spent the day after her father's sewing lace. Such restoration mended the world: her rooms stank of the cleansers which helped make her small fortune. White spirit and fine steel wool for removing the years of grime from small wooden pieces; white spirit for dipping jewelry and making *diamantè* gleam; white spirit for wine stains on lace. The scent of it hung about her, a sharp hospital smell, Eileen's own symptom of a clean, hygienic life.

CHAPTER FOUR

"Oh, I am not liking this: you know I am not liking this . . ."

"No, Stan, I can see you aren't. You sound foreign when you're upset. Calm down now, lad. It'll all be over soon."

Cool and weary sympathy from the jailer, not unkind in his reserve, keeping his voice low. Every one of them a lad. Stan here had been very excited. The valium had helped, but it probably wasn't enough. The prison doctor normally administered it with a shovel, but even he didn't seem to have taken account of Jaskowski's size. He was big, that was all, not fat or anything: quite a good-looking man in a way, like an extra-large bear, with his ugly neat hair sticking out over his wide forehead, with the very black eyebrows bushed above the piercing blue eyes giving him a kind of unconvincing fierceness. His hands were stubbily large and soft, the back of one more densely covered with dark hair than the other, and as they moved restlessly, looked fitter for gentle manual labor than savagery. Nothing sinister about Stanislaus: more like an out of place and gentle farmer, a man raised to raise children and build a roof over their heads. In one sense, Stan had done that, although lately the council had been providing the roof which was an improvement on some of the various other roofs he had known.

Perhaps not all of them, there being good memories, and bad.

"Stanislaus! Come back soon, and don't bring that damned magpie in the house . . ."

The first memory, a camp set in all those acres of parkland, where Mam and Dad had taken such pains with the coal-fired Nissen but which had been their first English family home. Heavily decorated, the tiny plot of land outside planted with flowers as well as cabbages, all in an effort to create the permanence of a home around a flimsy, draughty dwelling. Only later, after they had moved away to a proper house in London because of all the relatives and the work, could he see, because he was told so often, what they had done, those stubborn Polish refugees. Made a village out of necessity, insisted on thriving in it with rabbits and cats, pink-painted, jerry-built houses, gardens in the wilderness, and christening parties which lasted days. Only this son of theirs, when told of the hardships, and he was told all the time, did not see why he should spend the whole of this life being grateful. He had liked it, the camp and the empty green fields, and the pit where Dad worked. "Why do we have to leave?" he asked, and Mam had slapped him.

By the time Family Jaskowski was found in the metropolis, living far worse in a way, expecting better and laboring harder than a chain gang, they were achievers all, except the dreamer. "You'll never do nothing, Stanislaus: Why aren't you more like your brothers?" Familiar refrain, always in English, although Mam never spoke the English so good, and rarely at home. It added weight to the despairing scorn to say it in English. Why couldn't he be more like the eldest, Peter, the best of them, foreman clerk, fierce Catholic? You could take a problem to Peter: he was always ready with advice, and his wife even readier with tea and sympathy, moral spine to the family, steady earner. They had come a long way from the Nissen huts in the valley and the Red Cross boat from Poland, such a long, long way.

But for one cross taken away, said Mam, God gives us another. Gethsemane was an everlasting climb: you mustn't think you'd made it ever, since you never really did, even with the central heating, the church, the cousins, the new babies, as long as you had

Stanislaus sitting on your new chair in his silly shoes, waving his big daft hands, and telling you another wild get-rich-tomorrow scheme. Work's the answer, my boy . . . you'll find out. Build up gradual; don't you see your brothers, boy? They didn't expect something for nothing: they didn't chase girls, and spend everything on a stolen car. The police coming here, the shame of it. Go slowly, Stanislaus, and look for a nice girl like Peter's wife; she has nice cousins, you know. Ask her to introduce you after church. Stop saying you're going to have the biggest house in the world. You're nothing. Too lazy for anything. Oh, Peter, what do we do? Such a dreamer that boy. You speak to him. He won't listen to me. Says he has better things to do. What better?

Years passed in maneuvering Stanislaus into defeat. Marriage to the prettiest of his sister-in-law's cousins was only a preliminary to the most consistent love affair of his life, with his firstborn, Edward. For this son he worked harder, morning, noon and night, so that his family and the wife of his bosom breathed easier, until he was sacked for stealing booze from the warehouse. They nagged. He struck back, the real rebellion, cowing them all with his fury before he acquired the loan of that terrible shop full of old chairs he called antiques. God might forgive him, but Mam did not: first a thief, then a scavenger trading in leftovers, not even a colorful way to Hell.

But Stan believed, just as his small son Edward believed. "Better times are coming soon, my little man; want to come out in the van with me?" Edward leapt at the chance to roll round the markets with Dad, chunky boy and chunkier man, proud of one another. Having Ed made Stan swagger big, boastful and larger than life. Stan had always wanted to be brave, but only Ed could make him feel he ever was, and not even Ed could save him from the bailiff. By the time that man had come and gone, Stanislaus felt anything but brave with the weight on him of three children, the scolding world, and nothing else to show for forty years but dreams.

Indestructible nevertheless, since Stan would never lose the habit of dreaming, and when times were hard he simply changed the nature of the dreams. If not rich, he would be romantic. So what did he choose? Self-styled private detective: I ask you, said Mam, Stanislaus, detective, and him as clever as a dog? No joking, please, said Peter, afraid of another rage, let him be: I'll persuade him somehow. A tribute to Uncle Peter's interference, Stan becoming a hospital porter with the detecting stuff confined to a smaller part of his life, although not even Peter could persuade him to leave Edward out of it. How could he leave Ed at home when the boy wouldn't stay without him, even if it wasn't the boy who had the brain to suggest it?

"I love that boy better than the world, you know," Stan's confession as well as his boast. "Only there's times he worries me: too sharp, you know, he'll cut himself." It was a fear, although one he could hardly own. Ed ran rings around him and he knew it, but worse than that, seemed to have inherited all his father's fickleness with none of the inhibition; all mixed up with a terrible bitterness. Stan might have loved the idea of riches, but he could not hate the rich or anyone else for that matter, bowing to them rather than scowling. Not like Ed, the boy with the blank and unscrupulous face, whose pellucid eyes observed so much and revealed so little, while his nonchalant slouch hid the fists of rage curled inside the pockets of his fur-lined parka.

"Oh, I am not liking this."

Stanislaus had always been a man from whom sweat sprang with ease. Transferring to his cell, handcuffed on either side, he could be excused this moisture which steamed through the underarms of his winter suit and left him rancid with fear despite the meticulous washing and shaving he had been allowed. When he thought of Ed, the drops of perspiration rolled stinging into his eyes, horror for them both, incredulous that he had passed all tests so far, and never mentioned Ed to anyone who would like to know, even Mr. Bailey. Supposing they had found out about Ed knowing Mrs. Cartwright, about his awful, silent presence at those first two meetings? About him giving Ed the things from her car, or even worse, about Ed knowing so much of the rest of it, since he, Stanislaus Jaskowski, had been stupid enough to tell him?

Be quiet, Stanislaus. It is only you who talks too much. The boy will be quiet for his own good, but of all my badness, this is the worst badness. To have let him meet that woman, and to tell him about the money, the plan, looking for him to look up to me, you know? How could I be as stupid as that, push such risk on him? Only I needed to talk, and he said why not? It's only one rich woman, he said: it doesn't matter, they are all like vermin, you know? I didn't think so, but he thought so. He is not like me; he was not so afraid of Eileen. They could talk with their eyes, those two. She tells me, "Your son is a bright boy, I don't mind him listening." I think to myself, she likes him, and it's good for a boy to be liked by some woman with money, even if she is bad. But I shouldn't have; I shouldn't have taken him with me then, only I'm glad at least he didn't go with me to her home for the money, or with me on the killing trip. By then, I am frightened of them both, Ed, and Mrs. Cartwright, only I couldn't tell Mr. Bailey any of that. A grown man frightened of his son, you know? She will kill my others if I spend her money and do not do the work she wants, all of them except Ed. He thought I was a coward, "You won't dare to do it, Dad; you never dare do anything in the end." "Watch me," I said. "You will be proud of me and we will both be rich; of course I can do it."

Only make her go on like now, saying she does not even know me. If she does not open her mouth, and say, "That man had a son whom I knew also," then I can stand it all. If I knew that he would never again go close to her, I could stand anything, you know? I love the boy, but I don't know how bad he is, and it makes me want to pray. God help me until he is safe. I don't think he loves me any more. Father in Heaven, he is as hard as that wall. As long as she says she never knew me, she cannot say she knows my boy. My boy? My son? Oh God, he is like the devil, and I love him, my monster son.

Jaskowski, still muttering, irritated the jailer. "Try and keep quiet, mate, will you? Soon be over."

In the dock of the anonymous courtroom, the aching for the sight of a familiar face passed him, and he felt calmer after all in their absence. All out of his hands now, all of it, and all of them. He knew the outcome, hopeless enough to place him far beyond the reach of redemption, and there was huge relief in that. It was in part the retarded effects of the extra valium which so blurred his comprehension that he did not see Ed below his feet in the seat resting against the dock he occupied; might not have seen even without the drug slowing his mind and limbs to a quiet standstill.

"Guilty, or not guilty?" Of course it was guilty: it had to be guilty. Why did they ask? All he could say, everything he had been advised to say. He sat with his minders on either side, connected at the wrist, Siamese triplets, all of them large and empty, none of them showing a flicker of emotion. As the prosecutor recited the facts, it was difficult to know which of the three was the murderer.

". . . I did it, like I said to Mr. Bailey," he had told his solicitor. That simple statement should have been sufficient to explain it all, but obviously it was not. Nothing surprised him anymore. He had been too well briefed for surprise, although there was little enough they could do for him but advise him and prepare him, like a corpse for a funeral. "I'll give evidence against her. I want to do that; bad, bad woman," he had said when they explained he did not have any obligation to help the Law which destroyed him, "but I don't want my family involved." They had been kind. "But your family were not involved, were they?" "Of course not . . ." The vehemence of the protective reply surprised and relieved the lawyers. The man had a heart at least, and in the knowledge of how much better off he would be without it, they pitied him.

Stanislaus could see nothing of the judge apart from his wig, but this judge with hands tied to a mandatory sentence was far less terrifying than the next who would watch him giving evidence, weigh his words while Eileen watched from the dock. "I'm afraid you'll be on your own then," his solicitor had said. No more than now, perhaps: he would do it all the same. Bad woman. Stanislaus looked at the ceiling of the court, imagining it blue, finding that it removed his gaze from anyone in particular, tipped his head back and focused his eyes on the ceiling, he could escape. Back into the fields chasing rabbits, catching the hare, trying to teach his magpie to steal bright things in the hope that one day it would fetch him a diamond, and in all that time it provided no more than three treasured pieces of beer-bottle glass. Blue-gray sky of London, smelling the same smell he could smell on his own body now in the back of a borrowed car in a back street, straining his knees and thrusting between the legs of some moaning girl whose name he could not recall, not Maria; Maria had been too shy for that. Never again. He wished there had been many more women, and shuddered without real violence.

Details from the report of the pathologist intoned by counsel, poured over and into his head. So dry, these paragraphs on body fluids, the beaten flesh on the bare bones of the tale, repeated at length. Injury must be specified, justice seen to be done, and they must all know why his life was over to all intents and purposes worth remembering.

". . . I noted the following: ten horizontal stab wounds of different lengths on the front of the neck. These wounds were one-half to one and a half inches long, and appeared to go both backward and forward, indicating motions with a knife upward and downward, indiscriminately. The deepest cut had severed the left carotid artery. The left ear was split, there was one large, and several smaller cuts to the index fingers of both hands, considerable bruising to the knuckles, a semicircular tear, three inches in length, one-and-a-half inches above and behind the right ear. This extended down to the bone which was protruding, and was fractured. There were large splits in the left temporal region, with an underlying depression to the skull. There was extensive fracturing of the skull with numerous small pieces of bone dislodged, blackening around both eyes, bruising to the outer end of the left eye, where the outer rim of the eye socket was fractured. . . ."

Very dead indeed. Ach, poor lady. Stanislaus bowed his head in a moment of shameful pity. Poor, poor lady: rich lady, not vermin, like Ed had said. Just a body. If only it had smiled, or shooed him away like a farmer's wife with her hens, if only he had gone. Or stopped at the first blow. So much blood on the floor, more than he had ever seen.

He rose like a wooden puppet when the minders stood with him, everything glowing bright and blurred: the judge's wig a halo, his spectacles patches of light, his voice disembodied and carrying from afar, unimportant like the room itself and the cell to follow. Until he saw Ed, the bright head of him directly below his hands; touching distance without handcuffs. Then Stanislaus began to tremble, his mouth working silent words; not here boy, please not here, please, don't be such a fool, go home . . . The warders gave each other a fractional, experienced glance and braced themselves slightly as they noticed the signs of distress: don't bunk, or slump, Jaskowski.

Standing upright, it was they who were tall, attentive and respectful, gazing at his Lordship's sounding of formalized words as if their lives depended on it while the prisoner hung between them, his eyes fixed below, mouth twitching, large body bent in misery with the end of the best day-dream which had led him into this room for a jovial judge to say a mistake had been made and Mrs. Bernard had recovered; day-dreams he had known were false, but which guarded him from this foul reality and the sickening vision of all that blood seen through the eyes of his son. Dear God, what was the boy doing, was he mad? Why did he want to listen to this? Ed, son, why are you watching, risking this, testing me? Get out of here . . . get out, get out . . . Father stumbling away, pulled and pushed down gently, casting a desperate glance in Ed's direction, unable to see although he hesitated as long as he could. "Come on Stan, good lad," a polite, determined pull from the elder warder who spoke softly. "Come on, my lovely. All over now. Down you go." There was no wave, no smile of recognition, no effort of the head to show itself. He thought his heart would break, and his strangled voice would howl out grief and rage. Not for himself; for the boy who had not looked at him, the one he loved, his first born who would not take the chance of a last wave.

Until his father was out of sight, Ed was as still in his seat as the seat itself until the judge rose. No Maria. No Peter, or George, no elder statesmen, and no women. Simply Ed, unnaturally still, full of casual purpose, noticed in the end by more of those present than his father even in the subdued emotion which swept the emptying court. Helen felt sick with pity, a wrenching nausea of regret the way she always felt when she watched the sentence to long despair. "Poor bloody bastard," she told Bailey, averting eyes to avoid him seeing furious tears. "Poor man. Daft bastard."

"Just behind you, about seven feet away, there hovers that poor man's son," said Geoffrey evenly. "The only one of the whole clan to arrive." Helen turned and saw the boy fastening his cheap anorak, his eyes locked on hers in a long and innocent stare which somehow lacked the guileless gaze of youth. Involuntarily, she smiled. The smile was not returned. Silly, she thought as she turned away, why the hell should he smile at me?

"Hope that lad doesn't want to see his father," said Bailey uneasily, pity ill at ease with duty.

"Would it help if he did? He has to sign that statement. According to my orders, Mrs. Cartwright can't be arrested without it. Might seeing his son make him more amenable?" Even pity gave way to practical duty. Bailey hesitated. "No. It wouldn't help. Don't ask me why, but it wouldn't. Stanislaus clams up when he's mentioned. But if he wants a quick word with Father before the next prison visit, I shan't be able to refuse unless I've primed the jailer. Damn. He's asking counsel."

"Why do you think so? I know he's distressed; he seemed fine, then looked awful, but will it make any difference if he sees his son?"

"Yes." He smiled briefly. "The psychic detective says yes. Excuse me, but I'm not going to give it the benefit of doubt. I'll tell the jailer to refuse." With those words he moved, and disappeared beyond the baize door to the underground cells. Out of the corner of one pale eye, Ed watched him go while his ears took in the useless sympathy of his father's representatives, and having seen, he did not trouble them with his request.

Helen regrouped the papers listlessly, still full of the sick, sad feel, alone at the bench while Carey, prosecution counsel, talked to the judge's clerk and his junior talked to the defense junior in the general kind of club talk which preceded and followed almost any trial, even one as brief and predetermined as this. Tying the tape around one volume of statements, thinking ahead to the rest of the day in a cloud of depression, she was suddenly aware of two hands on the bench before her, young, male hands which were broad and powerful. Raising her head, the eyes still reflecting the tears she would never shed in the interests of sense, she found again the gaze of Ed Jaskowski.

"I just wanted to ask," he said politely, "when will Mrs. Cartwright be arrested?"

Startled, she replied with the same grave politeness, sorrow for him uppermost, sandwiched with surprise, underlined with dislike of the translucent skin and shining helmet of hair. The boy was so unlike his parent.

"That depends on your father, to some extent," she said carefully, still tying the bundle. "But I wouldn't be surprised if it was later today, or tomorrow. Maybe a few days. I can't say with any certainty, except that it will happen. Doesn't sound very helpful; I'm sorry."

"Thank you. As long as we know."

Embarrassment lowered her eyes. In the second it took for her to control her face and look up again to his, there was no need for anything more than relief. Ed was swifter of foot than his father, faster out of court than a sprinter.

"Damn the man."

They were grouped in the bar, scene of post-mortems. Crown prosecutors, dewigged barristers called to the bar in search of refreshment, a bad pun, often made but resisted in this gloomy company.

"Damn the man." John Carey, QC, took a sip from a murky half-pint. "He said he'd sign a written witness statement. Now he won't. Tomorrow, he says. Can't arrest that woman without it, the Director says. Worried by the number of cocked up prosecutions there have been recently, no doubt. Doesn't do to have another. My paymasters and yours, eh, Miss West? Can't fall foul of my orders. But what did you do to him, Superintendent?"

"Patted his shoulder. Patted his other shoulder. Let him cry a bit, as well he might. Asked him to sign the statement he'd been prepared to sign weeks ago, and he said, 'I don't think so, I am not liking this, you know?' I said, neither am I, and patted both his shoulders again, and asked again. Same result. Poor bastard. I didn't persist."

"Superintendent; you should have persisted. What's wrong with you? Losing your touch? You surely could have made him, guided the faint hand, so to speak. Eh, Miss West? Leant on him: I don't mean oppression, of course, well you know what I mean. Leaned on him. Come on a bit stronger. The firm hand of the law. All that."

"He was extremely distressed," said Helen defensively.

"Who? The Superintendent? Ho, ho." Carey laughed like an obscenely jolly comic at a funeral, deliberately obtuse. "He's a policeman, my dear Miss West. Policemen don't get upset. What a thought."

Helen could feel Bailey's hackles rise, and wondered, not for the first time, how a man as talented on his feet as Carey undoubtedly was, could be so insensitive socially, and she prayed Bailey would keep the silence he was obviously going to break.

"With respect," Bailey's courtesy was almost insolent, "I've never harassed a prisoner, and I'm not starting now. Not even a murderer. The man was distraught, beside himself with misery. I wish they wouldn't stuff the Category A's with tranquilizers, though God knows, he probably needed it, but it was more than that. You can't lean on a man who's just been put away for life and expect him to do anything but break. What am I supposed to do, with respect? Armlock for one hand, pen for the other, sign here? I haven't got the bottle. Or the inclination. He was beyond persuasion. I was sorry for him."

Carey looked uncomfortable, unused to being crossed. "But he's a killer, Superintendent."

"Yes. So he is. What does that have to do with it?"

There was a silence. The junior barrister, scarcely junior in years to his leader, smiled uncertainly at Helen. Helen sneaked a glance at Bailey, and they all took another awkward, simultaneous sip of their drinks.

"What do you think, Miss West?", Carey rumbled, anxious to restore a disturbed status quo and re-establish his team of minions in their proper places.

"I applaud Mr. Bailey. Jaskowski, we hope, will sign and tell us he's still willing to give evidence, and for now, it doesn't matter if it isn't today, although it would have been far preferable to arrest her at once. She seems to have decided against running away, and that was always the greatest fear. She'll stick it out. No real harm done in letting Jaskowski recover for a time. The powers of justice have just sent him away for thirty-three years. Why should he feel cooperative, even if he deserves it? What did we expect?"

"He says," Geoffrey added, "that he wants to know that his wife and family are safe. Not the eldest son; he's somehow not worried about him since he saw him, just the other two boys and the baby daughter."

"Where are they?"

"With her mother, the daughter and wife, that is. The three sons are all with Peter, Jaskowski's brother, and his wife. They'll redistribute themselves in time. Maria doesn't seem to care about keeping them together. The fight's gone out of the woman, which isn't entirely surprising. The flat's been burgled: they're like a crowd of vultures on the Hackington Estate. She doesn't have many choices."

"Did you tell Stanislaus where they were?"

"Yes." Geoffrey was scratching his brow, the irritation past. "He said, as he always says, I trust you Mr. Bailey. You go and see for yourself they're okay, and come and tell me, I believe you. I sign statement tomorrow. So I'll do as he asks. When I've finished this drink."

"Good man, Superintendent." Carey's heartiness in the face of unpleasant tasks delegated to others itched at Helen's scalp. She felt a familiar frustration at being so removed from the disturbing chores which were Bailey's, all in the province of the policeman, not the inadequate lawyer. How ignorant they were in comparison, how easy their role, shifting paper like ciphers, carried on the back of misery.

"It's all right," he spoke in her direction, interpreting the look of concern with his usual unnerving accuracy and a faint smile. "It isn't so bad. They don't like me much, but they won't be bad and if I tell Maria Jaskowski these days that her husband's concerned about her, she'll probably spit in my eye. She feels," he turned delicately to Carey, "that her husband has let her down. Failed to maintain standards."

"I can see her point."

Another, less awkward silence. One drink usually enough on such occasions; the conversation, stilted by their various preoccupations, drawn to a natural close.

"Must be off," said Carey, not reluctant to end the gathering. "You'll telephone Miss West with any news, I take it?"

"My pleasure, sir."

Carey liked the roles being carefully re-established with one word of respect. A grin in Helen's direction, and they all parted like children at the end of a lesson.

"Ed, what did Dad look like? Did he look different?"

"Shut up, I'm trying to sleep."

"No, tell me please."

"He looked fine. A bit in the dumps, but all right. What do you think he looked like? Same as normal. Now shut up. You can write him a letter."

"Will he be able to write back?"

"Yes." Ed's eyes closed.

"Ed? I don't like it here. I don't think Uncle Peter likes me."

"Don't be such a mug. He doesn't like any of us. Who told you you were going to be liked? It's a place to live, isn't it?"

"Ed? Dad, he didn't really kill anyone, did he? He wouldn't."

"Yes he did, idiot. But it wasn't such a bad thing to do."

"Why, Ed? Why wasn't it? Uncle Peter says it's very bad. So does the priest, he says. Shall I tell you something? The kids at school, not the ones you stopped, other ones, they still kick me because of Dad, but sometimes the teachers stop them, when they see, not so much now. Perhaps they'll stop now he's gone to prison. You're lucky not to have to go to school, Ed. No one hits you. Can I stop going to school, Ed?"

"Oh, for Chrissakes shut up."

There was an obedient, restless silence from Peter's bed.

"Ed? Where were you tonight? You were very late."

"Mind your own business. I was busy. Now, for the last time, shut up, will you. Talk in the morning. I'm asleep. I'm not listening to you anymore, so shut it."

"Ed?"

Silence. Deep, regular breathing. Ed could always sleep like a cat, stretch his limbs, find his threshold of comfort, and sleep through a storm. Deep in the darkness of his borrowed bed, Peter remembered he had forgotten his prayers, had even forgotten to ask Jesus to bless Dad, and save him from hell. He would go to hell himself. He would have liked to have asked Mam and Grandma if he would go to hell, just for that. Perhaps he could get out of bed and say them now: he wouldn't mind being cold, but Ed might be woken, and that would make Ed angry. As angry as Jesus and Uncle Peter, not a risk he could take. No one could say, no one would say, they were all like this, so angry, so frightened, while he was simply frightened. Why couldn't he stay with Mam? He'd help her, except that she was angry too.

Ed was snoring. Peter stuffed the sheet into his mouth. Bad enough to be a baby, more like little Stan, his brother, or Katy: forgiveness was not there for the asking should he act like one. Gulping into the detergent flavor of the sheet, head buried face down in pillow, Peter tried hard to think of one single good thing for the next day. A letter, a comic, a game, a race? From whom, with whom? Not little Stanislaus, snugly asleep with his favorite cousin next door, as complete as a pair of twins. Not Mam, or Uncle Peter, or Auntie Mary, who always complained about money. Perhaps Ed. At least there was Ed some of the time, but not much of the time.

No good pretending he wasn't crying, or trying to think he was winning, or that Ed would spend much time answering his questions when Ed had business of his own, just like everyone else. The sheet was up his nose, into his eyes, into his throat, muffling sounds of hopelessness. If I breathe, Ed, I'll wake you; please wake up without asking, please. One small hand out of the bedclothes touched Ed's shoulder in a single, tentative touch. Ed turned in his sleep, one massive heave toward the wall and the fingers shot back, electrocuted. He should have known by now, to keep his hands still, firmly held over his mouth, his eyes, and his ears, like the three monkeys.

* * *

Helen West had walked from Old Bailey to the Angel, looking for the market to paint colors on black depression. Crowding into her mind, there were the sad portraits; the man Jaskowski, the children, the wife, all those smaller and larger victims she would never meet apart from the unnerving boy. In the whole spectrum of things, there seemed no doubt who suffered most for the ambitions of Mrs. Cartwright. Sylvia Bernard was dead: no chance for her to mend her life, but her husband was left with his, however diminished. Helen disliked the sound of Bernard, and half-way home she had been struck by the worst of many morbid reflections when she remembered that he had not even asked for the corpse. Normal families clamored to bury their dead, but Bernard was content to leave his kith in refrigerated silence until told he could do otherwise and she could not respect him for that.

Murder was on her mind, visions of twisted attitudes and remaindered lives, fatal if she were ever to function for the preparation of this trial, the next trial, or the others after that. Jaskowski first, then Bernard, then Cartwright: pity and anger flourishing under her skin like a boil, telling her, as if she needed reminding, that she was not immune after all. Then there was the guilt, much more than usual. For being free and healthy, guilty for feeling guilty, and guiltier in the knowledge of the waste of it as she stood by a shop, gazing in with a fixed stare until she laughed at her own intense reflection, saved by looking ridiculous.

She should buy something, the best antidote to depression, something beautiful, and complete in itself, and designed to prove life exists to be preserved. Preferably a chunk of a thing with no practical purpose, but needing a good home. Suddenly purposeful, Helen retraced her steps, hazarded life in a sprint across the converging roads of the Angel junction, and entered the lane of Camden Passage.

There, dawdling before pictures in one window, brass fire irons in the next, she forgot Stanislaus Jaskowski for minutes at a time, drowned the over-hot courtroom of Old Bailey in the coolness of interiors glowing with extravagance. Friday stalls meant painted jugs and fifties' brooches, gramophones, discarded scarves, Victorian dolls, Edwardian prams and slides for magic lantern shows. Pictureless frames and unframed prints, copper planters and wooden boxes, silver spoons and glinting china; piano stools in faded velvet, spring sun on dusty, rainbow colors. And one old chair-back without the chair, saved for embroidery which glowed dirty and undestroyed from a battered gilt framework. There it was, the object to cure the ill, no useful purpose whatever, crying out for rescue from its own disgrace. A large piece of embroidery, designed to decorate a chair for a rich table, hours of work to be hidden behind a back. The patriarch who carved his meat while leaning from it had perished now with the legs and seat of his possession, leaving only a gold-mounted picture, vulgar in its own time, mellowed by age. Helen was entranced.

In the center of the embroidered picture were two women, back to back on either side of an apple tree. The full skirts touched; flowered hats carried blossom and each held the same posy as they turned their heads toward each other in conspiracy. One face smiled a secret, the posy held as if to shield the words: the other face showed mock alarm, as if the creator had stitched household scandals into her rich woolen threads, enjoying the last laugh at her lord and master's expense.

"How much?" Helen asked.

A bad day at the stall, feet cold, mind dull, had made business poor and his manners worse. "Thirty pounds," he said, cheeky with indifference, too tired for all the usual chat and makeshift history, beyond the point of wondering if he had been drunk when buying all this stock for a fiver a time, wishing he were drunk in the selling. A poor bargainer, she gazed in pretense at hesitation, tempting the man to speak in lower figures because of her silence, while he shuffled hopefully against his will, and Helen stayed bent toward the embroidery.

"I'll give you twenty-five."

She straightened, as if pushed between the blades of her shoulders by the gruff voice behind, looked questioningly at the man, who shifted further into his canvas seat and scowled.

"The lady's first, Mrs. Cartwright. Not seen you for ages. Thought we was too pricey for you up here. Not your kind of thing anyway, but there you go."

Helen froze, reluctant to turn, but having to look round into those stone black eyes. Recognizing the woman herself, she was sure that Mrs. Cartwright knew her just as surely from one brief encounter outside the Magistrates' Court a month before in that subdued, but definite crossing of swords. She spun back quickly, not quickly enough to hide alarm and repugnance.

"I'll take the chairback, please," Helen said.

"I'll give you forty," said Mrs. Cartwright solidly.

Stallholder frowned, irritation apparent in the hands which rearranged the bric-a-brac within reach. Some profit assured, the rest forgotten in a surge of dislike.

"This ain't no auction, Mrs. C. Lady was here first like I said, and I give her a price. Will that be cash?"

"Yes."

"Sorry Mrs. C. You can't win 'em all."

Helen reached for her purse and the clean notes from the cash-machine which should have been spent on groceries, all pleasure suspended in wanting to escape the force of Eileen Cartwright's eyes. She handed over the money, then turned with sudden resolve.

"Look, you can have it if you really want it."

The woman smiled, curving her wide, thin mouth in a brief spasm, pretending amazement.

"No thanks. What made you think I wanted it?" Moving off abruptly as before into her ordinary unhurried step, still holding the handbag as a shield; plodding away, obscurely satisfied by the conclusion of some battle she knew she had won. There was triumph in the stride.

"Take no notice, missus. Funny woman, that. Rich one an' all. Does funny things. Knows her stuff. If she was ready to pay forty for it, you've got a bargain." Happy at the upturn in trade, thirty pounds in his pocket, warmer by the second.

"Thanks. You were very fair about it."

"Make no difference really, does it? What can I do with a tenner? And a customer who wouldn't come back?"

"I'll come back."

"Good on you, girl, you see you do. Want it wrapped? Only I got no paper . . ."

The gilt chair-back with its secret-sharing ladies was surprisingly heavy. So was the effect of brushing shoulders with a manipulator under threat of imminent arrest for murder, who dared to march her way around her own domain as if nothing could ever curtail her liberty. There had been too many close encounters for one day. Thin and sharp, the hackles of alarm grew as Helen walked home, one eye behind her, one arm cradling a new, already spoiled treasure. She did not know if Mrs. Cartwright was arrogant, brave, or possessed of secret knowledge, but there was something granting that macabre confidence which drained Helen's own and made her want to run.

Beyond the Passage, turning away from Helen's progress to follow Mrs. Cartwright exactly as he had been directed, Ryan was amused. Poor Miss West. You could have knocked her down with a feather. Quite accidental really, but he doubted if his Superintendent would see the joke. Fancy them two shopping in the same place, for such rubbish. There never was any accounting for taste. Ryan's tastes were different. Love made the world go round, not things, although he had to admit, having the odd new thing helped. Annie liked the new car: so did his wife. Annie liked his new suit, but his wife did not. Such was life, very puzzling when he thought about it. But there were duller ways of spending an afternoon than following a woman, even if she was Eileen Cartwright. As for the evening, he would make sure it was an improvement. He trudged up the street behind her, thinking ahead, watching.

CHAPTER FIVE

Weeks after the end of Eileen's freedom, Michael Bernard came to believe in his own, and woke with the hope that the first day of summer would be an improvement on any which had preceded it since the death of his wife. He called it death now, rather than murder. Four months on, and he could almost attempt to think of her without nausea and disbelief rising in his throat as if his neck were held in a claw. The sickness persisted although the actual discovery of Sylvia's remains had been cool in comparison with the horror evoked in reviewing it. Despite that, and only in the security of his own bed, Bernard forced himself to consult the memory for accuracy, before filing it for future use, untarnished by more time. He did this to remind himself he was a disciplined man.

Arriving home after a day frustrated by canceled appointments, he had looked forward to the comfort of her presence. Two gins, a few light-hearted complaints with which she would sympathize in that absent way of hers. "Really, dear, you shouldn't let them treat you like that . . . ," music to his ears, even if the chronicle of her domestic triumphs and disasters which would follow was not. Scant attention would do for these and in any event he would have been amused if the saga of her afternoon included third-hand scandal about some marriage of their acquaintance learned over coffee or in the hairdresser. The evening promised less excitement than pleasure, comfort, predictable order, the apotheosis of an untroubled married life which ran on well-oiled wheels as long as she was not in her ambitious phase; not wanting another house or social circle where the accents were ever more clipped, the entertaining expensive, the women effusive and the holidays prohibitive. There dwelt a streak of meanness in Bernard. Children might have been cheaper after all.

The front door was locked. Perhaps she had slipped out as she often did in search of some last minute goody from the delicatessen, and he was pleased to notice she was beginning to recognize the risk of burglary. This was the last, satisfied thought before entering his elegant home where each observation and each step to follow mounted to a climax of appalling conclusions, beginning with the sight of his wife's feet facing him, her head inside the door of the downstairs washroom. (In pink, this one, with striped blind and matching paper, a bit overpowering he found.) There had been blood: he thought she might have fallen.

"Are you all right, Sylvia? What have you done?"

No light in the hallway, and the angle of body with hidden head made it difficult to reach for the switch in the washroom without planting his feet on either side of her torso into the increasingly obvious sticky fluid. A distinct smell rose from her, but no sound. In the dimness he could see her outline oddly slumped and twisted without any repose, a badly arranged doll placed on display by an unsympathetic hand. Bernard retreated slowly, conscious only of the slight gleam of the blood as sinister as her stillness. That, and the startling, mottled white of her half-exposed bra, glowing obscenely.

His hand was steady as he phoned for the ambulance, not the police since the fact of death did not occur to him at once. She had been alive in the morning, irritatingly so, with her early offerings of warm croissants, and it followed she was alive now. Standing away from her and waiting in the kitchen for the ambulance, he noticed the dirty cups and the crumbs on the wooden table, and from then on, he might have timed her demise precisely. He could have saved pathologists their trouble as soon as he saw this debris. Sylvia was so fastidious she never left dishes longer than minutes: they irritated her soul.

In the kitchen, and before the onset of panic, Bernard blamed himself for his failure to touch her but could not cure it. In furtive glances around the door, he could see the offending feet sticking forward, ready to strike out and kick him, the disgust and cowardice fueled by the realization of not knowing what to do. Better wait as he did wait, sitting on a kitchen stool biting his thumb at the end of each impatient circling of the room. Sirens: a blind dash to the front door, leaping over the legs to find the large men beyond, comfortably competent and uniformed. One firmer hand switched on the light in the hall: he and Bernard approached Sylvia, and Bernard saw the indescribable mess of her face, beaten features, holed skull, matted hair, and pathetic, pleading hands. Retching and moaning, he had stumbled back toward the refuge of the sink. The ambulanceman phoned for the police, and Michael knew then she was dead.

What wounded him most was, first, the thought of his own miserable performance, and next, all the other indignities which followed. He was not so insensitive as to feel no disgrace for his feebleness in refusing to touch her death before the authorities did so: rejecting that body he could still embrace with passion, reacting to the sight with none of their disciplined reserve, being sick like a baby instead. For all this weakness, he had apologized incoherently, but the shame burned fiercely even before it was reinforced by the poker-faced men whose eyes and voices spoke louder suspicion in asking why he had not called them himself.

"I didn't realize she was badly hurt, so dead, I mean . . ."

"Oh no, sir, I don't expect you did."

Tantamount to violent rape, this leveling treatment, beginning with the assumption of guilt, although it took less than twelve hours in his case before the finger of the dead wife wavered. Meantime routine enquiries included the stripping of his house, removal of head hair, nail clippings, items of clothing, fingerprints, and a dozen subtler insults. Bad enough with an easy conscience, intolerable without, as officers of the law neatly removed his dignity layer by layer, reducing him to nothing, without a friend for comfort. Even *in extremis* he had known of none who could endure such exposure or trust; was forced to conclude how shallow was his acquaintance, how tenuous his links with his own kind.

"Did your wife have any enemies, Mr. Bernard?"

The police detective, as long and thin as a spear, his pointed questions hidden in a cloak of innocence. The same Mr. Bailey who made him talk so fast, digested all his gabbling into information by the end of the night and day following, never stopped him or kept him to the point: found more of his life than any living soul, and although desperate to be liked, Bernard would never forgive him for it.

"Enemies? No. Why should she? She was . . . harmless." It sounded like an insult. "A popular woman, plenty of friends."

Defensive, as if to say, we might have appeared strange, but we are not, an infantile protest looking for good opinion. "At least," his lawyer's exactitude came to his aid, "if she had enemies, I do not know of them."

He knew nothing of Sylvia's life, less of her soul, and the ignorance added to the guilt.

"And her daily routine?"

Again, ignorance: nothing more than her reports, and he no longer trusted the reliability of those. "So you don't really know," Bailey had said, patiently repetitive, "about her daily life?" No, when he came to think of it, he did not.

Or her friends, apart from the sad conclusion that she had easily as few as himself. For all her industry, he had never seen how shallow was her existence, how superficial. Not the word he dared use, although it was the term in Bailey's mind.

"We were devoted to each other," he told Bailey half-way through the night, satisfying himself with this explanation. By then they were on more than nodding and smiling terms and Bernard's humiliation was advanced by the knowledge that the Superintendent did not believe a word of it.

"Have you any enemies, Mr. Bernard?"

Easier covering his own tracks rather than obscuring the trail of conclusions left by his wife. No, none he was aware of. Yes, his practice was mainly conveyancing and probate; not the kind of area where passions ran high enough to turn on murderous lines, although it was true that clients could become unreasonable in their expectations, absurdly disappointed in results. Had he any objection if they examined his office? Well, yes. There was Michael's face registering fear in every line, the specter of his conscience looming large, dressed in Mrs. Cartwright's clothing, ready to challenge him.

Since the very beginning of the questioning several hours before, there had flashed upon his inner eye so malevolent a vision of that lady that he had spoken yards of words to avoid speaking of her, knowing, as he had known when the ambulanceman had blocked him from the view of death, that she had been lingering there, somewhere in the background, a malicious shadow full of mute insistence on his silence. Deciding to disobey was Bernard's decision taken under Bailey's hypnosis, telling more than he needed to tell, not complete by any means, still too much.

All over now. A feeling of safety intervened to dull the memory of the shame. Silly fool to have held his breath so long while the bloodstained carpet was replaced and Eileen unfussily arrested, all this time postponing life and grief, no thinking of poor Sylvia submerged in the tide of her own death, pushing at his own survival. That large young detective coming to his door, "S'all right, sir. Thought I'd let you know, we got Mrs. C inside," grinning in triumph, expecting him to be pleased, which he was, but only now. Rising to make coffee far superior to Sylvia's, Bernard tried to feel the luxury of grief, missed her comforting presence, admired the reverie of his own sadness. Then he opened the post and forgot her again.

Brown window-envelopes usually signified nondescript contents and Sylvia had always dealt with them, pouncing on all the mail in the endless hope that it might contain a surprise, but any bill, however large, would have been preferable to this uncompromising order to attend the trial of *R.* v. *Cartwright,* Central Criminal Court, on a date to be fixed. Michael's legal expertise was not in such arenas, but he knew the witness order for what it was, a prescription for humiliation, an invitation to public cross-examination of his life. He had hoped his bald and guarded statement of facts which said nothing specific to influence guilt would be agreed, simply presented along with other innocuous evidence of plan-drawers and body-removers. Eileen's choice of revenge, complete with her hallmark: she had drawn blood, required more. If not your heart and soul, my dear, I'll have your reputation, and God in heaven, she had the means.

Bernard suffered sharp memories of cozy conversations with a witch.

"My wife doesn't understand business," he had told Eileen. "Refreshing to discuss things with a woman, you know. A woman who knows the terminology, as well as the art." In essence, it was true, with any woman who adored him; even a woman as plain as this was always a mild stimulant. Michael did indeed talk frankly of business. "All this is in confidence, Eileen, you know, you won't discuss it with anyone, of course." Heavy lunches and amusing tales, clients' secrets he had no business revealing, details of his own practices which unforgiving jurymen could only consider, well, sharp; certainly not blunt in the sense of honest. A few deals on property where he had taken advantage of his knowledge of an impending death and secured the pickings of death for the benefit of himself rather than the beneficiaries; a kind of insider trading in the estate of the deceased. Harmless, of course, only done where there was plenty to spare, not actually robbing anyone in particular, you understand. Eileen, scavanger of old lace and treasures from those who were indiscriminate through terminal poverty, understood the syndrome very well. Following hearses, she had said; and they had laughed about it.

Slumped at his breakfast table in the ruins of the day, Bernard would have given his heaven and earth to remove Eileen as she had removed Sylvia, began to understand the anatomy of hatred although he did not yet seek Eileen's remedies. Only the desire to kill was appreciated rather than the practice. He stood and threw the coffee cup against the wall with every ounce of strength, watched the stains appearing on the wood and the liquid dribbling slowly. The deafening crash of Sylvia's favorite china freed him for several panting seconds. But he was Sylvia's husband, and Sylvia's habits died harder. He bent, picked up the pieces and wiped the mess thoroughly and mechanically.

But as soon as he recovered, there was more. As he left his house he saw it on the branches of the shrub which shielded the entrance, one brightly colored glove, Sylvia's emerald leather glove, matching the emerald coat she had paraded for his approval the autumn before. Her winter glove blooming in spring, caught among the fresher leaves like a garish blossom. The shattered day collapsed around him, and Bernard, never a stout party, fell to earth with it.

In the general regime of Helen's life, nothing changed. Her phone was engaged every time Bailey rang, day and evening. On first acquaintance it had crossed his mind that she was busy to hide a vacuum: now he recognized another of the same breed whose acquaintances, colleagues, masters and servants would find the weak link of conscience. When finally they spoke, she sounded harassed, but to his relief the pleasure in the tone was unmistakable.

"Geoffrey! A sane voice from the wilderness. Don't tell me not to rejoice, I can't bear it. You're going to saddle me with bad news. The witnesses have emigrated, Ryan has foot-and-mouth, Mrs. Cartwright has mown down fifty warders with her submachine gun. I know it."

He laughed. "Well, perhaps the celebration Ryan staged when we finally arrested her was worth it."

She sighed, relieved. "Even you wouldn't be laughing if the news was that bad. I breathe again. What's up? Sad Jaskowski been any more trouble? Another change of heart?"

"No. Silence from that end. It isn't him I want to discuss. Something's been happening with Bernard. He asked to see me. I thought I'd better report the result."

"Will it take long?"

"Longer than a phone call, I'm afraid."

"Damn. I'm up to the eyes, court tomorrow. Look, do you mind after office hours."

"As long as I can drink as well as talk. No, of course not."

"It won't take that long. Any chance you could come to my flat about six-thirty? I'd say here, but I've got to be home to check up on my delinquent odd-job-man before he leaves. His work isn't guaranteed for longer than twenty minutes and it's easier to talk without the phone going all the time. If you don't mind, that is?"

"Fine. Yes, I know where it is."

Helen did not wonder how he knew as she replaced the phone, immediately half regretting the arrangement. A close degree of social contact with police officers was discouraged, even specified in the Service handbook, and while she had never found the rule difficult to follow, despite the open friendliness she gave and received, it was still a reservation to be held in the mind, a direction she regarded as inherently sensible. There was enough of the corruption of camaraderie in the ranks already; no point in adding to it. Policemen breathed a different air, not bad, or poisonous, or tainted, but different. Snobbery of a kind, she supposed, working both ways, but not as simple, more a question of mutually incompatible assumptions. Lawyers carried the mark of Cain, thought in riddles, believed in concepts, lived by analysis of the written word. Free of this, most policemen were freer of doubt or dogma, no time for thinking without specific purpose, believed in simple, physical solutions, and never looked comfortable in suits. For all the hours of conversation which she had enjoyed and endured while propping up cell corridors, jokes and stories which dulled neither affection nor respect for the breed, Helen always imagined closer personal contact could only be made through smoked glass revealing a stranger on the other side, prevented from touch. She had never tried, regarded the gap as one which could be spanned but never crossed: no need to question it. Life worked better when she did not.

On the other hand, never since the demise of marriage into divorce had her buried self responded with such awkwardness as it did now, with the pleasurable shyness at the thought of Geoffrey Bailey, which was not completely submerged in this innocent enjoyment of his company. She had not flexed the muscles of flirtation in a long time and did not intend to now, but the rules, spoken and otherwise, bothered her until she admitted they did. Then Helen thought of where obedience to conventions had left her and did not like that either. Time to engineer her own code, and having reached her conclusion, Helen felt secure enough to regard Bailey's businesslike visit with more than workmanlike pleasure.

Hurrying home, it was the kind of unprofessional anticipation which made her hope the flat had survived the onslaught of Mr. Ruparell, very odd-job-man indeed. The only alcoholic Pakistani of her large acquaintance; no task too great for perfection on a sober day, and none too small for destruction on the others. Mr. Ruparell, who was kind, funny and looked like a pickled walnut, had learned his carpentry from an Irishman and with it a certain fusion of habits, cultures and melancholy, so that employing him to make shelves and mend cupboards was always a risk worthwhile only on a balance heavily weighted by affection. Simply a question of preferring to pay him rather than anyone else who did not drink the profits within hours. On the one day when she would have liked to make a more efficient impression, the balance had not tipped in Rupe's favor. She knew it as soon as she entered the flat and heard him singing.

By the time Bailey arrived, Helen had taken the line of least resistance, paid Ruparell, whose singing had been the usual prelude to apologetic crying, told him, Never mind, Rupe, finish it another time. Look after yourself, Rupe, won't you? and was standing in front of sixteen crooked shelves marveling at his achievement. The kitchen cupboards had been the perfect work of the morning, that far off time in Rupe's life when the bottle had been full. The shelves represented the other end of the day. So did the plaster dust and woodshavings littering the carpet, footprinted to and from the direction of the source of refreshment.

"How," said Geoffrey in amazement, "did a carpenter manage to do that?"

"He drinks a bit sometimes," said Helen defensively.

"That explains a lot," said Bailey without a hint of criticism, "and he's left his tools. Here, I'll do them again."

"No, no, you mustn't."

"Why not? I'll talk as I work."

Coat and jacket discarded with actions swifter than promises. Helen poured two glasses of wine, listened and watched from her mahogany table, surprised into a complete and passive contentment while interruptions from the electric drill scarcely halted the flow of his story. Bernard had had a fit of doubt, did not want to give evidence; had told him that Mrs. Cartwright "knew too much about his work," and could embarrass him. That was not all: that did not matter for the end result of a proper conviction for murder, even though it would matter to Bernard, but then there was the question of the glove, a nasty, green practical joke, as if to underline a point, but what point, and who put it there?

"But Mrs. C's in prison. Who else would put it there?"

"I don't know. I'm always saying I don't know," Geoffrey answered, fitting another shelf straight and neat into its place. "A friend or neighbor, who had found it, didn't want to volunteer it, couldn't throw it away, who didn't want to speak to Bernard? Houses with murders are leprous: people leave them alone, don't like to have the possession of souvenirs like a glove left in a car. Put it on a bush? I don't know. I just don't know. But if someone was getting at him, they did well."

"No one could have known that he would find the glove on the same day as he received the witness order."

"No. But anyone with a brain could make a phone call and find out when the trial is due. Why? His evidence isn't crucial; discrediting him isn't crucial either. More like blackmail for another purpose, a softening up for something else. If it was supposed to influence the trial, this business with the glove, whoever it was would be better off tackling more important witnesses. Like the girl who took in Jaskowski's petrol-soaked money, for instance. I've checked them all. No approaches, nothing nasty at all. And I've checked with Jaskowski's family. Usual ecstatic response, but they say they've never heard of a glove."

"Do you prefer the first explanation, the nervous friend returning unwanted reminder?"

He hesitated. "It's as likely as any." The drill whirred. "But I have an open mind. Openly uneasy."

Helen was silent, oddly unconcerned at this development of a case which continued to disturb her so profoundly. She could not describe the concern, but could contain it as long as Bailey was there, tall and angular, creating space for precious books with competent speed. Engrossed in a task he enjoyed and pleased to display the competence, he knew a similar ease. When hands were busy nothing was as important as it might have seemed.

"My father was a carpenter," he volunteered, information following nothing, "about as successful as your Mr. Ruparell. For similar reasons. When I became a policeman, he was very disappointed in me."

"Not proud?"

"No. Never that."

"Were you ever expected to be academic?"

"No. Not part of their idea. Wish it had been. The Commissioner did that for me. Time off for a sponsored degree at the advanced age of twenty-seven. Wonderful. I spent half my time reading books outside the syllabus. Most people thought I was there to write a thesis on detective fiction. My wife hated it. Very juvenile, she thought."

"Still?"

"No. That's long in the past. But I told you, I still read detective fiction. It's better than the real thing, but more predictable."

"Wait a minute," Helen pulled toward him from a corner of the room a large box of books too heavy to lift. "Here you are. Designed for the shelves. Necessary furniture for any household. Complete Maigret, Eric Ambler, P. D. James, Nicolas Freeling. Take your pick, or have you read them all?"

"Ahh . . . ," the grin of a delighted schoolboy, bent on mischief, stooping before a box of treasures, straightening reluctantly. "No, wait, I've done the shelves; I'll complete the furnishing. Stack and examine at the same time."

A sense of order even in enthusiasm, she noticed. That was Superintendent Geoffrey Bailey in his disciplined element.

Three, maybe four hours gone if either was counting, and not a mention of Eileen Cartwright, or sad, twitching Michael Bernard in his nearby street. One bottle of wine gone, another tapped, floor cleaned, scrambled eggs eaten, bookshelves straight and full, and the air above the mahogany table rich with the satisfying smell of burnt toast, cigar smoke (his), cigarette smoke (hers): enough for the partial melting of two pathologically reserved souls, keepers of others' secrets, now open with their own, failures first, moving in easy domestic chatter from shopping to marriages.

"What's the worst part about divorce?" Geoffrey wondered out loud.

"Never feeling blameless," said Helen at once. "Always feeling it was my fault. That if I'd been wiser or something. Still stuck with the guilt, still let him manipulate me, because I imagine I could have made us both better. Arrogant, really."

"Hmm. You shouldn't think like that."

"You can talk. You know exactly what I mean."

"I suppose I do. Do you ever see him?"

"Sometimes. We're friends of a kind."

"Would he help with the shelves? Some do."

"Not mine." She laughed. "Do you see your wife?"

"Sometimes. Even though she remarried, I still mend things. A practice to be continued as long as she knows, and I know, that I'm free of other attachments."

"And are you?" An innocent question, a slight danger signal, ignored, then compromised.

"Oh yes. I don't mind the freedom. I like it. Too much, perhaps."

"Yes," said Helen, "so do I. Should I make some coffee?"

The danger zone passed, into a new phase of tranquility, another hour easily spent. He had admired her house, the opposite of his own with a genuine and curious liking, and mildly admired her. She had been grateful to him, and he did not want to leave. She would have prolonged it, but did not want him to stay, either. When he left, they were still as free, but curious.

CHAPTER SIX

There was always a breathing space between committal and trial. In this case a long delay. The trial of Eileen Cartwright to be postponed despite mutterings from the judge, grumbling from heavy chins, his contempt unmuffled by the wig.

"I do not understand why a lady who intends to protest her innocence is content to wait so long to do so, simply to ensure the services of counsel of her choice. With great respect to you, Mr. Quinn, there are other silks. Other equally eminent defenders."

"With even greater respect to your Lordship, I have done a considerable amount of work on this case already . . . many hours. It is simply, unfortunately, my commitments in Hong Kong."

"Yes, I know, I know. You've explained. I am not wholly satisfied. Delay and justice rarely coincide. I am even more astounded at the lack of strenuous objection from the prosecution."

Junior counsel for the Crown leapt to his awkward height, undignified by haste, anxious to deliver the token protest briefly, aware he had been expected elsewhere ten minutes since.

"I regret to say, my Lord, we are forced to agree, albeit with reservations. Mr. Carey, my learned leader, is away for the whole of June, and part of July, together with part of August, and in any event, we have some difficulty with witnesses in that month, and September. The holiday season, my Lord understands."

"Does he indeed? Yes, yes. I presume that doesn't apply to Mr. Jaskowski."

There was an obligatory smile in response.

"No, my Lord, but to several others. That is why we are content not to oppose the defense application."

"I don't like it, don't like it at all; but between you, you leave me with little choice. I presume," this with sarcasm as heavy as the humor, "that you will all be ready by October, so that I may at least fix a date for trial now? No more adjournments, not for any reason? Is six months enough notice for all your commitments?"

Murmurings of deferential agreement, dates noted, flapping gowns making way for more, Quinn urbane in minor triumph, others rushing, justice postponed to justice.

"Disgraceful," so his Lordship later informed Carey, as they sat in the Garrick, a fresh glass of claret each. "Disgraceful. Why does she want to wait for Quinn? And is Quinn so greedy that he's persuaded her it's for the best to wait, just for the brief fee? I know she's paying privately, but all the same, it must be peanuts compared to what he's getting from the Hong Kong bank for that fraudsman in the meantime. Why didn't you get your junior to fight it?"

"Well, John, because it suits me. Because my evidence is well preserved, not about to go stale; it's embedded in the minds of witnesses unlikely to forget it. That's my answer. I've got an excellent officer in the case, excellent instructing solicitor."

"Unusual, for the Crown Prosecution Service."

"Quite so. But between them, they'll keep it under control for as long as it takes. And Jaskowski's not going anywhere. I think the further he's away from the dirty deed, the better he'll be. As for Mrs. Cartwright, don't know her motives, do I? Not an easy case for us, relying on the evidence of a convicted murderer, but Quinn must have told her she's still got a very high chance of being convicted. Makes it easier to persuade her to wait for his services since she would have realized that the six months she spends waiting would be docked from her sentence if she goes down, and she may as well have six months in a remand prison than the same time in some high security wing. Privileges on remand, you know: visitors, better food. You can imagine the sort of thing. That's why half the prisoners like her are content to wait. Far more comfortable on remand."

"Good God. I'd forgotten. Shows how long it is since I defended and knew all the tricks. It's still disgraceful. So be it, George. I'm glad it won't be me who'll be trying the damned thing. Have you time for dinner?"

Carey, thinking of the taste of claret on his tongue, and the absence of his wife in the country far longer now than comfort demanded, debated the issue swiftly.

"Oh, I think so, John. Yes, I think I have, now I come to think of it. Might manage dinner."

In Helen West's office, there was a lull. Four pending trials, all major, all postponed; ten more in the pipeline, but far from crisis point, so that the quantities of paper were huge, with daily pressures bearable. The junior prosecutors were discontented to the point of rebellion so that all the symptoms of absence through sickness, backache, influenza were prevalent, and Helen was summarily loaned to the juvenile court. Her own work would have to wait, suffer for lack of care, but so did the system with its team lurching from one crisis to the next. No point protesting or stating how much she disliked the juvenile court. One perk of relative seniority had been the promise of freedom from it. She had not believed the promise then, and did not now.

Monday morning in Seymour Place, there to conduct the daily list, beginning with the guilty pleas, papers delivered late. Miss West, ensconced before the building opened, reading furiously while the police room gradually filled with witness officers, booking on to give evidence on cases which might or might not be heard. In the juvenile court, police inertia was seeping from the woodwork. No accolades for arresting juveniles and bringing them here for a finding of guilt and, as the police joke went, a tip for turning up. Traumatic for the new offender, the good boy, frightened by the high-bred faces of selected magistrates and the prospect of disgrace: easier for the recidivist lulled into false security by practice, sitting in the foyer eating crisps along with anxious parents and bored policemen. The list was too long: it was always too long in case it should be too short. Half would be sent away hours later, adult throats aching from too many waiting cigarettes, bellies rumbling from weak coffee, nerves blunted by the official rudeness of it all.

Struggling with the same indifference, the bloated defeat about the place even this early in the morning, Helen's eye was caught by the name of the fourth defendant on the list, and the name shook her awake. Edward Jaskowski, charged with carrying an offensive weapon, one small knife. She flicked through the flimsy papers, all in a mess of various, tired handwritings, and found a crumpled statement under caution.

". . . I carried the knife in my back pocket to defend myself—Had you ever been attacked?—No, but you never know."

Quite right, you never did, especially if your father was known to be in prison for murder, and you lived in the war zone, but it still didn't amount to a defense. First offender. Once might be enough. Probation might help. As long as the bench didn't worsen the situation by shoveling on a fine they couldn't pay. Miss West went out to find the defense, and found Jaskowski, mother and son, dressed in their Sunday best.

Although Helen did not ration compassion because she mistrusted the object of it, and tended instead to overcompensate for dislike, she could not help the slight shiver of recognition at the familiar sight of the boy, his jeans and leather jacket an almost dated attempt at adolescent glamor, his hair, longer than before, elegantly hung over one eye. Other attempts at sartorial improvement included one earring, but he shone with cleanliness, the white T-shirt spotless. Mother was less so, frayed around the edges, still fighting; whether with the boy or for him was difficult to tell, but both destined to draw the short straw, as on this morning, a pallid, unconvincing barrister who would do them no good at all. If anything was to be done to persuade the bench to the kind of leniency which would leave the boy without a record, Helen would have to do it herself. Not difficult once you knew how, to compensate for the shortcomings of the Defense while acting as prosecutor, something she had done more often than she could have counted.

It was a question not of what was said, but how it was said, in a quiet voice for the facts without drama or condescension.

". . . Edward admitted he carried the knife for his own protection, would have used it if necessary. Your Worships know that this is the full offense. However, it is not a large knife: it could be worse, and he did admit it. In all fairness the prosecution should add that it is within its own knowledge that this family have been subject to tragic circumstances through absolutely no fault of their own, and have attempted to make the best of it. Your Worships will understand if I do not elaborate on a sensitive issue, but while sentencing is no business of the prosecution, a matter entirely for the court's discretion, may I venture to suggest that assistance would be more appropriate than punishment to a first offender who is no stranger to suffering?"

"You mean probation, Miss West?" beamed the Clerk, not slow to take a hint. "Conditional discharge?"

"That is a matter on which the defense must address your Worships, of course."

Which he did, with uninspired hesitation. The result was more briefly written, with no column for fine or record, but one for conditional discharge and probation.

Mrs. Jaskowski was gathering bags as Helen emerged briefly from the room. She caught at her arm, a sudden awkward action, spontaneous, but regretted.

"Thanks, Miss. You done more than our bloke."

"No thanks needed. Only fair. How are you getting on?"

"Not so bad. You know about it all, then."

"Enough, Mrs. Jaskowski. You can't have had an easy time."

"No." There was nothing more to say. Edward, lurking in the background, reappeared at his mother's side, the hair brushed out of the eyes, the leather belt adjusted. Helen spoke, and like Maria, almost wished she had not.

"Adult court, next time, Edward. Won't be so easy. Don't forget to see the probation, will you?"

He nodded and moved away, half shuffling, half swaggering behind his mother. Helen required neither gratitude nor appreciation: no reason to expect people to be grateful for fairness, but she could have wished, as an alternative to reward, that she had liked him more, or could hope never again to see his name on a list. Unappealing, man-shaped boy; he must be sick of the sight of her, appearing at the back of bad news in miserable courtrooms on the two occasions she had ever figured in his life. If the dislike was so transparent, so mutual, she could not be surprised, but Ed in his wake left a prickle of despair.

* * *

"I don't know why," Helen later told Geoffrey, "but it seems my doubtful privilege to keep stumbling into the dramatis personae of this case. It's never happened before, but I keep colliding with them, saying I'm sorry."

"Bothers you, doesn't it?" He was sounding concerned, but amused.

"Oh, I'm sorry. I'm seeing the entirely different perception you must have of any case when you know all the people, spent hours with them, not just chance meetings and a view of the dock. It makes me feel so ignorant. I do nothing, feel a fraud, as if the brunt of the work never hits me."

"Helen, that's not quite right. You don't have to go to bed with them to understand them."

"Well, in Mrs. Cartwright's individual case, I'm sure you do, but not to be recommended."

"Bitchy, but mild. What's the matter?"

"I feel particularly futile."

"You mustn't. There's enough grief without that. It's right that you have your role, and the likes of me, mine. A silly, convoluted pattern, but versions of the truth often improve through translation, objectively assessed: that's where you come in, an assessor, it's better you don't know the people. By better, I mean, more exact in the long run. Does that make sense? Distance refining the understanding of the facts?"

"Yes," she said doubtfully, sipping her wine, unconvinced. Geoffrey finished his own.

"I wish you hadn't met the boy."

"I don't wish that. I wish he didn't have to suffer so much of whatever it is he has to suffer. Dislike, hatred. Something of the kind. He has it, like bad breath. It's almost tangible."

"Don't refine understanding too far. It doesn't bear so much. And Helen, that's enough. Six months delay, and we can't talk about this case for six months. I'm only here to distract both of us. I thought since you sometimes feel safe enough or desperate enough for the occasional post-work grumble in a pub with me, perhaps you'd like to come home for supper. I guarantee a slightly better stocked larder than yours."

She smiled, struck by a vision of her refrigerator, empty of anything more than four eggs and a stale loaf, all she had to offer herself or anyone else. A fridge like that, with a supply of wine and potato crisps by the sackful was a way of life. Helen hesitated, tempted to enter the shelter of his provision, curious, but careful.

"Well . . ."

"I'll run you home afterwards. You look as if you need an early night."

Light touch of reassurance, gently and adroitly given, for the benefit of them both. Armed with it, favored by it, they finished the wine, and left the artificial sawdust for homelier scenery.

All of them old, people like that, Ed thought; lawyers and such, magistrates and coppers. They did not, as a matter of course, give him anything on which to rely. What did they expect from him? Duty, gratitude, or something of the kind he supposed. Not that he thought much of them at all. Ed abandoned his mother on the courthouse steps, not rudely, but finally, went home and lay on his bed with his music connected to his ears. Ed was always plugged in by the ears; it was a new source of contempt that no one should question the source of the expensive stereo or the tapes which supplied it. He ambled round his city corners to the aggressive clash of rhythmless sound: he twitched to it in the Underground or on foot: on the bus, or in a shop, he listened to the music, his face vacant enough to discourage conversation, his step tuned to the beat of drums and shrill instruments. Ed provided the words, turning up the sound whenever irritated in order to irritate in retaliation. In such battles he had no equals. "He's very fond of music," Mary would explain to those upon whom the presence of her sulky nephew was inflicted by virtue of his unwelcome presence in her house. "Take no notice." What had been first a kind of plea for attention had become an end in itself.

He did not want them to notice in order to understand, or take him to one side and bore him to death with the very attempt to do anything so impossibly stupid, so insulting, almost as bad as their saying they would pray for him. Don't make me laugh, Uncle, you bloody hypocrite. It was more of a throwing down of a gauntlet—stop me if you dare, I only live in your house, I didn't ask to. More fool you for being dutiful, don't ask me to respect it, why should I? And in case you were thinking of treating me like a son, I hate you, don't dare do it.

Another way of defining that territory which was to be his: the territory of himself, what he wore, where he went, what he did, all to remain unimpeachable, as well as his territory over Peter. "Peter doesn't like fish," he would say, spokesman for the child's tastes, and Peter did not eat fish. "Peter is not going to school today," and Peter was not forced because of this strange parenthood in parenthesis. Lonely Peter was bound to his brother by thin steel threads of sheer adoration and loneliness, tempered by fine, but flawed intelligence, a pawn in everyone's game whenever he was not ignored, which was most of his life.

To Edward, he was not a useful tool: he lost his memory for instructions so easily, he was a dreamer, a bungler, a creature of artless sweet nature, with all the stupidity of innocence. To his aunt and uncle beset by many children, the contest for Peter was easily relinquished, Edward's challenge to their authority over either of them not so much battled and won, but never grasped, nothing but a cold and quiescent war where cease-fire was agreed before a single blow had been struck.

So complete was the bloodless rout, so preoccupied the adults and so intimidated, that even the most obvious questions were not asked with any regularity. When Uncle Peter had begun with a paternal quiz, a heavy-handed, well meant, badly executed duty:

"Now, Ed . . . we must think of a job for you," the answering eyes were uncomfortably blank. "So you leave school. What do you want to do? What do you want to be, Ed?"

"Don't know." Those were the days when he still answered at all. "A detective, I think."

Uncle Peter was confused and outraged. "All this we had, all this heartache with the uniforms, and you want to join the police?"

He was incredulous, Ed similarly so, that the man could be so dense. The glance of pale scorn arrested Uncle Peter's half-complete gestures of protest.

"Not that kind of detective," he muttered. There was nothing else to say. Ed's words had been given with the backward glance of leaving the room, closing the one and only discussion on the subject. After that, further debate was superfluous even had either party wanted to risk it. Ed would have done: Uncle Peter did not.

Formative years for Ed to practice all kinds of warfare. His tenth birthday found him setting a record: running the length of the dank corridor below Bevan House with a stick, smashing all fifteen neon ceiling lights without pausing for breath. He believed in learning how to be the best, and the Hackington estate was a hotbed of education for truanting children. It might have been designed for games with its interconnected units built round a square, so that children as well as adults could run from one to the next without effective pursuit, and the sound of domestic quarrels or lovelorn catcalls reverberated from one small tower to the next, echoing in the lift shaft, long since vandalized beyond repair. In the middle of the squalid square stood the garages, a centerpiece in concrete, ugly as sin and even more colorless than the surroundings. Those privileged enough to possess one of these kept it locked, but anything free the children inevitably found.

The first time Ed had sampled the delights of *Driller Killer* and other sadistic visual horrors, he had been in one of the Hackington garages with the video Tysall's son had borrowed from home, and the tapes Tysall's brother had purloined from the pub. Lying on the stone floor in his parka, fighting down nausea in the dark as the electric drill spun its way into the head of the victim, Ed had determined to keep his eyes on the screen while weaker Tysall failed, and after a few more sessions of acid thrown at babies or bodies slowly split by the chainsaw, eleven-year-old Ed could watch it all with enjoyable impunity, absorbed into the screams and blood-colored images, far more fun than that detective stuff he watched on telly with Dad. It was when Ed began to suspect that the stomach of the man would have been as sharply revolted as his own appetite was increased by the more brutal images absorbed in the garages, that he began that slow decline toward despising him. Not the whole story, but the beginning. Most was his father being the kind of servant Ed so despised, and Stanislaus could never have been anything else.

"Can I come with you, Ed . . . Please let me come with you."

"No."

"Why not?"

"Because it's late and it's cold."

"No it's not, and I'm very warm. Why not?"

"Because you can't. Nothing doing for little boys. Next time, perhaps."

"Promise?" A note of slight relief.

"Promise. Go to sleep." Useless to threaten to tell Aunt Mary. Peter knew that whatever else he did, Ed would despise him for that.

There was nothing doing for little boys, but more to learn on the Hackington and in all its surrounding streets with their newfound riches the older you grew, provided you never grew too old for all the nimbleness involved. Bigger thieves grew tall from little, never innocent, acorns. On the dreadful first, Ed surprised himself by his pounding heart, his own deafening footsteps as he neared the enemy car, the tinkling of the broken quarter light sounding like an explosion. Then there was the arm, shaking like the rest of him, thrust through the window, nerveless fingers fumbling with the handle, door open, contents of back seat scooped without examination, and he on his toes, running faster than he had ever known how to run, dropping things from the awkward bundle, realizing he had not even planned where next with his armful of incrimination, finally stopping in a churchyard to leave it all there. Amid the exhiliration which rose as the panic subsided on his self-conscious stroll home, came the treacherous realization of waste; all that effort, for what? Two coats, a couple of scarves and a briefcase, left warming the dead against the church wall, and himself cursing himself for a great big fool.

Technique was there for its own perfection: discipline counted, size helped, and companions never. Winter was best, with fewer bodies walking in the streets and all of them too cold to make accurate observations. Easy. Don't take it if it isn't useful; leave the tat for somebody else. Lucrative late nights and lazy days, and still Dad didn't notice. But even so, with his growing hoard in the garages, credibility with buyers and his dangerous self-respect, burglary was a frightening departure, a renewal of the old sweaty palms. Inside a block of flats, he treated the task like a workman, knowing from life in his own monster tower how little regard there would be for the noise, less for the result. Grateful he was if he had thought of it, for peoples' endless need for easily stolen goods. He wondered at their constant craving for such things, did Edward. He himself needed nothing he stole, or not with such critical need, one of many reasons why he so excelled.

Kids' stuff, all of it, crap for kids; his own words until he qualified for what he called the proper houses and learned all the rest, took in through his skin that septic hatred which grew with his size. Sentiments absent from the initial fumblings around flats as ordinary as the one from which he had embarked, but hatred found in the houses he came to know after these; houses with solid wooden doors, easier targets after practice, occupied by an alien breed who took holidays, abandoned ship for whole weekends, had predictable lives, and left exposed to him the treasure trove of their houses, from which, in the beginning, he could find nothing to steal.

He hated them for having nothing to remove, with their cash buried in the brickwork, sunk into immovable carpets, solid furniture, and thousands of books he would never begin to read. Edward knew he observed whole lives and casts of thought light years beyond his grasp or comprehension, all of it enviable and frightening. No word or action of his own could describe the loathing. As a grown child utterly frustrated by knowledge he could not share, Ed understood with complete clarity all the defecating, spoiling breed of juvenile burglars, who would have cut the paintings with Stanley knives, aerosolled the walls with obscenities, fouled like dogs on the carpet, saying in obscene gesture what they could not say in words, envy and hate thrown at the old lie of equality. Ed understood it all right, felt it rise in his own throat like the vomit of despair, the bloody pitiless unfairness of it all, but did not react in the same way, his hatred too acid and extreme for temporary relief. He wanted to spit in their food, murder their animals, but did not. Instead he planned his own route and began to follow his plan. Ed would not bow to this, or serve it, and in finding these houses, he left behind his father.

"You're different, Edward," she had told him, and he preened at the flattery. "Most people fall into this. Thieves by habit, see? Not you. You've planned it, haven't you?"

"Yes."

"Good boy. And you understand, don't you, that a first class criminal must have no scruples, none at all, must regard every law with equal disrespect? It's no good doing it otherwise. There has to be no person you wouldn't bribe, no weak links, and no being sorry for anyone at all."

"Yes, I know that."

"Well then, you've got to educate yourself to the top of the tree. That means trying everything, and I mean everything."

"Yes. Before I'm twenty. Beginning now."

"That's it, Edward. You've got the idea."

On balance he was pleased, even with his mistakes: even if he had been caught that one and only time, burgling Eileen's house. By Eileen herself. Following from such nightmare, he could never be afraid of anything as banal as a policeman. Not bad, his humility on that arrest, and his ingenuous version of truth, he thought. Try everything. She might have been proud of him had she known of it, and known of his purpose. Ed slept, not without dreaming. You bastard, Dad, you stinking daft bastard, you sodding feeble liar.

"I love it here," said Helen. "Can't help saying it again and again, can't help thinking it either. I like all the bits and pieces, but I'd like it even without them, but not as much. It's not a surprise. When we came upstairs, I wondered where you were taking me."

Geoffrey smiled, pleased the impression should have been so much better than he had hoped. Like me, respect me, like my home had seemed a workable formula since his home, after all, was his closest and most consistent friend, the only one for whom he sought approval.

"I'm glad you like it," was all he said. "Perhaps you'll move out of a basement, and copy me. Live on top of the world, drowned out in summer by the smell of the river."

"Don't joke like that. I'm too impressionable. Every time I see somewhere I like as much as this, it makes me discontented with my own. At the moment, you see, I'm under the influence of yours, toying with the idea of spending the weekend painting all my colored walls white, throwing things out although I'm quite happy with it. There; now you have some idea of my inconsistency."

"But you won't go home and paint it all again?"

"No, of course not. I'm not quite so fickle. I like it really. Homes matter far more if you live on your own, I think. You have no excuse not to like it because you can't blame anyone else. I found I was tired of waking up in places which made me depressed. Hence the poverty of a huge mortgage, and all those colors."

"Well, I agree with you, but I keep my domestic enthusiasms

close to the chest. The details of my life would be difficult to share since I can't have the same view of necessities as most I know. I'd rather have the drafts, the incomplete kitchen, and go out and buy something absolutely useless. Don't entertain colleagues because I can imagine what they'd say on their way home. They'd try and sort me out a suitable companion for a new life in a house the way I lived once. They could be right. I just don't want to measure the opinions."

"Oh, don't you think you misjudge them? Anyone would like it here."

"Like it? Yes. Approve? No."

"Why did you choose it then? Most people, including me, choose their places with some thought of approval in mind."

"Not me. I'm more of a fish out of water than you think."

She was tickling the balcony cat which had adopted her: he noticed that she seemed neither to mind nor notice the sooty fur graying a once white blouse.

"How does a fish become so far removed from its element?"

"Ah, that begs a life story. It's late, and there isn't time." He wished it otherwise. Relaxed into his battered armchair, Helen curled into its companion sofa a few feet away, he knew he had already talked too much, and did not care, or at least cared only enough to be concerned not to bore her, indifferent, for once, as to what he might reveal. She looked at her watch, sensed the nature of the real concern, compromised.

"Oh no, don't throw me out. There's time for wool-gathering, surely? Tell me something I'd like to know, a really clichéd question. Why a policeman?"

Now his own silence had been broken so recklessly, he could not resist such a question and she could tell he could not.

"Oh, a long progress away from respectability. Dad was a drinker, my mother the ladylike one of the whole arrangement. I can't find it in me to like her, even now, long after they're both dead. She compensated for the downward spiral of circumstances by always pretending to be above it, which, to be fair to her I suppose she was. That meant doing good, always visiting those she called the poor, though most of them were scarcely different from us. Me, as a kind of boy-bodyguard, not that you needed one then, not in Mile End. It disgusted me, all of it; I wanted nothing to do with it."

He paused, sipped from his glass, lost for a moment.

"But you adopted it, all those needs and miseries, or the symptoms of them. How?"

"By accident. I was allowed to be idle, you see, preferred to be known as daft Bailey's son than good Mrs. Bailey's boy, and apart from that, didn't know what the hell I wanted, finding most things a joke, like my father, who always saved his best ones for policemen and vicars. Still like the booze a bit, not as much as him, still like talking too much when I can get away with it."

He grinned ruefully, ashamed at the length of speech.

"Not too much. That's your mother talking. Worried about the impression you make."

The grin returned.

"Right. Anyway, at sixteen I'm loafing around with my dad full of artistic dreams, a contemptuous little sod. Then one evening, mother collared me to go with her on one of her wretched errands of mercy to see some nice old boy in a tenement. Respectable poor, bombed out. We found him dead. Hit once over the head with a piece of pipe, sitting in an old chair, reading his paper. My mother behaved better than me."

"Why? What did you do?"

"Cried. Touched him, and cried. For the picture he made with his whole life around him. A few good sticks of furniture, old rugs, but good: photos of his dead wife and children, reasonable books. Dressed properly each day, you know the way people did, some still do, cavalry twills, sports jacket, very worn, made to last forever, always a tie even if he wasn't going out, keeping up standards even for his own company. Dignity, I suppose. And some drunk lout had killed him for tuppence, hit him when there was no need. That's when I decided to be a policeman. My mother was furious. She wasn't really that public-spirited at all, she was a snob. My father thought it was hilarious."

"You became a policeman because of him, the old man?"

"Yes. Nothing to do with idealism. More a determination that if anything could be done to prevent such a death, I should do it. Hence police cadet, aged seventeen. No one could stop me. I must have been easily moved."

"But you don't regret it, do you?"

"Only for the reasons which make me so deficient, too insular;

hopeless as a member of any club, and worse than that, I'm not at all interested in the good of the public, only individuals. It's easy to distinguish the two, I find."

"Very easy. Even though there isn't any difference, not when you think of it. Only in practice." Helen smiled. "You can only serve the public one by one. Go on."

But it was enough without reciprocal secrets and there was no time for those.

"No. I promised you an early night. I'm taking you home now, or you won't be protecting any interests tomorrow. Least of all your own." She knew better than to prompt.

"I'll take one last look at your river before I go. Come on cat, get off. Find another warm place."

Bailey noticed that the gray of the once pristine blouse was more apparent than ever: could not suppress a feeling of satisfied pleasure in the fact that she had clearly known from the start how dirty was his borrowed cat, and had not cared. What strange judgments he was imposing on her, and if she realized, she failed to resent. She was unaware, but wary of his observation, not knowing how shy he was of hers.

"There are a few small privileges left in being a policeman," Bailey remarked as his car rolled through the lurid lights of the Blackwall Tunnel. "One of them is knowing my way round in the dark."

"I'm afraid of the dark. Even more than when I was a child."

"That, Miss West, is entirely sensible. So am I."

They were still free, and she was yawning nicely from the car. "Thank you. I've enjoyed it." Awkwardly formal again, as they were most of the time. "I owe you a better meal than scrambled eggs."

"You mean the shelves are still standing?"

"I mean I'd like to repay. Perhaps we could try the local auction sometime? Woodworm, followed by antique cooking?"

"I'd like that. I'll phone. Goodnight."

He drove home, faster than he should, homing pigeon to base, to sit on the balcony, watching the sluggish river, listening for all the calming sound of the night. So unusual for him to feel dissatisfied with solitude that even the cat, suspicious of his restlessness, moved to another squat for the hours of his wakefulness.

He had told her he was interested only in the fate of individuals, and wondered with all the nagging doubts of his own honesty, how much of that was still true. For the moment he thought nothing at all, and considered himself a fool to imagine he missed her.

Helen opened her window to the warm air of the garden, stung by the silence of the place, grateful for the muted sound of traffic, the distant rumble of a train, the comforting presence of humanity at arm's length. She was not always afraid of the dark. Only most of the time.

CHAPTER SEVEN

A warm morning, but not warm enough to explain the temperature in the offices of Daintrey and Partners, solicitors these days to E. Cartwright and many others less capable of paying the fees. It was Cyril Lawrence, junior partner, who looked after the lady's interests in particular, and he had reached the conclusion that asking the advice of his senior, Paul Daintrey had been ill-advised, judging from the reaction reverberating round his room.

"I really think we should tell them. I mean, it's ridiculous. Where the hell did she get this information, how did she get it, and what's she trying to do? I don't understand. I've only met the woman once before she latched on to you, couldn't handle me, and said so very abruptly I seem to remember, but at least she didn't want to leave the firm. That apart, I wouldn't have said she was a philanthropist, not by any stretch of the imagination, and yet here she is sending money for the Jaskowski family. The family of the man telling lies about her, whose word'll put her inside for the rest of her natural . . . and she's sending money for his kids, for Christ's sake. Fishy? It stinks."

"But it isn't only the Jaskowskis. She's asked us to provide for her two friends, the ones who've been running the shop we haven't managed to sell; she's asked for other generous bequests with her cash. Perhaps it isn't odd at all. Perhaps she's just got a conscience."

"Oh come on, Lawrence, what color are my eyes? Green as grass? I mean, listen to this, listen to this crap," he picked up the piece of closely written, closely lined, exercise-book paper, embossed with its prison crest, ". . . I would like you to deliver the sum of five thousand pounds to Edward Jaskowski. I believe he is the eldest son of the family, and must be in charge of it in the permanent absence of his father. His father is telling lies about what it was I asked him to do, but I am nevertheless, as a Christian, sorry for any family which has been broken apart by such wicked fantasizing, and although their position is not my fault, I should not like them corrupted by their father's lies. I would like them to know that I do not bear them a grudge . . ." He stopped himself tearing the paper, threw it down instead. "I mean, can you credit it, I never heard such rubbish. She's trying to buy them off."

"But why? I don't believe she could be as stupid. She isn't a stupid woman. And anyway, even if she sent the Jaskowskis money, how would that help her? Short of them telling their old man what a kind soul she was, how would that help? It's no particular incentive to him to withhold evidence."

"Of course it is, Lawrence, don't you see, you great idiot? He'd think keeping quiet was a condition of support for his family; and she'll have bought him off by providing for them."

Lawrence rubbed his wide brow nervously. He ached to believe well of human nature, especially the samples of it who were his clients. He did not like Eileen Cartwright: he did not fully believe Eileen Cartwright or even half believe, but he needed to convince himself she had some goodness in her and it pleased him that the letter, fulsome and suspicious though it was, gave him some good grounds for doing so. He tried again.

"If you'd only take the trouble to read the rest of the letter, you'll see she's doing her best to take it out of the realm of bribery."

The older man was exasperated as usual with Lawrence's willful naivete. "I can scarcely read her writing," he growled. "You read it to me."

Lawrence was happy to oblige. He cleared his throat, insensitive to the anger of his companion who found his very presence an irritant and was wondering why it was that all the calculating, complicated clients were drawn to Lawrence, who was least equipped to deal with them. Do Lawrence good to be mugged, he thought savagely. Might make him less of a sucker for lying, bleeding hearts, and all the vicious pretenders who conned him.

". . . I do not wish it to be thought that this gift of money is designed to influence the trial in any way." Lawrence looked at his senior partner with significant triumph. The reward was a snort of contempt. ". . . It is made from altruistic motives. I would suggest therefore, that no payment is fulfilled until the end of my hearing in order to make it clear that it is not dependent on the outcome. In the meantime, I want Edward Jaskowski to be informed that he is to receive the sum for the benefit of the family, and also that it will not be paid until my fate has been decided; not at all if he breathes a single word to his father in the meantime. He must promise not to do so: that is the only condition, but he must know of it as soon as possible, since I know the family are in straitened circumstances. He can then plan for them accordingly."

"Straitened circumstances? How the hell does she know?" demanded Daintrey. Lawrence blushed.

"She asked me to find out, so I did."

"From who?"

"The prosecution. Nice woman. Very helpful. I asked her, and since I suppose there was no harm in my knowing, she told me."

"Well. Doesn't the bloody Cartwright woman have her letters read?"

"She's on remand, not under sentence. Letters to her solicitor aren't read. Nor ours to her. You must know that." Lawrence was smug in scoring a point, and Daintrey's irritation became more obvious.

"But it's monstrous, the whole thing. Obscene. Bent."

"I don't see why. A little unusual, perhaps."

"Unusual? Is that all you can say? A little odd? Putting us in the dock for attempting to pervert the course of justice? Interference with witnesses, promising money? God, I don't know, I really don't. We've got far too much on with that woman already, what with a Power of Attorney to sell her shops, her house mortgaged to pay for Quinn's fees, and Christ knows what else. Bloody woman."

Lawrence was riled. Correct, in the limited book of his mind, to think ill of your client, indeed it was difficult to avoid it most of the time, but incorrect to say so, preferable by far to speak of them with the respect you would at least give to the dead, and besides, they were occasionally innocent. In his own cases they were always innocent: the best complexion must be painted upon their requests, however bizarre, and in Daintrey this morning he scented the naked dislike of himself which normally went clothed. Attack became preferable to defense.

"She's not that bloody woman. She's our client. Our paying client, not even legal aid, and one way or another, giving us plenty of business, all that stuff she used to give to Michael Bernard's firm included. We've got to do what she wants."

"Tell the prosecution about that letter," Daintrey interrupted.

"Why should I? Give them the chance to cross-examine her at trial about something she's written in confidence? Lose Edward Jaskowski five thousand pounds which he probably doesn't deserve, but that's not for us to judge, is it? No, I won't, I damn well won't. Why shouldn't I just obey her instructions? How can it be interfering with witnesses when none of the Jaskowskis are witnesses, except the father and he's in prison already? She's not offering him money, and she's covered the possibilities of the payment being treated as corrupt. Why the hell shouldn't I just do as she says?" Rage turned his voice into a shrill and aggressive whine. He tried to calm it. "Anyway I should point out, I was only asking your advice. As I see it, the interests of the client come first and foremost. I'm hired to protect those interests, nothing else. If she wants me to do something which isn't blatantly illegal, I should do it. For God's sake, Paul, you've banked money for robbers before, and while this is certainly more eccentric, it isn't nearly as below board. At least we know this time whose money it is."

The general division of labor in the firm was something of which Paul Daintrey disliked reminders. By and large, he dealt with the professional criminals, while Lawrence dealt with those loosely described as amateurs. Daintrey did not doubt which he preferred, and although he was a man of selective conscience rather than no conscience at all, to the extent that he was almost, certainly occasionally, trusted by the police, especially when he had done their conveyancing, there were several areas of his work where he would have preferred the finer details to remain unknown. Quite unwittingly, since he was not overendowed with either wit or judgment, Lawrence had hit upon the weakest of many Achilles' heels, and the senior partner's insistence deflated as suddenly as it had arisen.

"Oh, do as you think best, whatever that is. Write to her first, though. Ask her if she thinks it's a good idea to mention it to the boy before the trial. Point out she might think differently afterwards, might be sorry. I mean, why should this kid keep quiet?"

"Because they won't get the money if he doesn't."

"Yes, yes, I know that, but it's a test for him all the same. How old is he, seventeen? Christ. At least ask her to wait. She'll quarrel about the bill if we do something she regrets later."

"I thought of that," said Lawrence coldly, stung by the insinuation he had not covered all the angles. "I'll write, if you insist, but I doubt it'll make much difference. She seems to have considered it carefully already."

"But you'll write? Before you act? Not after?"

"Yes."

"And for God's sake, at least tell counsel. He'll have to know."

Honor was satisfied. Daintrey had given his advice and obtained at least the one concession. Smiling affably, he changed the subject. Other cases, other dilemmas emerged for ten soothing minutes, leaving Lawrence convinced he had won not only the point but a renewal of esteem. As his clients had found even more often than his peers, Lawrence was easy to placate and easier to fool. They may have needed drugs, violence, theft and forgiveness: he had an equal craving to be liked.

Not inclined to think at speed, he was still capable of it, so that the moment Paul left, he was thinking hard before lapsing into reverie. He was given to monumental thoughts, imagining how he would explain his reasoning aloud at the same time as formulating the reasoning itself, a sort of speechless thinking on his feet which encouraged him to walk around his room casting himself in an Oscar role as advocate for the exclusive audience of himself. Unfortunately a role for which he was otherwise unsuited, not for lack of words: more for lack of presence or any element of humor, and a complete insensitivity to the character of those addressed. There was only one style in his repertoire, a kind of elaborate pomposity, heavy Dickensian condescension which had failed to earn either the respect of the local magistrates or local villains, and the failure pained him still. Broad hints from an ungrateful audience would not have forced him to retire from the stage with the single court appearance which had scarred him for life, although it had been the one which most endeared him to his public.

Spindly, unprepossessing, thirty-three going on seventy and ignorant of youthful indiscretion, Lawrence had done as Lawrence misguidedly did in court, stood thinly in a fat man's stance, legs astride, watch chain resplendent across concave stomach, thumbs hooked into the lapels of his waistcoat, jacket hanging off his shoulders, while he intoned on the law for twenty numbing minutes, revealing throughout at armpit level a large and well chewed lump of Farley's rusk, perfectly preserved in the saliva of his youngest child. A devoted and liberal father who was proud of the fact that he bore so many of the domestic burdens of his two children, nevertheless the hideous spectacle of himself decorated with their souvenirs while in all the uniform of his dignity quite destroyed his confidence to the unsung relief of many. Lawrence abdicated with elegant excuses, persuaded himself he was too refined for open conflict, but still spoke and thought, not in jotting phrases, but always in fully grown sentences as if he were making a speech.

"What in these circumstances, is my duty to my client? To do as she directs, of course, but advising caution . . . A matter entirely for her, of course. Her barrister, senior though he is, will not be informed," and there Lawrence paused to dwell on his dislike for Mr. Quinn, whose condescension was a thorn in the side "unless I am instructed to do so. I am sure Mrs. Cartwright will understand. She and I have a perfectly good understanding, a meeting of minds." In the aftermath of a disagreement with Daintrey, and at the merest thought of Quinn's contempt, Lawrence warmed to the thought of his client as though they were the allies they might have been, if not the way he had come to understand it, and his letter was genial.

Eileen knew she had already achieved her object. Lying on her bunk, she tore the pages into shreds, the only way to preserve it from eyes both prying and bored, and wrote her reply.

"Dear Mr. Lawrence, Thank you for your letter. Please do exactly as I said in the first place. Yours, Eileen Cartwright."

She knew all about it, knew what a solicitor should be and shouldn't, when they were naïve, and when not. Entering Michael's office by chance to sort out the meager bits and pieces of her husband's estate, it had been quite simple. He had been pleased to see her, admired the brooch on her lapel, expressed curiosity, flattered her. Noticed her white spirit smell, contrasted it with the sweeter perfumes of Mrs. Bernard, and still admired. In the wide world of her charmless life, he had gone to her head like a pint of brandy, an intoxication which survived all sickness.

Poor Sylvia Bernard: so very far from the wicked creature Eileen had come to imagine. The lady was a trifle silly, was all: restless and bored. Michael had wanted a good little, pretty little wife, and that was what he had got. Sylvia died in the end after Eileen changed color, forgot the original jealous impulse, and simply found it intolerable that she should stay alive. Hate conquered love without anyone realizing, Eileen least of all, but she found it quite possible to be objective, whatever the object.

Helen West knew all about objectivity, and knew that its only virtue was as a discipline to make her consistent in action, since it was quite impossible to be consistent in opinion. She had long since abandoned the notion of equality with which Lawrence was infected: knew, as he did, that the power of the client she did not like was greater than the power of the client she did, simply because of a small factor known as guilt. All that cant about legal objectivity was so much rubbish: it simply meant she would work harder for untouchables because lack of affection toward them must never show. Helen was thinking wildly and idly, the irritating mish-mash of thoughts just before sleep when molehills become mountainous, clutching at stray thoughts to keep the rest at bay. Looking at self after midnight was always a bad idea. Especially when you hated what you saw, the virtues in particular, since virtues were unloveable assets. Helen was wishing she had the strength of wickedness with none of the instinct to be good.

Duties—life was fuller than ever of duties. Functions, office parties where absence would be an insult, gatherings where absence would be a denial of friendship, days out endured in the desire not to offend because no one deserved it. Time-consuming guilt, wanting to be liked, high-stepping funny chatting through hours of painful boredom, nicely nicotine-stained, without the faintest idea why she had bothered in the first place, knowing she was superfluous.

Going to dinner with ex-husband and fiancée had been such a duty. Zoie, she had been called, sweet, glamorous model, good for

Hugo's image, bubbling with the relief of one who was finding a difficult evening far better than she had hoped and was content to share the honors, but not all of them. Trying to be mature, visibly relieved at the sight of Helen's older face, handsome still, but nothing like her own juvenile perfection: she needn't have worried after all. A well-handled initiation which had taxed Helen's charm and left her boiling. And now another invitation, far worse, and despite the anger at her own weakness, she felt utterly obliged to attend. Standing on the sidelines at the wedding of a former husband to a younger bride had all the conventional ingredients for a crisis of confidence, but it was no simple recipe which so turned her insides upon themselves. Hugo insisted on the invitation for several reasons: first among these was the desire to show the world he was an admirable man without enemies, whose friends included an ex-wife who forgave and supported him, and it was this which infuriated her most since she did not entirely forgive him. Why not admit at least to himself that it was his wife who had prevented him from stealing from his clients, instead of pretending none of it had ever happened, not even the infidelities and the lies? She would have liked him better and kept all his secrets as she always had, but this was galling: she would not, could not do it. And knew she would, not out of love, but out of the daft desire to be stronger, and kinder, than she felt.

She closed her eyes and concentrated on what to wear. Planning an outfit was much less depressing than examining life, so that when she heard the faint and puzzling rustlings in the garden which were now so familiar after dark, her mind was geared to other things, which skirt with what, and since the sounds were acceptable by now, she was content to ignore them.

Sitting in his own Ford, converted to the occasional use of his employers and the glee of his children who liked to play with the radio, Ryan gave up the slow addition of his mileage expenses beneath a street lamp, wondering how it was he had drawn this particular short straw, this game of monkeys, and how soon he could stop. "One or two nights a week for the next five," Bailey had said. "I'd like to see if there are any comings and goings. Bernard's house, and the place where Edward Jaskowski lives."

"But why?" Ryan had asked, truculent at first, bitter against his normal willingness, taking Bailey's hesitation as a sign of weakness, knowing him well enough to suspect it was not.

"Why? A very slight suspicion. I can't even call it a guess; some suggestion that life has not entirely returned to normal in either of those places? I don't really know why."

"How are you going to justify my overtime, sir, on a hunch?"

"With difficulty. Which is why some of it will have to be night duty. Only some."

Ryan tried again, with the control of one who knows it is already hopeless. "I still don't get it, sir. Either there's something to see, and we observe all the time, or nothing which watching some of the time wouldn't miss."

"No, it isn't quite like that. I'm looking for the consistent things, not the odd incidents. Movements in or around either place, who shuffles round in the vicinity, when they turn their lights off, which of them comes home late or not at all, does Bernard put out his milk bottles, and does Edward Jaskowski come home after midnight. I only want to know what someone watching either of those households would see on normal nights: I'm not expecting anything dramatic."

"Is that all?"

"Yes, that's all. I'm not hoping to find closet murderers. More a question of loose ends."

Man must have lost his marbles. There they were both of them, that monster Cartwright and the idiot Jaskowski in the slammer, done, finished unless the jury stayed drunk, and Bailey was carping on about loose ends, like an old woman with her knitting. Mutiny had been apparent in his face.

"Just do it, Ryan, will you? I'm sorry to ask, but I think it's necessary. Someone may be getting at Bernard, for what little that may achieve." He smiled, and Ryan saw the order in the smile.

". . . And while you're at it, could you check on Mrs. Cartwright's address? It's been empty for three months, but if she has friends looking after it, or it's for sale, or whatever, I'd like to know."

"The local police station would tell you that."

"Probably," said Bailey mildly. "You'd better ask them. And let them know you're there."

Ryan had done both, with a surliness which provoked less help than he deserved. Detective constables on peripheral murder enquiries were privileged animals. Let them find out for themselves: no one tells us anything, and then get off our patch.

Lighting a cigarette in the darkness, he knew he would not have objected to any of this in most circumstances, accustomed to fulfilling orders beyond his comprehension, including those which were silly by any standard, far worse than these only mildly uncomfortable directions which at least allowed him to remain warm and dry. He was no professional moaner, normally cheerful with observations in the freezing rain, all-night stands by the canal which flanked the rear of that warren of empty warehouses, waiting for the expected outside a house. He could doze with his eyes wide open, watch with them half closed, hear through the clothing layered around his head. He knew that habit of slight, silent, persistent, movement which could keep alert the muscles which screamed for rest, was half used to functioning in fatigue, the way of life of it, where sleep assumed new proportions of sheer delight.

No, that was not the point: nor was it the point of his objection that this current kind of desultory watching had none of the advantages of his former employments when all the misery of it was shared, pooled and dissipated in the early hours grumbling and blowing on hands, and the after-hours joking even in defeat, with all the others equally raw, cold and hungry; nor did this, unlike all the similar tasks, have the dim prospect of an event, a conclusion, an arrest, or even a single moment of drama. He was watching streets, and all streets were basically the same; so were all houses when there was no purpose to it but the satisfaction of a senior officer's whim, a work-creating scruple which was wasting precious time, and what was more, ruining his love life. That placed any other objection into a milder perspective. He could stand all risks to boredom or sanity, but she could not.

The love life of an active, thirty-year-old detective constable, generally working hard under the anonymous cloak of central London, can be complex, and in Ryan's case well beyond his own understanding. First, there was the wife, married when he was twenty-one, and she twenty, amid great celebration, the obligatory disco, and a carefully chosen dress, a marvelous do, they had all said, nothing spared. He could still smile at the memory of it, never wondering why they all took weddings as seriously as they did, there being so many. Even Clarke, smallest man on the division, was married twice before he was twenty-four, big party each time, and the second wife leaving after six months. For that he had received the proceeds of two collections, and plenty of sympathy for his optimism and all the expense. Nothing at the end of the day more romantic than a copper. Wives were inevitable; you had to have one, and it was in the nature of the beast that it never understood what you did with your time, not even a WPC; never came close to knowing what it was like, never knew that the excitement of a new bathroom, a new car, or even a new baby, could not compare with running in fury, stalking in cold blood, questioning with cunning, pursuing if not glory at least satisfaction. Nor could she ever know that the trust you placed in her was minimal compared to the trust you placed in Bill, Tom, Dick or Harry to arrive when he did, to know when you needed him and he needed you. How could she know she existed at the fringe of a life so much more pressing than hers, not even a competitor with the other kinds of loyalty? She might once have heard the truism that good policemen make, of necessity, bad husbands, but not when she was nineteen, and if she had heard, would not have believed it. She wanted more: they always wanted more, and wanting an indefinable, impossible, first place in his life, was forced to ask for payment in kind instead, first sign of discontent in a second class citizen which had given them entry to the age-old, Blackmail–Overtime Tunnel.

"I never see you: you don't even know your own kids. Don't say you're not going to be back this weekend, it's his birthday . . ."

"I know, love, but it's overtime . . . there's that new carpet . . ."

Without answers to that, Ryan's once pretty and adoring wife stayed fighting, simply for his time, for some prominence, some relief from one-parent child-rearing, but not the same kind of war she had once fought. She had accepted substitutes, carpets, an extension to the house, a reasonable wardrobe, a garden, holidays, occasional meals out, and given him in the process a defeated alibi for all his non-official absences.

He was wrong in assuming that she never guessed when the overtime excuses were working overtime themselves, since the method of his lying did no credit to a detective. He was right in assuming that she no longer cared, having educated herself and the two children into a state of semi-contented self-sufficiency. He was right, too, in the knowledge that apart from his pay packet, he was redundant in his own family life. Not introspective, far from analytical, as opportunistic as the next with a thousand-and-one examples to follow, it was then Ryan had started to keep his eyes peeled for all the other more demanding, less demanding women. They were not difficult to find. Making the choices was harder.

Pubs. That was where you found them, hunting in pairs, you with your mate, she with hers, bored husbands finding bored wives, but not always, and pubs with music were best, mating corners, not just for the lonely. He had met the first in a pub, all drowned in sound and crowd, happy with beer, eager for jokes, loving each other, more than content to meet again another night, same place, same time, same row, same masks. Night three, by prearrangement with your minder, unless he was having less luck, you paired away, and found somewhere, there was always somewhere, women out for a good time could always find you somewhere. The soullessness of it never occurred to him, nor did the fact that the designs might not have been common, to say nothing of the desires, but he was too good-humored to encounter much resentment, too ready with laughter, too lacking in embarrassing insistence, and if there was a hint of pique, there were always other pubs. The moving tribes of London moved, stopped for a week or two, then moved on, not without accidents of unreciprocated lust which he learned to avoid. "Never tell them your real name, or where you work, and never tell them you're married," was the sterling advice he invariably followed. With scant enough information to equip pursuit, and all the inhibition of wounded pride or possessive husbands, Ryan's ladies had left him fairly free; those, that was, who had never wanted more than he offered. Perhaps in a year or two the circle would become too small, but already he was finding the lack in it. Practice was not making perfect, conquest was not its own reward: it was Romance with a capital "R" he craved rather than exercise, and all of Ryan's uncharacteristic sulkiness was because of the awful fact that he had found it.

Possibly the pubs themselves had made the more complex version of love so unlikely. Legs might have revealed themselves in pubs, but hearts did not above the pulse of sound and clichéd words, and all the smells of the wilfully, temporarily homeless. Maybe Ryan had needed a quiet meeting, one to one, in order to find Romance. As in pleasant house-to-house enquiries in the days after Mrs. Bernard's death, leading him inexorably toward the nanny two doors away, who had greeted him in company with two baleful infants, quickly informing him they were not hers. That was Annie, whose face was not worth the launching of ships, nothing splendidly slim or awesomely statuesque about the body either, more like the one worn by his wife, but younger. Twenty, to be exact. She was no legendary Swedish au pair, no pouting French help, but Annie from Bristol, soft West Country accent, first job away from home, missing her mother, kind lady employer, but lonely all the same. "It's big, London, isn't it?" was the first remark which enchanted him, the second her statement that she only knew boys below the age of three, but of course her most interesting contribution, if only initially, had been the description of the man carrying the gift-wrapped parcel. "Very funny, that," she had told him, "very sloppy, you know? If he'd wrapped it himself, he needed lessons. Could have done a lot better myself. It was a funny shape, and he looked worried, big fellow. You don't suppose it was a gun, do you?" Ryan had reported back, returned to take a statement. "Come up to my room, will you?" And to her room, private from the rest of a liberal household, Ryan had been returning again and again, armed with gifts and flowers, light on his feet as he bounded up the stairs, blessed by the lady of the house who considered that a happy nanny would stay longer. The odd part about it, and the facet of it which he considered least, was the fact that she recounted all the tales Ryan's own wife might have loved to have told once, given the chance. The only difference was that Annie and he lay naked on a bed too narrow while Annie regaled him with stories of precocious two-year-olds, and he listened to the domestic triumphs and disasters of her day, spellbound by traumas he would never have credited. "It's a very responsible job, you know," he told her, "looking after kids; I mean, I never realized . . ." Ryan's wife would have wept. Ryan's murder enquiries lasted all night. The lady of the house smiled indulgently: Annie bloomed out of her state of almost complete ignorance of the opposite sex, and wrote her mother that she had fallen in love. Ryan told no one, and his condition was agonizingly similar.

Evenings had become sacrosanct. For Annie, now that the worst of the murder enquiry was over, and it was not, as it had been, weekend inclusive, allowing him the odd visiting hour, the odd Sunday stroll, he had invented a figment known as weekend duty; for his wife, the necessity for overtime prevailed. Both were unquestioning, one out of admiration, the other out of suspicions she preferred not to define. But recently, Annie had changed perceptibly, not because of him, only because of a new-found confidence in her adopted town, new friends in the nanny sorority, new things to do with her evenings, more excitement than waiting for a boyfriend to cease working, or waiting in by the television. It was this threat which made genuine overtime such a burden. Not only did Ryan have to compete with fresh entertainments, but he had also to contend with the fear that the local talent halls would contain local contemporaries, and that by some awful, accidental means, the truth of his adulterous history, as well as his marital status, would out. Not yet, he prayed, not yet, not until I've explained, as if it could be explained, the love and the mess of it all. He could almost deceive himself she would not mind, but for the moment that was not to be faced, could not be endured, the thought of losing her. The only way to minimize either of the risks was to be with her, since as soon as he appeared, with or without warning, late or early, she forgot everything and everyone else, fussed, fluttered with pleasure, made him tea or coffee, drank the wine he had brought with him although she disliked it, and drew him down on to her bed with a sigh of relief.

"We don't have to do this every time I see you," he had mumbled once into her thick, baby-smelling hair. "Oh, don't we?" she said with a giggle as soft as the hands unbuttoning his shirt. "Who says we don't, officer?"

In the car, outside Bernard's house, knowing she was at home while he had genuine leave of absence from his own, Ryan scratched his chest in mimic of her hands, and sighed at the memory of her touch on the buttons. There was never anything hurried about her: never grasping, open-mouthed, crude, never a hunger he did not share. Slow in the casting off of clothes, his and hers, each time a seduction as if it had been the first. His tie, his shirt, her blouse, his hand beneath her skirt, hers unbuckling his belt, touching and stroking their way to nothing but skin, exploring with mouths, still slowly, more giggles, more words, love, admiration, falling away into all those subdued sounds with himself feeling massive inside her smallness. No hurry still in the undulating closeness: she was supple, moved like a passionate angel while he waited, holding back for her, damp in the whispering warmth, legs entangled long, long after. She it was who made him so skillful, so generously complete. He could feel now the softness of her buttocks, the full bosom crushed against his chest, and shivered, agonized and embarrassed in the darkness. No doubting where he wanted to be: quite simply, he had never known anything like it, not since an adolescent in love, new to the feel of another body.

Instead, he was outside Peter Jaskowski's mean, terraced house, at odds with its gentrified neighbors for garish paintwork and ugly double glazing, looking at lighted windows, a closed door and a blank wall. Who would know if he stayed there or not, or moved to the front of Mrs. Cartwright's empty maisonette to sit there, just as still, as bored and as cripplingly frustrated as he would be when he parked outside Bernard's, two doors away from Annie? Who would know if he ignored Bailey's foolish suspicions, which were simply designed to destroy the greatest treasure and pleasure of his life? Five weeks was a long time for such a girl to live on short rations. Too long, too much, even for a sense of duty as strong as Ryan's. He started the car, and did not stop until he reached the house where she lived.

Summer advanced.

"I saw your DC Ryan, steaming through Islington near Bernard's house quite late the other night," Helen told Bailey. "At least, I think it was him. Pursuing further inquiries?"

"I hope so. I asked him to keep an eye out. He didn't seem as keen as usual, so I'm glad he's doing as told. He's a bit off-color lately. Domestic difficulties, I'd guess. Observation duties might distract him, but I doubt it. Anyway, he deserves the overtime. He works hard. By the way, he got those extra forensic reports. All the notes we recovered will smell of spirit forever if kept wrapped. Added weight to Jaskowski's evidence, added effect for the jury. Same chemical as the stuff found in her house."

"Is that what you phoned to tell me? I hoped you just wanted to chat. Might have known better."

"So you ought. The reports can wait. They only say in three pages what I've just told you, and I've warned the scientists we'll need them for court. No, I was just wondering if you'd like to browse round an Antique Fair, sort of auction? On Saturday."

"Oh, yes, I would. I'd give anything to browse round an auction instead of what I've got to do. That would apply to most days of the week, but this Saturday in particular. I've got to go to a wedding, obligation, not pleasure. My ex-husband's, in fact."

"Why do you have to go? It seems odd for them to invite you. My ex-wife certainly didn't, but I would have gone if she had. I sent them a present instead."

"I think I'm expected to do both."

"What, a sort of no-hard-feelings exercise? The seal of understanding and approval; him showing that the old and new order don't conflict, nothing in the past but pleasant bygones and honest mistake?" She had told him something of her marriage, turning it into anecdotes, and was pleasantly shocked by the understanding.

"Something like that."

"Will it be hard work?"

"Very."

"Well. I can see why you'd consider yourself bound to go, sometimes best to give people what they want, however unfair, but all the same, I wish you didn't have to. Something more relaxing would be better for you."

She liked the genuine concern, the luxury of his reassurance pushing a new thought into her mind.

"I don't suppose you'd like to come with me? It's only a buffet thing. Moral support?"

Damn! Wishing she had left the thought where it belonged, stopped it dead on its insolent way through her mouth. Presumptuous, even to a friend of far longer standing, to suggest a chore so personal, an entertainment so close to home, even though she had felt with the words what a relief it would be, the mere idea a comforting cream on inflamed skin. She waited for evasive refusal, irritated response to embarrassing request, prepared herself to make a joke of it.

"Yes, of course I will, if you really think it would help."

There was no hesitation whatever, and no laughter either.

"Well, it would, and I'm grateful." She was stuck for the phrase to describe how grateful, how much lighter the day had become.

"No need for that. What time shall I pick you up?"

"A lift as well? Eleven-thirty? Wedding at twelve, champagne and bits immediately after. What time's the Fair?"

"Three-thirty. Shall we do both in our finery?"

"Even better; no lingering over the sparkling once I've been seen to do my duty, and you've been scrutinized by the laser eyes of my ex-mother-in-law."

He chuckled. "I'll enjoy that. How do you want me to be? South

London yob, with connections in the motor trade. Or severe, tight-lipped, disapproving, teetotal, officer of the law? I have suits for either role."

"I'll leave that to you. Wait till you see her. Don't know what I should be."

"Whatever they're least likely to approve, I should think. Can't expect you to turn up, salve consciences and behave well, surely? Put your hat in the Fair later. See you eleven-thirty."

Suddenly the Saturday prospect was relieved of all anxieties, a pure penance turned into a pure pleasure, no fears or reservations for her small uncomfortable place in the limelight of the has-been. Helen smiled, stretched, ran her fingers through her hair so that it stood inelegantly upright. Yes, that would do. Pulled a face at the wall, canceled the plan to buy a dress, and dragged the next set of papers toward her.

Ryan kissed Annie, loving the reaction of slight shyness, the usual little reserve of her delighted greeting which revealed the fundamental innocence of her and made him so protective. His woman, he called her. Then she put her arms around his neck and kissed him again, longer and even sweeter, swaying together in the doorway of her room. Meetings confined to late at night had a sharpening, clandestine air; they spoke in delicious whispers as if they could be heard.

Peter Jaskowski Junior slipped in through his ground-floor bedroom window, clearly visible from the street, whose indifferent observation he would not have minded, but free from the view of his aunt and uncle, which would have been more awkward. It was the same window he used to get out. He knew that Ed would not be there until long after midnight, if at all.

A light burned in Mrs. Cartwright's house, unnoticed by uncaring neighbors as Edward left his own additions to the collection, more familiar with it now than he had been when he first discovered it, more careful not to disturb familiar patterns in the arrangement, aware of occasional checks by the police and a man from an Insurance Company, never at night and never thoroughly, only for omissions, not extras. A safe house for a long time now; he liked its brooding, old-fashioned darkness even more than he had liked it when she had showed it to him such a long time ago. Even Ed, with his peculiar memory, chose not to remember the details.

Helen had long since decided that the peculiar rustlings and signs of movement in her garden were more than her cat, or even a confederation of cats. At the same time she had decided that whatever it was, it carried no threat of harm. It was a secret, was all: not a threat, but not to be told.

CHAPTER EIGHT

If they had chosen to ask him why he had begun to watch her, he would have shrugged his shoulders; standard reaction dreaded by teachers and uncles, who saw it as insolence or indifference, qualities he recognized but rarely felt. Far from hostile, this shrug of his, only an alternative to speech, quicker than searching for words suitable for adults. In his twelfth year, Peter withdrew from older company, making noise only with other boys whom he chose deliberately for their failure to question him. He was accepted in turn for his energy in games, liked for his reliable determination and his disinclination to challenge leadership. Peter arrived unaccompanied for school or football: participated, departed without trace of curiosity. Second school after Father's scandal: gossip faded into indifference, and he was always useful to a team.

Alone in the streets he whistled for company, looking for none. When he saw her for the second time walking in the street parallel to the playground, he was whistling toward evening football practice, and she caught his eye with more than vague familiarity. He could not have described what made her special, not beauty, age or color of hair; simply the fact of her passing smile, not issued through him or over his head, but into his eyes, and he smiled back, brimming with the warmth of it, glowing with the comfort of approval, turning to look long after she walked on. Then he remembered: she was the one Ed had showed, pointing at her in the distance with one stubby finger.

A long interval between that time and this, all time eclipsed since Dad went to prison: Mam indifferent and himself nagging Ed for company. Ed had protected him from the Uncle and Aunt, which was something, but it meant they had no time for him either. Baby brother Stanislaus was twinned with his cousin, baby sister was a blob, and he was the odd one out. Let me join in something, he asked in those days when Ed was still trying, and it was then he had been shown the house where she lived. One spring evening they had stood at the far end of the street and watched her come home, smart in a black coat, carrying a case, not like anyone he knew. Ed had told him it was all for fun since he had nothing better to do, a remark he resented while knowing it was accurate. When he was grown up, he was promised he could help Ed be a detective. That was why Ed stayed out so late at night; learning.

"If you want to be useful," Ed had informed him, "you can watch her. See when she comes in and out, how she locks her door, who comes to visit her, and when."

"Why?" Peter had replied in his most irritating refrain. "Is she nice?" a question of such naïvety Ed almost struck him.

"You don't ask why, and it doesn't make any difference whether she's nice or not. People like that never are, anyway."

"People like what?"

"I knew you were hopeless," said Ed, suddenly relieved to have an excuse for argument, "hopeless and stupid. You never understand anything. Nothing at all."

"I do, I do," Peter had cried. "Tell me what you want me to do, and I'll do it, Ed, please." But Ed had seen the unreliability of any ally foolish enough to question and young enough to speak if ever questioned himself. Better not. Peter would be as obvious as a flag, as reactive to the breeze.

"Forget it."

"Oh, Ed."

"Forget it, I said. Come on, I'll buy you some chips."

Peter was easily seduced. He had forgotten, accepted the bribe instead. Ed gave him a pound to go home. Ed was always giving him a pound to go home, just like his father. Mam occasionally managed ten pence, which reflected the size of her pocket rather than the extent of the guilt.

Then he had seen her again, the lady who smiled, and at first, that was all. Not significant, more than enough. Hours of life intervened before the next football practice, hours of school and home where the door closed on them all and harassed Aunt Mary was happy to accept his preference for his own company in the confinement of the room he shared with Ed whenever Ed was there. In its conspicuous tidiness the room paid tribute to the effort both made to control their own uprooted lives and keep them hidden, while Mary took the unnatural order of it as the only sign of consideration they gave her apart from Peter's distant politeness, which was preferable to Ed's silent challenges. Pete and he were an odd couple in an odder union which, for all its fragile consistency, was not unsociable or even insecure, a mutual lonelines both dignified and undiagnosed. To some extent Peter relieved his peculiar isolation by reading anything and everything, gathering a disjointed vocabulary which owed more to printed pages than speech. At school he submerged himself in teams and games, survived the rest, but all the same, as the woman who smiled would notice, he had mastered remarkable powers of quiet concentration.

No more than accident, and a kind of benign envy at first which drew him to watch her, not because Ed had told him to do so long ago. That was forgotten. After the smile, he arrived early at the empty playground with his own ball and kicked it aimlessly while waiting for the others. Slowly at first, then harder for the satisfying sound of it. Idleness turned into energy: finally one massive kick lobbed it over the wall which separated the ground from the back of the houses in the next street, and he watched in disbelief as it sailed out of sight into silence, knowing it was a good ball and he would not get another soon enough. He stopped for breath, then ran at the wall, scrabbling up to the top, pulling himself astride determined on pursuit, paused instead, paralyzed with pleasure when he saw what met his eyes.

The houses in the street beyond the playground were large, split into generous flats, but it was only the garden he noticed. One of his shoes was entangled into the branch of a huge climbing rose which seemed to escape rather than grow in its impatience to be seen. Ignorant of gardens as a child of the tenth floor, his muddled notion of plants was derived from books, photos of formal arrangements, tedious lessons and one school outing, none of which meant much and had led to no sense of wonder before he saw this luxurious wilderness guided, rather than controlled by human hand. Rich and small, enclosed entirely by walls, a mass of shrubs and flowering plants paying tribute to generations of indiscriminate planting on rich soil; a garden which required hacking back to save it from choking, now at its fiery best on a warm summer evening when the light exaggerated the color and contour of it all, and the heaviness of the air emphasized smells.

A sunken area of cracked paving stones led to the only exit at the door of the basement flat, and even these stones were decorated with flower tubs spilling with life beneath the russet creeper covering the walls. These had been Helen's only contribution to the garden: the rest she had found, and kept on finding in her ever increasing love and conflict with all this determined life. A cat basked in the lowering sun: traffic sounds, any sound was dim and distant, and there, half turned from some business about the tubs, trowel in hand, was the woman who had smiled into his eyes.

"Do you know, your ball gave me a fright," she had told him in her pleasant voice. "I thought it dropped straight out of the sky, a message of some sort. Then I hoped someone would follow, and here you are."

She showed no sign of alarm. Tongue-tied, he nodded and smiled, gesturing stupidly at the football which lay by the door, watching as she obeyed the mute request to retrieve it, laughing as she pulled a face in throwing it toward him and over his head, waving in response to her grin before he disappeared back the way he had arrived over the wall.

The vision was beyond his control. She haunted him as he ran, caught, kicked, shouted, she and the cat and the picture of that sanctuary. As darkness fell, he wondered if she could see from her flowers the lights of the ground, guessed her work would be complete and the garden empty. Pushing and shoving, the boys left the ground, teacher last, checking for litter and abandoned clothes. Shouting faded across the road before Peter emerged from his dark corner, climbed the wall cautiously this time, dragging against the roses as he slithered through the other side. The habits of silence were instinctive, and although fear contorted all his movements, he could not have stopped in the face of a dragon.

By night, the garden was better than he remembered, heavily scented, completely quiet, another world from his own. Light from the basement's uncurtained windows made glowing squares around the tubs, giving them new and brilliant charm in the spotlight. Peter ducked beneath a bush and lay flat on his stomach, sweating slightly, suddenly unafraid in nerveless contentment. Resting his head on his hands, he fixed his eyes on the windows and waited for nothing. A large cat surprised him with a soft sound of curious welcome which concerned him until he raised a tentative hand to touch her, the touch becoming a stroke as she purred and curled against his hip, warming him.

Then she came to the window, sat looking at pieces of paper as if perplexed, familiar flimsy sheets which he recognized from his own household as bills. On the days when one of these windowed messages arrived from the gas or electricity, the adopted Jaskowskis and their cousins endured a range of angry noises from Uncle Peter and for some days after, heat was at a minimum, blankets were worn at supper, and light was rationed with such severity that Peter read with a torch and all of them washed in semi-darkness before Uncle himself lost patience with austerity, and the mood passed. Here, light glowed sinfully generous from every window, revealing rich colors inside, different materials in the half-mess of a bedroom, a kitchen of red and white with wood among it, chipped and cheerful as an old postcard, the small room she occupied full of books, an old desk, a green reading lamp, and herself as centerpiece. No comparison with the place he was obliged to call home, none at all, not even a passing resemblance to Mary's gleaming surfaces, closed doors, the clean and comfortless froth of her bedrooms, and all the pale business of the papered walls. No plants like these in various states of growth in every room, no dozens of tantalizing pretty details, no kind face. He imagined her waving toward him, and shrank back, half wishing she could see him, terrified she might, determined to stay where he was.

Long after the chill of the ground had stiffened his limbs and the warmth of the cat had ceased to protect, longer after she had disappeared from sight of any of the windows, Peter moved out of his daze, returning silently over the wall, out of the playground, running the easy mile home.

There was no need to explain his long delay with more than a mumble: football practice was regarded as flexible, but he was already rehearsing unaccustomed lies for use on the many other occasions he would need to excuse his absence from the house so long after dark. By nature a child of transparent honesty, Peter became cunning in his invention of friends and his appealing description of their families. "Nick's mum works in a bank; he says, can I go there after football, but she says I have to ask you first," hinting at all the normalities they would have approved and were scarcely able to supply in so crowded a household. Without such approval or alibi, he simply retired to bed and left his room secretly by the front window, and unnoticed after football, after nightfall on other evenings, he kept his watch in the garden.

Again, if asked why he continued, he could not have answered. There would have been the shrug. It was not perversity or vulgar curiosity which made him seek out the playground, climb the wall, stretch out his undersized body on the ground, or sit behind the shrubs looking into that world of warmth of which the garden was only an extension even in summer. It was herself which drew him, slender and beautiful in his eyes, graceful and untroubled, and it was to Helen he came to speak in silent dialogue as if he knew her; she who would welcome him without challenge, understand everything he thought, approve everything he did, whose acceptance he trusted with a blind, unreasonable instinct and loved in return with a fierce worship all the better for her unreality, the more intense for never being tested. Artificial, but truer than Jesus was his belief that the woman and he could look after one another entirely as fate decreed. Only another oddity of a barren life for this to be such an unspoken arrangement, or that he, so used to the stifling of affection, should be happy to dwell in this silence of intensity, but he was content. He loved the very sight of her, wanted to protect her, and although he longed to touch, feel her ruffle his hair as Mam had done in that other lifetime, knew his limitations and did not presume on dreams such as these. Prone in the garden night after night, warm or cold among tickling grass, whispering insects, unfamiliar earth and silent life, he was content to see all he could see, watch as he would, know what he knew and imagine the rest. Speechless guardian of her calm, he was Helen's private army.

The interrupted vigil became familiar as weeks passed a hot city into a stormy summer, days of rain, miraculously dry darknesses if he had noticed, which he scarcely did. He so relaxed in the garden that once, instead of the shorter nap he might share with his companion cat, he slept for three hours and woke so cold he could only move like a puppet as he scrambled up the decaying trellis over the wall in a slow, dazed, clumsiness, arriving home at a walk, legs too stiff for running, faint and sick as he half fell through the window. And on that rare once, Ed was in residence, sleeping or pretending sleep. Peter was exhausted beyond caring; if Ed saw, let him watch him aim for his own uncurling space, where nothing short of earthquake would keep him conscious.

Ed had been waiting, simple procedure compared to the unthinkable alternatives of waking the household or alerting fussy adults by the sheer betrayal such a step would involve. Brother was part of no other lives and although he might not have wished to exercise care himself, would ensure no one else did. He turned as Peter's sleep grew profound, and stared at the ceiling, his hands cradling his head. Little sod: where had he been?

Wary laziness made him resist the impulse to shake his companion and pull from Pete an account of this rebellious independence. Laziness and pride in not displaying curiosity, accompanied by the sneaking fear that his authority might be questioned. Ed closed his eyes, listening to the noise of the other's sigh. The kid was tired. A girl? Was that the explanation? No, too young: to say nothing of too small. Friends, mates of the late-night kind, but what kind? Watching from his pillow as the curtain moved over the open window, Ed was jealous of the company his brother might have acquired by stepping outside the charmed circle of his influence. He did not want Pete's needs supplied elsewhere, required no rivals for Pete's irritating respect, and loathed Pete having secrets which were his sole prerogative. Anger quelled as only Ed could quell it, along with the anxiety which feared itself; as much an example of love as Edward knew toward any breathing creature, a love nevertheless capable of strict control.

Enough. The questions would wait for morning: Peter was his and remained his. Ed ordered sleep, obeyed his own orders.

The day was hot and breathless when Peter woke to notice the grime of his hands transferred to his face and the sheets of his bed, omen for a day of trouble. Ed was up first, watching as Peter sprang from bed, thinly naked, late, groaning, scrabbling for clothes.

"Get in the bathroom, Pete. Wash your face. There's no one in there. Be quick."

Peter jumped, struck by Ed's laconic words which were less of advice than command, words which summarized all his own guilty awareness.

"Go on. I'll turn the sheets. She," spoken with the indifference of dislike, "won't notice. Do your feet as well, for Christ's sake."

Peter shot from bedroom to bathroom like a rabbit, stood in the bath splashing away the remnants of Helen's garden in guilty fury and shallow water, bracing himself for further shock, bolting back to the room and into his clothes. Aunt Mary regarded it as the pride of duty to provide clean shirt and socks every day, and for once it occurred to him to feel grateful. Ed, sitting on his own unmade bed, smoking toward the window, glanced at the closed face of his baby brother, and debated the wisdom of silence.

"You weren't in till late, Pete. Where were you?" Ed was sounding mild and disinterested, but Peter knew better.

"Football."

"Don't be stupid. What do you take me for? Football finished by half-past eight, not bloody midnight. Where were you?"

Mulish silence, the face shut, Peter turning away, folding his clothes as Mary liked, stuffing pens and unnecessary bits into the bag for school. He felt Ed behind him, towering, hands on his shoulders, large hands on small bones.

"Where were you, Pete?"

"Nowhere."

At the back of the house was the clatter of voices and breakfast arguments. Peter's left arm was twisted, deftly doubled high over his back, pulled tightly, bending him forward with a low, quick, scream of agony.

"Where were you, Pete?"

"Nowhere."

Ed sighed, pushed the arm higher with greater strength than it had ever been pushed even in all those playground and back-shed bashings which had been endured in the days and weeks after Dad's well publicized arrest, days when pain at home was a relief from pain outside it. Peter's shoulder ignited with agony, and even as his mind drifted into the vacuum of it, he remembered how Ed had saved him once from the same bullying, identical means of torture to those inflicted now, the same humiliation, and a similar gasping conviction that in a minute, the arm would snap.

"Where were you, Pete?"

No louder than before, softer if anything.

"In a garden. Hiding." Ed recognized victory, enough of the truth to release the hold. The pain was momentarily worse, and the water of shock in Pete's eyes became tears of outraged sorrow.

"Doing what?"

Rubbing still averted eyes with one hand, moving the nerveless arm, keeping his face from inspection, Peter found a new cunning hidden in contrived hesitation.

"Looking into windows. Watching girls. Those new flats in Sotheby Road, you can see in their bedrooms . . . I fell asleep."

"What were they doing?" Ed was relieved rather than avidly curious since it was now the telling which mattered far more than the tale.

"Larking around, three of them. Trying on clothes. I thought I'd wait until they'd gone, but I fell asleep."

"That good, was it? Good enough to make you sleep?" Ed jeered. "Come on. What do you want with tits and bums?"

"Only watching," mumbled Peter, content in his relief to feign shame.

"You stupid sod. Leave it out, will you. Who do you think'd believe you if you got caught? Not the Old Bill, they'd beat shit out of you first."

He reached for another cigarette, a sign of relaxation and the cross-examination ending.

"Happen often, this, does it? Spying on girls?"

"No. Sometimes."

Ed snorted. "As if it's worth it. Watch it. I'll get you a video if you're that bloody curious. And next time, don't make me twist your bloody arm. Just tell me, right?"

Peter had nodded, grateful for the end of the interview, the beginning of other endings, the shock of it driving him to school in a state of grief, edges tinged with disappointment, triumph, and loss. The loss of Ed, and the loss of himself to Ed was uppermost, as if Ed had wrenched away the arm instead of merely hurting it. Then there was the factor of fooling his omnipotent brother simply by using half a truth which was so far from the truth to achieve an easy deceit where he would never have tried to deceive. Peter would never become accustomed to lies; they made him twist and turn afterward, and these unprecedented lies to Ed were the worst of the few he had ever told, but the greater misery was Ed's behavior. It was not the persistent stiffness of his arm which brought the disgraceful tears to his eyes in the privacy of the school lavatory, only the thought of Ed inflicting the pain, twisting the arm so thoroughly, Ed condemning him to that, treating him like the enemy, leaving them both diminished. All that trust exploded like a light bulb in the moment he had known one flash of hatred for the man-boy twisting his arm into pain and his mind into lies. If wavering before, he was lost now, if sinking, he was drowning: there was nothing but this aching confusion which he could not explain to himself and would never be asked to explain to anyone else. He would have liked to be allowed to cry, was all, to cry and be silly, to talk about anything at all, know someone would notice and not mind, not treat him as an obligation or threaten him to say what he needed to hide. He did not know what he wanted, except to know he had nothing he wanted, nothing at all. Except the garden and the Lady. He would be going back, whatever Ed did. There was nowhere else to lose himself, and the room, with or without Ed, would drive him mad.

Helen had found the boots in the garden on the morning of the wedding when she had escaped the flat to delay the still not final decision of what the hell to wear, a conclusion postponed by too much thought, and complicated by the promise of blinding heat. In only the second summer she was too new in her garden to have survived the novelty, still guilty for her ignorance, besotted with the freedom and contrasts so swiftly formed between winter wilderness and summer promise, reluctant to leave on a free, dawdling morning.

There were the boots underneath a bush, dampened by more than a day, the grass flattened around them: football boots, with laces tied together for easy carriage, neatly placed and forgotten until she hooked them over the branches where they hung oddly lifeless and decorative, toes turned in, dead without feet. It was the boots themselves which surprised her, not the implications of the boots, which forced no new conclusion on a mind already anesthetized with the sun, since she had realized for quite some time, weeks in fact, that the province of her garden had ceased to be her own exclusive domain from time to time. What perplexed her more and nagged her still as she sat in the garden with Geoffrey the same evening, hoping he would not notice the bizarre blossom of the offending bush, was the fact that she could not bring herself to mind. Whoever he was, the intruder who flattened her plants and comforted the cat, he meant no harm, and although that reaction was entirely subjective, based to some extent on a fear of finding out otherwise, she had promised herself to abide by it. At first, the rustlings and the obvious presence had alarmed her long before the sounds of him, never close, always noticeable, merged with all the other sounds of the evening, less predictable but only as alarming as the worst of them, friendlier than many. Perhaps her determination to leave it at that and hope that the interloper would return to recover his boots was based on the clear impression, gleaned from she knew not where but confirmed from his footwear, that she was not dealing with anything fully grown: more like a child, and only one child. All right, maybe a juvenile burglar, or midget rapist, perhaps the height of folly to make any other assumption, but for now, she was content, much to her own surprise, to give him space, to believe better of him than he might have asked.

And then there was the rose bush. How could she have believed there was anything intrinsically harmful about this trespasser after the rose bush? Two days after an earlier summer storm, when the largest bush, almost a tree of brambly roses, shaggy from too little pruning, certainly none by the present owner, suffered from having its overlong branches all splayed, some broken by the force of wind and driving rain, the roses themselves blown into a heap of pock-marked petals in a sad trailing petticoat around the roots and across the grass. On inspection of the damage three days after, Helen had found the petals in heaps, tidily gathered as if to preserve them, and three of the broken branches bound at the fractured point with Elastoplast. The hardy bush had reflourished the way things did in this garden, and she had hoped he had noticed its response to his futile but loving care. Since then, she had never minded his intrusion. He who would give first aid to a rose bush would not wound its owner.

Although she was well aware that of all eccentric introductions to the many facets of her life, Bailey accompanying her to the wedding of a former husband was odder and more personal than most, a gesture of peculiar trust and confidence on both parts which had been amply justified, she was not prepared to explain to him either the history of her intruder, or her reaction to it, suspecting he would prefer the explanations and precautions of a policeman, rose-surgery regardless. At the end of a long and successful day, there were other and safer topics. In the moment when the football boots caught her eye, Geoffrey and she were midway through post-mortems of wedding and Antique Fair, with the spoils of the last at their feet—one clock, not working, Helen's purchase, to be his repair, both shaded from the last of a sticky, hot sun, both decently half-way out of all the impediments of formal clothes. He was reduced to open-necked shirt, trousers, no shoes, she to the rolled sleeves and crumpled skirt of the suit which had been the wrong choice after all. The wine was not cool enough; there was nothing cooler, and it did not matter. Nothing mattered. Helen felt she looked a mess, had laughed too much to care. He thought she had never looked prettier, had surmised the husband was no great loss, even accepting that he was in no position to judge, nor wished to do so. He wished he had cauterized his own past far sooner, and reviewed it all in a garden like this.

"You were right about the mother-in-law."

"But I didn't tell you anything about her. Gave you license to behave as badly as you liked, told you she had eyes like lasers, the biggest snob unhung. What did she say? She cornered you for all of ten minutes."

"I enjoyed the ten minutes."

"You what? How could you?"

"After I'd told her I ran guns for a living . . ."

"Geoffrey! You didn't!"

". . . and told her, no, we didn't have any plans to get married; you didn't believe in any of that anymore, but we might reconsider after the baby."

"You told her that?"

"Why not? She deserved it."

"Couldn't have done better if I'd turned up naked. You're the best alibi I could have had: my name'll be mud. What more could I want?"

He had been pleased with his own invention, relieved by the fluency, pleased to make her laugh. A relaxed silence, sip of warm wine, a celebration of not being an in-law, or the victim of one.

"I wonder what a gunrunner does?" was Helen's only lazy inquiry, her eyes caught again by the boots on the bush, wondering why they were the only thing after this day which she would hesitate to explain to this man.

"Why are there football boots in that bush?" was his only hand-pointing question, a mind-reading exercise in the same silence.

"Oh, next-door's boy . . . he comes in sometimes."

It might have been true if she had known of the existence of any next-door boy: Helen and Peter shared the same embarrassment with lies and Geoffrey was better able than Edward to detect them. And to know, at this particular moment, when to let them go.

"Food?"

"There's an idea: long time since canapés."

Bright things on toast, glazed to an unappetizing sheen like half the guests, he had thought, and she had laughingly agreed. The sandwich later had been preferable however curled, and even that had passed beyond memory as dusk began to fall. Lazy debate on food, culminating in the indecision of salad things, a kind of picnic, eaten in the still warm out of doors, colder wine, talking with the softness dictated by light on summer darkness. Talking of the cameos of the auction Fair, the ferret-like dealers with all their subdued rivalries, beautiful, wonderful, enviable, ugly things for sale, the way liking for one of them prevailed over all caution, and how it was that an old prize, paid for in the same money as the dull necessities felt more like a gift snatched from fate. Late talk, better, slower, until ending became inevitable, sultry warmth gave way to less continental chill: they shivered, lingered to talk of summer places, moved indoors with plates and dishes, he in search of jacket and the duty of parting. Again. Friend and friend first, still lawyer and policeman in that other life, dictating a whole plethora of inhibitions, buried deeper than bones, accepted for more years than the weeks of their acquaintance.

But he kissed her. He altered it all; he could not help it, no more could she, nor the manner of it, out of doors again, by his car, somehow safer, and just before it was too late to kiss at all, unbearable to leave without some signal of mutual trust, or fail to place some floating mark on the undercurrent. Her fault; it was she who had touched his shoulder, brushed his cheek with her own, saying thank you without moving away, so that she was still close enough for him to pull her closer, hold her face in both his hands and kiss her longer, not on the cheek, but on the soft and willing mouth, feeling her arms circling his neck, slightly uncertain, not much, with her tasting of coffee and wine and everything he could ever remember wanting, a lengthy kiss, like a slow electric shock.

Driving home like a boy racer, forty-six-year-old child, nothing new under the moon, happy as Larry, knowing none of this would be pursued. She would retreat, and so would he, for now; all wrong, and all so right, while she was indoors furiously happy and embarrassed, wondering if the blush was permanent, and how she would never let this happen again even while her face was blazing young in the usually cruel bathroom light.

Only in the morning was she relieved that no one, in Geoffrey's presence, had arrived to collect his boots. And with all the mutual liking, knew she was right; he would not have accepted with her equanimity the visitor to her garden.

If little Peter was hurt beyond redemption, frightened by now into almost total silence by Ed's defection to the ranks of traitors, then so was Edward worried by what he had done, defensively concerned by the completeness of his brother's new reserve, a refinement of the old to the extent that they did not have their impatient exchanges in the middle of the night, nor any of the normal few words in the morning. He missed it. For days afterwards, there was suddenly no pleading from Peter, no "When shall I see you . . . can I come and find you after school? Please, Ed, let me . . . ," pleading which Ed regarded as whining, but led in the event of a Yes, to occasions which Ed suddenly realized he actually enjoyed. Perhaps once a week Peter would be allowed to meet with his hero brother in a café: they would mooch around shops, nose to windows in Holloway Road or Chapel Market, Ed conducting a slow monolog, making Peter listen to music in HMV or comment on whatever Ed wanted to buy. Uninterested in either music or clothes, Pete tried anything for the sake of the company, hearing new tapes with every sign of pleasure, shaking his head as Ed appeared from a changing-room in too tight trousers which he knew Ed would not buy. Edward liked expensive gear: but it would be a giveaway. The pretend evening job might have provided some excuse, but even with that he could not wear suits worth a hundred pounds without a more legitimate source of funds although he looked at them all the time. Peter glanced sideways round the shops, trying to avoid eyes, grinning foolishly, not quite pretending he was alone, but almost; still proud of Ed and wanting to be there rather than elsewhere, wishing the pleasure was less pain as Ed proved too big for slender modern clothes, his father's son in that respect, solid-thighed, broad-shouldered and chested, a challenge to the fitted shirt, a joke in a double-breasted jacket. In the end he concentrated on the purchase of things which did not reveal their own value, good shoes, belts for his wide waist, jeans which actually fitted.

"What do you reckon, Pete?" turning in front of a mirror, while Peter, relieved at the imminence of a real purchase, always agreed, delighting in Ed's more carefully controlled pleasure, nodding vigorously.

Buying was invariably followed by treats, usually food, with Peter relieved to break the monotony of Aunt Mary's provisions, and able to eat everything on offer in whatever enormous quantity provided.

"You've got a worm, Pete, you really have," Ed would say, watching the slender wrists at work transferring egg and chips, ice-cream, buns, toast, sweets, into the gaunt little face, and this was as far as he would ever get in words of admiration for the boy. No one would have diagnosed their brotherhood on first sight; Peter so small and tinny ribbed with legs like sticks, sharp shoulder blades, wispy hair, wide, permanently creased forehead and huge-eyed gaze, next to stocky Ed, low-browed, thick thatch, small, puffy eyes. But in overhearing the sparse conversation, you would have known they were brothers. Mere friends could not have tolerated all those silences.

Now there was nothing, not even the familiar, taciturn ease, and it was Ed who missed it most. Through all his cool plotting, exerting authority over gangs challenging his one-man band, with all the envy and hatred he excited, Ed was by force of circumstances completely alone apart from Peter, and, like Peter, immune from every human contact. The fact that he had chosen it, with the isolation descending on him bit by bit, month by month, did not make it any the more palatable, since even Edward needed some voice to blend with his own, some corner where he could touch shoulders without threat in the intimacy. The room which Ed could have left so easily had been kept for the unconscious purpose of listening to another's breathing, and even though he regarded

Peter's adoration as a chore and his company deficient, he had not known, still did not know, how important it had been.

The state of frustration remained unanalyzed.

"Look, I'm sorry," Ed had shouted on the second day of silence, "You should have said where you'd been . . ."

It was a churlish apology which rebounded on itself. Peter's silence, even his nervous half smile and his it-doesn't-matter-forget-it gesture, so infuriated Ed he almost hit him again, and both of them had recognized that violent temptation hanging in the air like a nuclear cloud. However much Peter struggled and mumbled, "S'all right," managing it once or twice, it was the most he could do before speechlessness descended again, and Ed's rage dragged him out of the room or numbed him into sleep. Perversely, he came home more often, drawn by the nameless need, both of them turning in their own grooves with the air electric around them. The only thing which Ed understood absolutely was that Peter would need from him something far more precious than gestures or gifts before he would ever again nag for company, trust him, plead for his time, instead of bolting away like a rabbit from a fox. Ed had nothing of the kind to give, nothing sufficiently precious except his own secrets, and finally, after two weeks of screaming frustration, surrendered these, crashing through every rule in his own book in sheer desperation. If Peter's intention had been to practice blackmail through silence, he could not have been more effective, although nothing had been further from his injured mind than the baring of Ed's soul. Peter's wishes were never fulfilled. He always got the opposite. This time it was alien, self-indulgent words, designed to restore comfort, but destined to terrify.

Late at night in the dark room, Pete's silence pushed Ed to an orgy of words.

"I'll be able to look after you one day, Pete, I really will . . ." In the telling which followed, Ed could not resist the boasting. "One day, I'll be rich, Pete. You know how Dad came to get into prison, Pete? Well I do. He got frightened, and he got caught; he didn't have the bottle, couldn't have learned, he weren't clever, not like me. You know that Mrs. Cartwright, the one who got him to do in that stupid woman for her?"

Peter did, but scarcely. The details of his father's disgrace were hazy since no one had ever explained it all; everything he knew was eavesdroppings.

"Dad thought she got his name from the book, but she didn't. No one knows, but I knew her first, see? I got in her house, two years ago, and she caught me, see? Didn't call the police, nothing like that, just sat down, talked to me, told me I'd got no choice but talking back. I thought she was mad, but she isn't, she's clever. She let me go, but she made me turn out my pockets, tell her where I lived. I can't tell you what she's like, but she got me so frightened. I hated her at first, but then I didn't, I got to like her, and after the first time she made me go back, I didn't mind going. She got me to say what I did, all the thieving I done, and she clucked her tongue, I thought she'd say she'd stop me, but she didn't do that. She just said, 'Well, boy, it's as good a career as any, no one owes anyone anything these days, but you're wasting your time. What are you, fifteen? And you haven't even started learning anything yet. If you're going to be a criminal, be a good one, and learn to do it proper.' She said she wished she'd done that, instead of spending her life trying to be good. She said, 'Let's talk about this.' I said, 'What?' and she said, 'About being a proper crook, that's what, and not being afraid of anything, being ready to do anything. You can't be a successful villain if you've any respect for the rules, you could have a team in the end to do it for you, but you must have done it all yourself first.' Then I pinched some stuff for her, good stuff; she flogged it and paid me fair. 'This is the kind of stuff you need,' she said, 'not all that old rubbish, tellies and all that stuff,' and she told me where else to go with it, names, people who had it in their houses, stupid rich gifts, we used to laugh about them, we really did."

Ed was enjoying himself. He was not deterred by Peter's silence, knew he had his attention.

"About every fortnight I'd go there. Make yourself at home, Edward, she'd say; always Edward, formal, but I didn't mind that. She was the only one who listened to anything I said, she made everyone else look like idiots. Sit down, she'd say, and tell me what you've done. Everything. What's the point going to school, she'd say. Look at me, it got me nowhere. You can always come here, or to the shop if you want to learn something, get to know a good thing from a bad thing. Only deal in quality, nothing else is worth the risk, she told me. She's right, you know; she's always right.

"But she wasn't so clever about Dad, was she? 'Now,' she said to me one day, 'now for something entirely different. You know how I told you you had to learn to do everything, not stop at anything? Well, I'm wanting to practice what I preach. I want somebody knocked off, not by you, don't worry.' She must have seen my face . . . , 'but what about your dad? He's a private detective; don't private detectives do that sort of stuff sometimes, or know who does it?' I'd told her about Dad, all about him, how he wasn't really good at anything, what he tried to do, about me going with him sometimes, watching people. She'd said, there was no money in that: I told you she was always right. You want to be a detective, she'd said, only to find who needs robbing, that's all. Anyway, about Dad, she said to me, would he do it? I couldn't let her know how I thought about it, shit scared I was, and I said no, straight off, no. But there he was, bellyaching on about being so big, and all the time being so poor, and I thought again, and then I told her, he might, he just might, you never know. 'So,' she said, 'I think he might if you push him a bit; I'll ask him, but not yet. He can do some work for me first.' She didn't need to tell me not to tell him I knew her, and she didn't say anything more about it for a bit, and I didn't ask, but I knew she'd got him when he started going round all worried and mysterious. Then the gormless idiot took me with him to see her. I just sat there, kept quiet as if I didn't know; then I had to listen to him all the way home, and every night afterwards and I thought she's right again, it isn't such a big deal to knock off some silly woman. Shall I, shan't I, he went on and on, even after he'd been watching the woman for all that time. He made me sick. Remember the time I had that black eye? Well, I lost my temper, and he lost his, and then I really got to him, got his goat. 'What are you, Dad?' I said, 'what the fuck are you? Go on, hit kids . . . hit me again, hit other boys . . . I'll line them up for you. S'pose you can make money hitting kids, when you haven't got the bottle to go near some silly rich cow who could buy and sell you with her money . . . Go on, you pansy . . . Go on!' In the end, he did it."

The silence no longer mattered, and the response was less important than the talking even into a vacuum. Ed had despised his father's confessing, but there he was, isolated with the audience of one horrified child, victim to the same desire as Dad to have a witness for his tale whatever the consequences.

"She knew, you know, I'm sure she always knew, that she wouldn't get away with it, but she didn't seem to mind, as long as it was done. Not at the last anyway. She said, 'You never know your luck, but I know mine, and your dad's, not so good, either of us. I hope you don't mind.' 'No,' I said, 'I don't mind, but what do you mean?' 'He'll blow it,' she said. 'He'll blow it sky high, and I'll come down in pieces unless I'm very lucky and I'm never that lucky, even though I never stop fighting until it's all finished.' 'No,' I told her, 'you won't get caught.' 'Just watch,' she told me, and I did, watched what happened, and I hated Dad for being such a cretin. What could they have done if he had kept his big trap shut? Nothing is what, sweet nothing.

"I saw her then, and no one knew, after he'd been booked and they'd had her in the first time. I'd go to her late, the back way. She was sort of resigned, you know, not giving up, not hopeful. It was odd the way she didn't seem to care. I knew what she'd promised Dad, and they've even got most of the half she paid him. It's not fair, they should pay it back, he earned it. Why should it matter how he earned it? I said I was sorry. I was embarrassed: She said, 'Don't be, I did what I wanted, don't mind me. Try and stop your father if you can,' was what she told me to do, but if I couldn't, which I can't, not to worry, just play a joke on a man called Bernard, put this glove outside his house, and she'd think of something to look after herself. Bloody worth it for her, she said: life didn't matter, but she told me she wanted me to do all the things she'd never done, and she'd give me money . . ."

Ed faded into silence, swallowed bitter saliva, summoning strength for the worst which was yet to come, remembering the mesmerizing face in the firelight, fanning the flames of his own ambition with her hot hatred, making him shiver with a strange heat, the thought of her, the only one who began to know him. In the same moment, he was aware of the utter futility of telling Pete. Poor Pete, who was stranger to all her lessons of trusting no one, telling no one. Poor Pete, but it was too late: he had begun, could not stop himself from slithering further.

"She said, she said to me, 'Your Dad will probably have me, but not you, and you can have what he won't get.' The other money, was what she meant. You know, what Dad was supposed to have got after he done the job."

Peter did not know, but he was sitting up now, arms around knees, eyes on Ed's face, his own face as pale as death in the light through the thin curtains.

" 'Money,' she said. 'Your Dad's share first, and more.' But first you see, I had to prove I was worth it, worth the effort of being given a chance, by showing that there was nothing I wouldn't do. A proper test, she said, and she told me how, and told me who, just before they arrested her the second time. Ain't seen her since. 'No need to kill her,' she said, 'not unless you need to. But you have to hurt her, hurt her so it shows. You have to take a risk. You have to show me,' she said very loud again, 'that you can do anything. Or what,' she said, 'have I ever achieved?' "

Peter shook his head, mouthing confusion. Ed was unconcerned. He could not go back for explanations of what was so entirely obvious to himself, and it was only for himself he was talking at all.

" 'They'll put me up for trial, I know they will,' she told me. 'They're only waiting, and at the end of it, I'll get the money to you, once you've done as I said, and I know that you have.' I pretended to laugh. 'Ahh,' I said, 'but I've learned from you, it was you warned me not to trust anyone, so how would I know you would pay when you can't do nothing in prison?' 'Oh, yes you can,' she said, 'that's what lawyers are for, and I'll know you've done it. You just be sure you understand. No job, no money, just like your father.' Then she showed me her safe, gave me some things, and said, 'Goodbye, Ed. You are like the son I never had, a real man, you'll do well,' but it wasn't soapy, or crying, just saying it, telling me. 'You can prove you can do anything, then go on and be the best, and this'll have started you on the right track. You'll win, Edward, as long as you never get a conscience, and you haven't much of one now. If you do like we've discussed, I shall know I helped to train you.' 'Is that all you want?' I asked her. She said, 'Yes, and that's enough for someone who's wasted their life trying to be good. Plenty enough, raising a bad one who wins. You can have all my revenge for me. I'll know I've made them pay . . . the bitches, all of them!' I wasn't sure what she meant . . . What do you think she meant, Pete?"

"Mad." Peter forced out one, hoarse word, then a grimace or two, followed by phrases difficult to decipher.

"Don't, Ed, please . . . Help Dad . . . Don't, Ed, please . . ." and the slurring of the wandering words, the concentration Ed needed to translate, brought an end to his catharsis. He fell back against his pillows exhausted.

"I don't know if she'll do it," he muttered for his own benefit.

"Do . . . what?"

"Pay me."

"Good."

He was outraged.

"What do you mean, good? Five thousand pounds for the asking, and you say, Good, if I lose it?"

But the boy was crying. "Not true, Ed," he blubbed. "Not true, not true, Ed's silly," speaking like a backward child, until Ed, purged of his own knowledge, felt the familiar, restless return of the old intense irritation. With it, as he lit another cigarette, a guilty relief in the realization that Pete had not begun to comprehend what it was he had been saying. Thank God for Pete being so simple: the tale had been beyond him after all.

"All right, all right, not true, made it up, a story, to make you talk to me," he soothed, giggling at Peter's face.

"Not true, Ed . . . You couldn't make Dad . . . do that . . ."

"No, no, no. It's okay, I didn't. Only a story. But don't tell."

"Oh, no. Not ever. For always." Promises of sheer relief.

"All right. That's right. Tomorrow we'll go to the shops. I made it all up. Only a story. Go to sleep. Nothing. Only a story. Go to sleep, Pete, good boy."

The crying had stopped.

CHAPTER NINE

Ryan was the carrier of bags, again, and it seemed to him that in the months since they were first assembled, they had reproduced themselves into twice their own size, a pregnant volume. Depositions tied and indexed running away to four hundred pages, copy exhibits, three bundles, none of them light, all those as well as sets of photographs for the jury, six copies each, what a mess, and he'd probably done them wrong. Three sets for the defense, three for the other side, one for the judge, one for the witness-box. Why hadn't they decided to distribute them free to the public gallery, hand-outs to the crowd like give-away magazines at Tube stations? Ryan was not objecting to his lot in life as he loaded the car and flexed his arms. "Mustn't grumble," he'd been advised early on, and copied his father now only because it was too warm a day for any other sentiments. No chance of parking inside the Temple, and Mr. Carey's room was up three flights of stairs, full of uncomfortable chairs when you reached it. Even if he secured a seat by the window, and watched the river gleaming, imagining himself outside with Annie, time could not pass soon enough. Already he was missing a chance of seeing her and two hours hence he would have to turn homeward to a houseful of relatives, not a prospect designed to improve his mood. The wife was suspicious, putting strictures on his time, school holidays giving ample excuses for expecting him sooner rather than later. Perhaps the conference was not such a bad way of hiding when he came to think of it, better than being in the dock at home or fending Annie's increasing questions. Cross-examined by two at once with answers for neither. Bitter, even on a day as glorious as this.

Bailey, launched on another murder enquiry, albeit as short-lived as the life involved and needing little detection, arrived at the conference from a different direction, leaving his sergeant with all the weight, for which he had the grace to apologize as Ryan remembered, slotting his car into a semi-legal space on the Embankment. Stepping from the Tube station, Ryan saw Miss West as heavily laden and unaided, and that cheered him. Nice, Miss West, nicer as she put down her bags and waved at him, all the better for carrying her own kit. The guvnor was sweet on her; you could tell, he was sort of over-respectful, suddenly pausing at the mention of her name in the last week. Ryan smiled to himself: he wasn't the only one with a weakness and the knowledge of Bailey's raised him in his estimation. Wonder if they did . . . ? No, they wouldn't: they'd just talk about it. Not like Annie. There was no one like Annie.

Carey, wearing his size well, laconic, expansively good humored, less condescension than usual to the group which had somehow welded itself into a team, seated them less tidily than a tea party, and as Ryan noticed, provided tea, or rather clerk provided tea. Conferences with counsel, always scheduled for four-thirty after court, inevitably beginning later, when the Temple became alive with scurrying gowns and the buzz of voices in summer from open windows: footsteps through cool archways into hot paving stones, black, ant-like traffic past the Fountain, through Pump Court, skirting Temple Church, and on to the fine façade of King's Bench Walk, Paper Buildings, Hare Court, old descriptions on walls, a warren of tiny streets and courtyards hidden from the world, enclosed at night. Inner Temple, Middle Temple, retreat and center of the Criminal Bar, a thousand barristers' syndicates where privilege jostled alongside struggling rank and file, a crowd of discreet fighting sparrows clinging to an overcrowded tree in cramped but tasteful chambers. Mr. Carey, Queen's Counsel, had ceased to cling, if not to crow: there was no need, but he would never cease to work like a well trained hound.

The Chambers clerk treated Helen and all solicitors who provided work, and thus his commission, with sedulous courtesy. Nice day, Miss West, how nice to see you: Uriah Heep incarnate, better dressed. She could feel the smile as she saw Geoffrey; Ryan saw it too; harassed junior counsel, late from Acton Crown Court, missed it; and Carey was indifferent, anxious to begin, but not to end.

Case conferences, the bane of life, accelerating in number as a major trial drew close, a few weeks to D-day, and the team in harness to ensure nothing had been left out, to see Carey QC was as fully equipped as possible, the prosecution machine well oiled in the best sense, and the truth dressed in her best clothes. Sorting out distortions and clangers which tended to linger through inumerable revisions and ruin the whole aspect. How to use the order of witnesses for the maximum impact, which witnesses were unpredictable, how much should a jury be asked to take for granted, methods of avoiding confusion or over-simplicity. Had they crossed all the Ts and dotted all the Is? Each had a contribution; some needed to speak more than others, and it was mandatory that Carey QC should speak most of all.

As Helen had promised, he was thorough. Not exactly pleasant, but efficient. An hour passed deciding which witnesses, although there were less of these than there might have been since no one denied the death or the perpetrator of it, half the evidence to be read to the jury like a complex story with slides, omitting the nastier pictures. "Photos of the inside of Mrs. Cartwright's place—can they be color?" Peering at the black and white version. "Christ, what a gloomy room: like a funeral parlor," his remark a lighter moment for brief laughter, but not enough to hinder progress, and so it went on.

"How much proof should we adduce of Mrs. C's obsession with Bernard?" Carey had asked, genuinely fishing for ideas. "All of it," said Helen. Including the neighbor who had seen her sitting outside the house; the waiter who saw her outside restaurants waiting for a glimpse of the beloved; the receptionist at Bernard's office, who knew just how often she had called, left notes, waited in vain, but hadn't liked to say; the incomplete, embarrassingly passionate letters found in her house, but never sent; all the photographs taken by the first detective, stored and labeled, Michael and his wife, from every angle. Poor Bernard, he hadn't known the half of it, hadn't known the fire he handled, still didn't know. Should he remain in ignorance? Yes, he should, let him appear as disingenuous as he could, don't frighten him more.

Carey had paused. "Any more on the green glove, Mr. Bailey? Miss West told me," he looked at her large sheets of instructions, "you were concerned about it. Thought our friend had acquired a practical joker, perhaps a revengeful Jaskowski? You had them watched, I believe? I must confess, I applaud your caution, but I don't quite follow your reasoning."

"Not so much caution; precaution, I think," said Bailey. "DC Ryan did the watching."

All eyes on Ryan.

"That's right, sir." He swallowed. "But nothing odd, sir, absolutely nothing. All very quiet, all the time I've been observing."

"How often, Mr. Ryan?"

"Oh, three nights a week, over five weeks."

"How tedious for you, Mr. Ryan . . ."

Another passage of polite sympathetic smiles from Counsel for the worker, poor victim of an over-fussy government. Ryan gripped his pen, and made a scribble on the corner of his paper. Bailey shifted, watched, and shifted again, brittle with a sudden suspicion, almost dismissed at the sight of Ryan's sturdy, conscientious face with its hidden expression. Surely not; even though Ryan would always have been the first to join in with a joke at Sir's expense, and he was not smiling now. Bailey had not asked him for written reports as proof of duty; he trusted the man, but nothing to report? No household, not even solid households, remained as lifeless or free of normal movement. Bailey volunteered no more and the conference moved on.

And on, until at last before the thirsty meeting shuffled once more in surreptitious consulting of its watches, there came the chapter of inspired guesswork on the tactic of the defense. By and large, they were pleased with progress, could afford to indulge themselves with ideas. What if . . . what if . . . ? If Jaskowski came up to proof, like a good wine matured, if he kept his promise to tell the truth, and did not fade away, scream, cry, deny, retreat in the face of ruthless questions; did not explode on being called a liar so often. They had to rely on him for an Oscar performance of memory, but after Jaskowski, and his dreadful damnation what would the defense say? Would she more wisely concede the sad devotion to the wicked married man, admit its madness and shameful purity, confess the employing of Jaskowski to follow the beloved, but add that she never intended more; while he deliberately exceeded all his relatively innocent instructions, chancing his arm on reward or blackmail for a killing she could never have ordered or devised? Most likely of defenses, more plausible to admit one madness, but point to Stanislaus as the maddest, bent on a murderous frolic of his own, tempted by nothing more specific than the prospect of riches from her hands, or Bernard's? Not more than that, no real joint enterprise.

"I just don't see how she can defend it all," Ryan announced, firm in his optimism and aware that his opinion had never been asked.

"We're relying on the evidence of a convicted murderer, don't forget," said Carey drily, wanting no one to downgrade the nature of his task, "so it's certainly worth a try. And Mr. Quinn, QC, is not without certain skills." The last was snapped, before the wide mouth closed into a narrow line. No love lost there, Helen guessed. Silks so aptly named, prima donnas of the Bar, ruffling their feathers toward one another before judge and jury, settling old scores with new virtuoso displays: better that way. Greeting as friends, each feeling his weapons, sizing the other for strength, pretending the last crossing of paths was forgotten, although Carey for one, never had, remembered every triumph or disaster with a perfect recall for humiliation. Last time with Quinn, Carey had been defending, and Quinn, little whippersnapper, ten years younger, two stones slimmer, had won.

He opened the straight line mouth. "Another conference in three weeks, if you please. Miss West, you'll arrange it with my clerk?"

His Cheshire-cat grin appeared, a sign of approval of Helen West. A good instructing solicitor, collating, organizing, gathering anything but wool, she was a lynchpin of the case, and he could not resist the hope that Quinn was less well equipped. As she left the room, he felt lonely.

"I wonder," he said to his junior as the door closed behind the last of his departing troops, "what they can say, Clive? What might they have we don't know? It worries me."

Clive Barrow was rearranging his papers, appreciated a cry for reassurance and able to provide it.

"Oddly enough, I doubt they've been able to arrange much yet. You know Quinn's been in Hong Kong, only returned last week, I understand. Saw the client once before he went, but that's all. Very good junior, but still . . ."

"Good God, leaving it a bit late isn't he?" Carey was delighted with the news, while the junior failed to point out how in the general run of things, especially with the razor-sharp Quinn, there was probably as much time as they needed.

"Well, well; we'll see, we'll see." Carey's chuckle caught the edges of cigar-coated lungs. "Come on, Clive, let's have a drink."

The junior sighed, and like a good junior, obeyed.

In another public house, free from all the distinctions of Fleet Street legal gossip, free from any advantages at all apart from its position as the last island in the traffic mid-way from office to home, Lawrence sat later than usual in his regular six-thirty refuge between the pressures of the one and the eternal hysteria of the other. He hated conferences, threw back one half-pint in the time it took him to order a whole, worried by heat, prisons, particularly upset by Quinn, supercilious bastard. How was a man as awful so popular with the establishment? Quinn's nonchalant composure, his genuine, enquiring charm and his over-abundant skill was in itself the source of the irritation, together with Lawrence's own failure to respond with anything other than his normal prickly lack of grace. Faced with truculence, Quinn had been . . . nice, consistently, politely, patiently nice, all day, and every minute of the day, effortlessly agreeable, until Lawrence could have screamed at him to be the opposite.

They had begun their meeting in the grim ante-room to Mrs. Cartwright's prison quarters, which Quinn graced like a lord, ended it in Counsel's chambers, Lawrence jotting Quinn's suggestions, discussing the mountains to be moved before trial, wilting with heat and anxiety with Quinn still smiling, fresh as a spring daisy, skin healthy brown, apologetically telephoning his wife to enquire who was coming to dinner, while Lawrence sat in the spotlight of sun from the window, too awkward to move, surveying the enviable elegance of the room, scratching a prominent spot on his pale skin.

Second galling feature of the day had been Mrs. Cartwright, reacting to Quinn's appealing smile and extended hand with more gratitude than she had ever shown to Lawrence who had been her link with the world for months. Quinn's second meeting with the client unbent her more than Lawrence had done in six, and it hurt. Laboring for two hours in an ill-ventilated room, he had watched Quinn taking apart Mrs. Cartwright's line of defense, and putting it back together again into a jigsaw puzzle of stronger if still imperfect fabric after his discreet and clever treatment. He drew it from her so nicely—she remembered better under his care—she had told Jaskowski why she had wanted Bernard's wife followed, told him she was rich, might even have suggested Bernard might be better off without her. But Jaskowski may have come to her house, might then have taken his lethal direction himself, perhaps seen the rich pickings there could have been in a bereaved, unguarded home. Ah, yes, said Quinn, that explains it, I'm sure the jury will see the feasibility of that.

Lawrence wrote it all, wondering how it was Quinn could humble himself to the role of the client's interpreter with such bland dignity, renewing the client's confidence without ever making a promise or telling a single lie: full of innate reassurance, conspicuous authority. Not even taking off his bloody jacket, a fine, light-weight, well-fitting garment, probably made for him in Hong Kong out of his enormous fees for whatever enormous fraud, while Lawrence wilted in his ready-made synthetic, horribly conscious of the damp armpits, the slightly gluey smell of his deodorant. "Warm, isn't it," was Quinn's only soft complaint, while he himself scarcely glowed.

Ms. Sissy Malton, junior counsel for the defense, had warned her learned leader from weeks of fussy experience, that Lawrence was, in her own words, a pain in the neck. Quinn had bent over backward, contorted himself with charm and appreciation to relieve the pain, and failed. Lawrence, picturing Quinn in Chelsea with his gin and tonic, ordered another pint.

Used to his own fury when paired with the glamour of Quinn, Lawrence might have coped far better without that other debilitating worry of conscience. He had been told so often by his senior partner in no uncertain terms, that if the bloody woman insists about the money, don't forget to tell counsel; he has to know. Lawrence had not forgotten and had not told. There had been the moment in prison when Quinn had asked, "Now is there anything more you would like us to do for you?" and Mrs. Cartwright had told him, "We have covered it all, Mr. Lawrence and I. Thank you," his one triumph of the whole day, although her glance in his direction suggested conspiracy rather than gratitude. Too late to tell now: he had already done it, executed the first part of his suspicious orders to the letter, and met Edward Jaskowski. Thinking of it now quickened the desire for another pint which would leave him less relaxed than he had been before the first. Something there was with the junior Jaskowski which made oblivion impossible.

He did not like to call it reluctant admiration. Lawrence preferred the downtrodden; even liked his own wife best when she was thoroughly depressed, and before meeting Edward at all, his sense of romance was caught. Then Edward appeared, solid and surly to answer his appointment, and on sight of him, Lawrence found fellow feeling for all pale, unattractive teenagers everywhere, since at thirty-three he was still in the same mold himself. He admired Ed not only for a shared condition of life, but for Ed's stubborn self-possession and stunning lack of gratitude in the face of it. No thanks for the Cartwright generosity; no expressions of surprise, anger or any one of the gamut of emotions Lawrence had expected. Instead, Ed shrugged his shoulders and sat volunteering nothing as if it were all his due, no more than could be expected, and why not after all, it was only money? At seventeen years and now, Lawrence still wore the imprint of the last person who had sat on him, while Edward did not, leaving Lawrence gabbling in response to the silence, repeating his message and all its strictures three times over, stung into volubility by the boy's stillness.

"You understand? Don't you?"

"Yes."

Lawrence cleared his throat. "Do you . . . do you wonder why my client is making you such a gift?"

"No. Why should I?"

The lad was intimidating. Lawrence found himself copying the infectious shrug before he explained it all again. No contribution whatever from the boy apart from a promise that they would correspond after the trial.

"You'd better open a bank account," said Lawrence, unable to allow Edward to escape without some piece of advice.

"I've got one already, thank you."

The beer, fizzy and warm, inflated stomach and ego. He was like a ship, filled with water ballast to ride rough waves, stabilized by the intake, readier to sail. Bugger Quinn. Let him work it out for himself if he was so bloody clever, and besides, what harm in it, this rich Cartwright eccentricity? Maybe she would be free with her cash in his direction for the unquestioning loyalty of his service. Lawrence composed himself, fastened the top button of his shirt and straightened the tie, swayed from the pub fit for another quarrelsome evening.

Going home alone after dark was the essence of being single, the very nub of it; often pleasantly lonely, sometimes nostalgic, this evening, neither. For once, an evening on her own had been an unbearable prospect, driving Helen into another house as soon as the telephone gave acceptance. A restlessness incurable without pleasant company found and given before walking home alone, slightly ashamed to be seen in need. There was a moon above the trees in a newly dark sky, serenely decorative over the imposing Victorian houses she passed on the mile home. Ahead of her, a man walked slowly in isolation, reminder of the dangers of the night which made her develop her storm trooper walk suggesting resistance to any interference, an air of confidence not always genuine but convincing.

Alongside the doorway of an ugly public house, a man and woman sat on a wall, arguing furiously in low, bitter tones—Go on, tell me, what have I done?—the quarrelsome voices undermining the order of words. Only as lonely as everyone else. Bypassing their misery and turning into the other tree-lined street which held her own home, she was impressed by the fully dressed branches, and recognized her own loneliness as preferable to most, far from unbearable by comparison, and in spite of that conclusion wished above anything else she had been able to speak to Geoffrey after the conference, wished she could speak to him now.

Stepping between the cars, eyes fixed on the ground, she found herself dawdling, avoiding the cracks in the pavement like a child, afraid of what might or might not happen next between them, angry with him for the mood he had created, knowing he would have all the same reservations, a badly bitten, twice shy pair of people, outwardly confident, inwardly terrified of ever again crying into the pillow. Wise to run before it was too late to restore the hard-won equilibrium of their lives, since this would be no peccadillo, no laughing kiss-and-tell, no one-night-stand. Fear and cowardice: she did not know which afflicted either of them, could forgive the first, not the second. The gesture would have to be his and his was the greater barrier to cross. If he did, for all her agonizing, she knew exactly what she would do however much she might contemplate the opposite.

Opening the door to the flat, the telephone tailed into silence. She sorted clothes and papers in preparation for another day, wandering from room to room, silly with pointless sadness.

Then she heard the sirens. Looking through the window, she sensed movement in the garden, the same rustling, and a small sob of sound, coinciding with the sudden roar of engines in the street at the other side. Keep down, she told him silently, whoever you are, you little idiot. Hide . . .

It was his garden: his, hers, the cat's, space also provided for birds, flowers and all those live creatures who belonged as naturally as himself; no one else's garden, his second home in the few weeks since Ed had so effectively destroyed the remnants of the first. In Ed's view, the confession had re-established the balance of brotherly discipline in allowing him to stay away until the early hours and remain as ignorant of Peter's whereabouts as he was of his mind. Peter's silences were disguised in smiles and surface serenity and the deception worked well enough to allow him to adopt his resting place within view of Helen's windows as often as he pleased. Familiarity bred carelessness: so did his sense of belonging, and although he needed no reminder that his presence was an intrusion, once hidden he immediately forgot he could be watched as well as watching or that his freedom was not one which all observers would take for granted. Down in the dark he could tell himself, no harm: the lady had given him prescriptive rights to admire her flowers, stroke her cat, mend the bird with the broken wing, wonder at the trees, anchor himself to her island, sometimes noisily.

Far too noisily on this occasion for the nervous couple one door down, two floors up, who saw him entering the garden to wait for

Helen's return. The intruder, they said to the telephone voice, might have left already, but he had been there, they had better look in case the lady in that flat is not in. Helen's arrival within minutes had been visible, Peter no longer so, and the men in uniform, so many of them—what a waste—were referred to her doorbell. Her problem—we merely called you—nothing to do with us. They did not really care for the police.

Poor Peter. Siren sounds were not infrequent, but there had been a tone to these which marked them as the baying of his own hunters. He had been lying on the ground, the cat in his arms, kicking his heels, humming to himself, hoping she would come home soon, alive with sudden pleasure when she did, settling himself again when he first heard them and recognized the stiffening of fear. He might have run at the wall immediately, over and home by any route dark enough to take his shadow, but he could not. Movement was beyond him: peace had become the paralysis of a blacker terror than he had ever known, even at the hands of father, brother or baiting contemporaries, and it denied him the option of escape. By the wall furthest from the door he shrank behind a blooming camellia bush, his back to the worn bricks, curling his small body smaller, fist in mouth, the other hand pulling thin knees to thin chest, watching and listening for the car doors closing in the street beyond. High and low voices, calm and authoritative, and Helen at the window, appearing to whisper something before she disappeared from sight while he stifled a scream. Still time to run: too late to unfold such frozen limbs which he contracted instead into an agony of tension. Longed to close his eyes, unable to grant relief, watched instead for hour-long seconds until finally the door from the basement opened. From it she led three uniformed men, speaking to them cheerfully with an insistent politeness. In the light from the door which made his eyes as shiny as diamonds, the garden seemed tiny, bare and innocent.

"I'm sorry you've been troubled, really I am, but there's no one here. If there was, I'm sure I'd have known, but do look."

She moved casually before them, and stood in front of his hiding place, almost touching him, brushing the bloom. The cat had emerged toward her, rubbing at her ankles as the men strolled a few steps, absurdly large in that smallish space, reassured by her nonchalant protest. One searched the edges, the others shuffled and gazed.

"Nice garden, miss. How do you find the time?"

"Well, I don't really: you know how it is. I'm lucky, it just grows."

"Wish mine did. Mostly it just dies. Summer like this doesn't help."

Muted agreement and chat on the subject of plants. She managed to move without moving, pointing to things, talking quickly and easily, making them at home.

Another spokesman, "Your neighbor might be right. Someone's come, and someone's gone, by the looks of it. Nothing missing?"

"Nothing to take."

"You'll call us again if you hear anything?"

"Yes of course; I'm sorry, they're a bit nervous upstairs."

"Better safe than sorry. You do have window locks? Now those who won't call, there's the problem. Never mind. What plant's that? My mother has one."

Unhurriedly, conversationally, all four returned into the house. Peter heard them retreat without haste, feet on stairs, civilized goodnights, hunters heading toward another scent, no rush, no trouble, adrenalin on the ebb. He remained as still as before, aware again of the chance to run, equally unable, crouched like a statue with the silence hammering at his ears through a pounding heart, blocking even the rustle of leaves. Stay he must for the very horror of running; frozen by shame and the terrible end of all his dreaming. Peter bent further, sobbing into his fist for the sudden awareness of his own oddity, his freakish, silly presence in her garden as if he owned it, for the stupidity of hiding, fooling himself for all this time that she would not, could not, hurt him, knowing now how she would be the last of many to find him stupid, inadequate and naked to whatever she would inflict before sending him away. He was more used to being discarded first and only struck as last resort: the order of it did not matter, only the sickening familiarity of rejection.

He could not close his eyes even to compress the tears, but kept them fixed open, watching through the new dark as the basement door reopened. She emerged, slim and upright, her dark hair silhouetted by the light as she moved the two steps toward the flower tubs and stood with her arms folded, speaking softly and clearly without even looking toward him, addressing the night at large without hint of accusation or anger in the soft voice he remembered so well.

"I think, don't you, that it's time we two met. This is silly. Can you stand up?"

Peter paused, betrayed into movement by a sudden shock of hope, quickly dismissed, still reluctant to face retribution, but without choice. He uncurled and stood by his lair.

"Come here," she commanded.

As he moved into the light, she saw his clothes were damp from the earlier rain, streaked with the color of the grass. Furrows of tears ran down the cheeks of a thin face rigid with pride and despair. He stood like a sad boy soldier, trained never to ask favors or expect either concessions or understanding, ready to take punishment without a word. She had known for the weeks since she had sensed his presence, that he was neither fully formed or capable of doing her harm, this friendly alien whose company her cat preferred. Apart from the first anxious curiosity, it had never occurred to her to be afraid of his presence, but faced with him now, she was simply surprised to find him as small and defenseless, so dignified and resigned in the defeat of his whole bearing. A beautiful child, larger than an infant, all the more pathetic for that, the saddest child she had ever seen, and her heart overbalanced. Even the pity puzzled her, but she could not have rationed it, could not have betrayed him, knew she would have lied for him more than she had done already, and should the need have arisen, pretended she knew him well. Which she did, in a manner of speaking.

Expulsion should be immediate, with a slap. She should send him home like a peeping Tom, full of threats and public disgrace. The thin body of him, held in control for too long, shook with cold: there was no shrug, no bravado, only exhaustion, which made strictly rehearsed words irrelevant. Of course she should send him away, now: tell him never to return, how dare he, to her garden or anywhere near it. Any adult with half a brain cell would do precisely that.

She fished in her sleeve for a handkerchief.

"Look at you," she said. "You have the dirtiest face I've ever seen. Gently, she wiped some of the grime from it. "And now, what do we do with you? It's warmer inside, you know. And the front door much easier. Time we learned to talk, don't you think? I don't suppose you're hungry, are you?"

The immobility altered, only to the extent of a nod. The eyes, fixed on her face, refilled with tears, brushed away.

"Do you have a name?"

The head shook, anxious, but adamant.

"All right. We'll do without names then. Come on."

He nodded, crumpled face alive with an awestruck smile as she took his hand and led him in through the glow of the doorway. The cat yawned, stretched, followed.

In the kitchen, she invited him to sit while she continued a stream of soothing chatter. From another room the telephone rang, and she watched him poised for flight but yearning to stay, wondering if it was Geoffrey's call she had missed again. Either speak to a precious friend, or cater for this frightened imp: no choice. The loneliness of the child, nothing else in him afflicted her more, the glaring loneliness of him, he wore it like a birthmark. Who had dared leave a small boy thus? Busy with hands, with food, with smiles, she boiled with anger, stroking with meaningless words, watching him calmer, eating with nervous haste, finally rewarding her with words.

"I like it here," a quick earnest sentence, hands pressed between knees with the effort of it.

"Well, I'm very pleased you do. I like it too. You must come here often. Is it better than home?"

"Oh yes."

"Where's home?"

A shake of the head, a pleading look. Please, please, do not make me say . . .

"Don't want to say? Well, don't then, pet, if you don't want to, but I'm worried for you . . . How do you get there? Walk?"

Nod.

"Aren't they worried about you? So late, I mean."

He was puzzled she should think anyone worried. Why imagine anyone was concerned to look into his room, let alone notice? Helen suspected no one noticed: he had that look, the appearance of one neglected in clean clothes, not an obvious target for the indiscretion of Pity.

He stood, suddenly, pointed to the clock, this boy of so few phrases, apologetically anxious with a smile which transformed his features and she knew further questions would be useless. He was warm and fed now, little else she could do, and restraining him would destroy that little achievement like hitting a wounded dog in the first moment of recovery. Besides, he would manage: he had left alone before.

"Going home now?" Very casual.

"Yes. Thank you for . . ."

"You're very welcome." They were, strangely, smilingly, well-mannered.

"Again?" he said uncertainly.

"But of course, my pet. I hope so. Could you come and help me in the garden tomorrow evening? I could do with it, you know. It's getting out of hand. You know it is."

The look of pleasure was starlike, the nod this time so vigorous his hair stayed on end, although she had been allowed to comb it without protest.

"By the front door, do you think?"

"No. Wall."

"Whatever suits you best. Goodbye then."

From immediately below Helen watched him, shinning to the top of the wall as agile as the cat on a good day. Up to the brink, he paused and waved, and only then was she reminded of where she had seen him before. After the wave of hand, he pointed to his chest, looking down at her smile, granting in his happiness a sudden accolade of trust.

"Peter," he said, "is me."

CHAPTER TEN

Hallo, Clive, Sissy Malton here. Do you have a sec?"

"Sissy! For you, all the time in the world." She still had that rich chuckle.

"Good. I don't actually need much of it, but I do need some. Hasn't anyone told you I've been pursuing you for days? Blank negatives from your clerk—Mr. Barrow's out, Miss Malton—the world's best traveled man, found anywhere from Knightsbridge to Snaresbrook with every Crown Court on the south-eastern circuit in between. How's your learned leader Mr. Carey?"

"Lusting after you. I've told him you're consumed with desire for his perfectly formed body."

"Don't. I've forgotten all I ever knew about lust, and it would take more than Carey to make me remember. Quinn might, but Carey never."

Clive did not believe it.

"Do I take it from this you've only phoned to discuss the drudgery of the Cartwright case? I mean, is that really all? I thought you might be offering me alcohol. Or something." He smiled at his own hands, remembering how Sissy had been such a frightening lady.

"Can be arranged, I suppose, but I was thinking you might like to haul your papers across here, or invite me to you. We've got to sort out which witnesses you want and we need. You know what Quinn's like, swanning off to Hong Kong to earn more in three weeks than I could in a year, leaving me with all the spadework. Now he's back, and nothing's altered, three weeks to go before trial. Your nice instructing solicitor keeps badgering mine, who is absolutely cretinous, for a list of witnesses. You need to know who to warn, after all. I thought it would be quicker if we sorted it out between ourselves. Has Carey decided?"

"Sort of. I suppose you'll also want to pick my brains over recent developments?"

"But of course. Are you coming over or not?"

He had never been able to resist Sissy's will, her cut-glass voice, or her handsome size. Few could: most ran to her bidding with the same speed as himself, arriving in her chambers a few minutes later.

"You bully," he greeted, grinning at the sight of her.

"Handsome as ever," said Sissy, businesslike as ever. "Witnesses first, gossip later. The tea's filthy."

Junior counsel for the crown against Cartwright bent his graying head toward Sissy's carefully preserved golden one across her large desk. The familiar Temple shuffle had begun outside. Junior counsel for the defense was brisk: the long list of witnesses was soon noted and decided with few surprises.

"Why are you calling forensic stuff? No, don't tell me, Carey's idea, I can guess why. How do you think your man Jaskowski's going to perform?" Sissy sat back. Late motherhood, the expansion of an already large frame, early middle age and the slight fraying of her once immaculate edges, suited her well.

"Oh, he'll do fine. He knows his lines." An unconvincing confidence in his voice, guessing she was fishing. Barrow had loved Sissy once in the distant irresponsible days of pupilage when she could outdrink them all. He had once woken up in Sissy's bed, long before marriage intervened for them both, and since she could still penetrate his caution if not quite overthrow it, that was all he was going to say about Jaskowski.

"Why are you calling Bernard?" he countered.

"No secret there. I don't mind telling you, but use your discretion about what you tell Carey." The sudden confidentiality was alarming: there would have to be a *quid pro quo.* Sissy never gave something for nothing unless she was slipping. Come to think of it, she did look tired.

"Quinn wants to make some mileage with Bernard. That bloody man obviously gave our Eileen some encouragement, and if the jury sees that, they might have some sympathy to spare. You know, poor widow, led along by rich lawyer, you can imagine the kind of thing."

"Bit far-fetched, isn't it?" Clive would certainly tell Carey.

"Could be, I don't know. Quinn's sometimes too clever for his own good."

"And a bit hard on Bernard, if you see what I mean. The man might have flirted a bit, but he didn't deserve to get his wife murdered."

"But my client is innocent," said Sissy with a wink.

"Sissy, all your clients are innocent, unless you happen to be prosecuting: prisons are full of your innocent clients."

"Okay. My client tells me she's innocent, and that's all I need to know. All Quinn knows is that she's going to need all the help she can get. You haven't met her yet, have you, but you'll see what I mean: she's hardly a cuddly woman, doesn't exude warmth, especially not in my direction, and she hasn't been to charm school either. In fact, it's fair to say that what with her and her solicitor, who is a creep of the first order, I've been run off my feet, and I'll be glad to see the back of this one. It's so much easier when they're approachable, and she isn't."

"Sissy, you aren't asking me to sympathize, surely?"

"Yes, as it happens. And warning you to wait for fireworks. Quinn has a thing about Carey. He won't pull his punches."

"You don't need to tell me. The feeling's mutual. I can't guarantee the behavior of either of them, but I still don't see there's much Quinn can do with this evidence."

"Nor do I," said Sissy, "but he'll have to try, won't he?"

"And if you're good, he'll let you go out and buy his sandwiches. Or let you read a statement from time to time, so that the jury can see you exist." Quinn was renowned for ensuring that his juniors received no share of the limelight.

Silence fell. Sissy eyed Barrow from beneath her still long lashes and recognized a touch of the depression this damned case always inspired, feeling old despite the boisterous children at home. Perhaps she could give up being calculating for once, perhaps not.

"Now, how about that drink I was supposed to suggest? El Vino's?"

"No. I'll stumble across Carey."

"Somewhere else, then? Or are you expected at home?"

She made it sound like a challenge, subtly recognizable as such, politely put. Remember me? Look at me if you dare. And with equal understatement, he rose to it.

"Anywhere you like, Sissy. Are you better at choosing wine than you used to be?" Then, attempting to even the dangerous keel but not trying too hard, he added, "You can tell me about the children: how old are they now?"

Sissy's handsome hips filled his vision as she bent to retrieve her bag. He caught a breath of far more expensive perfume than she ever used to wear. "I'm looking forward to hearing all about yours," she said sweetly. "And all the gossip. And yes. I'm far more discriminating than I used to be. About wine, I mean."

Woken by another woman's snoring and dreaming of women, Eileen did not know why she had thought of women so rarely until now. Women were the real enemy: she should never have bothered with punishing the men, killed all the women instead. Tossing asleep, half confident Edward would do as he was told. Something there was with that woman who gave her orders, the one who wanted Michael. Hunting for Michael she was, buying pretty things to please him: Eileen had known it as soon as she saw her that second time. Setting a trap for him: she had those kind of clothes, that shape, like his wife, but not fair in skin like that diseased thing, not so small, but even so, the same woman. Pretty enemy. Women it was who had ruined it for her all along. Edward will see to her. The legs or face, she had told him. Mark her at least. Edward was the only one she did not doubt, a good boy. Hurry, darling Edward: let me sleep better.

"Women!"

"What about women?"

Bailey found Ryan crashing the phone into its cradle, a modern phone not proof against such treatment or sufficiently satisfying an object to hurl across the room, no weight to it, no potential injury.

He was forced to sit instead with his fists clenched, tongue hissing on words like a curse.

"They're bloody impossible, that's what. Bloody impossible," and no, he did not want to explain it, but wanted to shout rather than cry, could manage neither. "Excuse me, sir, I'm going out for some air."

"Sit down." Bailey's calming hand was on his shoulder, not restraining but not to be brushed aside. Ryan sat, the rage expelled all in one breath leaving him white and shaking.

"You don't have to tell me, but there's just a possibility it might help. You've been like a bear with a sore head for weeks. You're a first-rate copper, Ryan, finest kind. I can't be seeing you miserable—even if I didn't have so much time for you. Now what's the matter?"

Confiding had no place in Ryan's life: he would never analyze whatever pained him, he would pick himself up, run headlong at the next brick wall, fall with a wounded skull, recover after a fashion, look for another brick wall, and run at that. Hurting at the moment, smarting with worry, unable to take the lid off his emotions, incapable of keeping it on. *Cherchez la femme,* Bailey had decided, familiar with all the symptoms. The poor bastard's in love. That makes two of us, and I doubt if he'll confide in me any more than I could in him, but I wish I suffered from his lack of caution, and I'd like to help.

For once, Ryan was ready to look for help. As masters went, he was as contemptuous of Bailey's idiosyncrasies and status as he would have been of any, par for the course, a mere habit of rank, and not inconsistent with the enormous respect and grudging affection he had come to bear for the man. Bailey did not claim credit for success; he let Ryan take it with the lion's share of interesting enquiries, made him learn, never once told him to do what he himself was not prepared to do, and always thanked him. Ryan had taken more from this enquiry than any other in his career, and, while not admitting it, was as grateful as he could be, bearing in mind the sad state of his conscience, without which he might have stripped the bones of his not uncommon dilemma immediately, with the guvnor as audience, believing he would listen. As it was, he hesitated.

"Problems at home, sir," he mumbled. "The wife says she's leaving me."

"Why? Because of the other woman you've been seeing?"

"How d'you know that?" Rudely and abruptly said. He might as well have asked him to mind his own business, but that was not what Ryan wanted; he wanted Bailey to pry into his affairs although he was the last to be able to ask.

"It didn't take much to guess," Bailey was saying. "You come in one day as high as a kite, the next looking as if you've been hit by a bus. I know your duty states, and I have a rough idea from what you wear whether you've been home or not. Obviously not as often as your wife expects. The rest I can only guess from the fact you've been tearing yourself apart. How many kids do you have?"

"Two."

"And the girl? Married?"

"No."

"Decent girl? Forgive me, but I can't see you getting yourself into such a state about someone who wasn't."

"Sir, she's marvelous, bloody marvelous: she's a great kid. Shit, I can't describe her, but she's no side to her, none at all. She didn't know, you see, about me being married, she wouldn't have . . . she's not that kind of girl. Now she does. Know, I mean. I had to tell her when the wife found out: she's been crying for a week, it makes her thin . . . I can't bear it, she's been so good to me, says she loves me anyway. The wife stopped even thinking that a long time ago: it's not like going home when I go home, no one comes near me; I may as well not have bothered."

Scenes crowded into his mind and into his mouth, the worst week of his life, all because of that bloody anorak. He'd kept two, a nice division not entirely dictated by prudence, something more to do with fixing a barrier between the two lives to stop them touching, one coat to go home and go to work, another separate coat for seeing Annie, who would take it from him and hang it up as if its condition mattered. In the pockets of that coat would remain all the detritus which revealed her existence, silly cards with kisses added, tickets for a film, lately a packet of Durex and a lipstick from a spilled handbag. Access vouchers for places of which Mrs. Ryan knew nothing, receipts for admittedly modest gifts, but still not gifts for Mrs. Ryan. And, dummy he was, he had walked into his own house with all that incrimination on his person, and left the wrong coat for her to pick its pockets when she was looking for cash for the milkman who was never paid that day after all. On the way to work he had realized, knew what would happen, nothing he could do, what could he have done, telephoned home and said, "Whatever you do today, don't look in that coat, you won't like it and neither will I?" Half of him had been relieved. Only half: not enough for anyone to have called his carelessness Freudian. Although he knew the inevitable, he had still sped home as early as possible (Bailey was more than reasonable on the subject of hours) in the hope of forestalling it, aware as he stopped and started down the Lea Bridge Road that his appearance two nights in a row would be suspicious in itself even if she had not discovered any other cause. Any lingering hope was dispelled when he let himself into an empty house. "Gone out," announced a note in the kitchen. "Back later, in case you needed to know." On their neatly made bed in a room so devoid of frills it stood in stark contrast with all Annie's glorious feminine clutter, lay all the evidence. She had even kept sweet-wrappings from the pockets, distinguished for their innocence, since sweets were not one of Annie's vices. No bluffing this away as the Commissioner's jacket.

By the time she came home, he was slightly drunk, not much, enough to turn a summit conference into a battlefield and the living room into a scene of carnage long before he was consigned to sleep in it after every insult, especially those unfit or unjust for the flinging, had been exhausted.

After several nights on the grimy floors of friends who were not recommendations for divorce, Ryan cracked, told Annie the full particulars of his double life, and then his die was cast. Darling Annie, looking at the face of him which had aged a century in less than a week, had at least cried in his arms and refused to send him away even when he offered to go. Impossible then to make his wife the one statement for peace, namely that he would never see Annie again. Long term deceiver though he was, he could not adapt his conscience to that, could never fly in the face of forgiveness, and if only Mrs. Ryan had known, was bound to stick with the one of them who offered it.

Now he camped with the beloved, uncomfortably, forced out early, leaving himself with a couple of hours to kill in lonely streets before presenting his harassed face at work. He accumulated six new shirts, underpants, socks, in as many days, and desperately wondered what he was going to do with his laundry as he sat in early morning cafés, drinking coffee he did not want and smoking cigarettes he did not like, suddenly aware of the fringes of life which colored such places alongside him. A strange dawn breed sits in cafés at seven o'clock, men who breathed in a twilight zone, cleaned offices, swept roads, delivered papers, towels or petrol after a hidden fashion, leaving a world which only turned into color after they had disappeared. Creepy monochrome men.

Ryan learned from rubbing their shoulders what it was like not to have a home, and saw a chasm before his feet, the vision only suppressed in Annie's arms and alive in the red-rimmed eyes which faced Bailey. The question of his laundry, stuffed in his locker with increasing difficulty, to say nothing of the cost of buying a shirt a day, loomed large in his mind, symbol of all the other necessities. Today's shirt was revolting, all he could find in the High Street at 9 A.M.; blue and red stripes, a foil for his blotched complexion. He had never been so tired.

"Don't seem to have anywhere to go, sir." Ryan straightened up stiffly to remove the impression of self-pity from his tone, aware it was there, ashamed of it, rubbing his forehead in the relief of the telling, almost tempted to make a bad joke of it, not expecting sympathy, hoping for a measure of understanding, preferably without judgments.

"You look horrible," was Bailey's contribution. "Seedy. You're no good to man or beast in that condition. You're a bloody fool who needs twelve hours' sleep." He fished in his pocket. For an awful minute, Ryan thought he was going to offer him money like a beggar being given a tip to go away.

"Here," the extended hand offered him keys, car keys and house keys instead. "You know where my flat is? You've given me a lift once or twice." Ryan nodded. "Well, go there. Clean up, eat, whatever, but for God's sake, go to sleep. Ten hours minimum before you can make a decision of any kind. Tomorrow, we'll talk about it. Use the bedroom, then I won't disturb you when I come back. Oh, and phone the women first, will you? In case they think you've opted to go under a train. Why they should bother is beyond me, but they will."

"No need, sir," Ryan mumbled. "They're neither of them expecting me."

"Are you sure?"

"Sir."

"Go on then. There's food in the fridge, and the washing-machine's in the kitchen."

The man was uncanny.

"Thanks." Ryan felt the prospect of untroubled sleep make him buckle at the knees; but hesitated, aware he should confess and refuse.

"Sir? Those observations. On Jaskowski's sons and the others . . . I didn't really . . ."

"I know. Was it all of them you missed, or only some?"

"I did the first." Ryan was dismayed to find tears of shame pricking his pinkened eyelids. Silence, as he prepared to hand back the keys to sleep.

"Go and get some rest, man, before you hit the traffic or the floor. Get out. I'll book you off sick, and see you later." The quietness of the voice was not a dangerous softness, no threat in it. Ryan's half-hearted, sheepish smile was met by a rarer smile conveying the resigned forgiveness Bailey half felt, but not the chronic unease which lay behind it as Ryan gratefully disappeared.

Who to tell of this nagging, nameless doubt, this niggling dread of nastiness in the streets daft Ryan had failed to watch, and who would understand the frustrated sympathy he felt for him, a pity not born of approval, but the same old crippling pity he felt for anything alive and in need? Oh, for anger, for the luxury of banging a table with a fist and wanting to strike the man or woman who let you down, instead of his own pathetic blandness, feeble forgiveness, acceptance of all shades of gray without black or white. Ryan made Bailey feel wretched, frustrated by irritation and the urge to help. Felt himself a cold fish who never shouted, never even objected, never needed enough himself to do so until now. He sighed, tempted by the telephone. Phoning Helen was becoming a habit, but she always knew what to do.

Ryan slept, coasting into dreams of awkward, guilty, erotic thoughts of the road where he lived, his wife biting the pillow and calculating alimony with sixteen shirts on the line; the street where Annie dwelt, still crying in her bed. May he be saved from such awful powers to influence lives.

* * *

Passing through Annie's street, Edward walked as he had walked for an hour in square circles, plotting a route, mapping the landscape like an explorer, adding and subtracting the distances, looking for trees and shadows, never far from target, planning the best way home, the best way in, so much more scientific than his father, less clammy in his clothes, using planning as a way of postponing, unscientifically afraid. Papa Jaskowski had retreated and advanced on the prey even before she had assumed the status of a sacrifice, he had been terrified of the dark: while Edward was in his element, one advantage over Dad, as well as freedom from all the moral inhibitions Dad had acquired with years. Not the inheritance of a son who cared for nothing, respected nothing, hated the existences he envied, knew no law which made sense, and no reason to regard life as precious.

The very shape of his tutor pressed on him, walking beside him like a guardian angel, protecting him from the desire to run away, hiding him from any chance of failure, encouraging the self-conscious professionalism which made him want not only the end result, but the achievement of it in a series of tidy steps, each boosting confidence. An endless conversation in his mind, less lonely than addressing all the tactical issues to himself: Edward, how can you be so foolish, clever boy like you, you know you must make a swift escape; you know you can not walk out of the front door after like any casual visitor, find another way. Don't go home tonight until you do, especially not my home, I would despise you. I do not pay you for stupidity or laziness.

Armed thus, he first found the way out on the seventh casual circle of the block. Through the iron railings he could see the lights on the backs beyond, marveled how they even illuminated the right house for him, counting the numbers carefully from the bottom of the road. All the rest would follow sooner rather than later, but then there was this sudden floppy tiredness, the knowledge of not wanting any of this until he was far older, braver and less ashamed of the fear. She was waving its red flag in front of him like a challenge, sneering at him. Cold, but too late to turn back: he would have to conquer it, but it chilled him to the marrow all the same.

He rewarded the effort; pizza from the takeaway, with milkshake. Jaskowski Junior, impure child, measuring his own pace, granted himself small bribes for his own achievements.

* * *

Peter's breathing was labored with the effort of thought. His brow was creased, tongue caught into one side of mouth as his face twisted in concentration, but despite it all, the egg yolk slipped from the half shell he had been using to catch it, leaving the white in the other half. That, she had explained, was the idea, although it did not always work. The yolk slithered: he tipped it deftly into his palm, and looked up at her with a half smile of regret, and a mouth of mild distaste at the slimy feel of it.

"Never mind. You've managed to save the white. Here, put the yolk in this cup. You did wash your hands, didn't you? You did? We can still use it. Okay. Now, what did I say we had to do next?"

The face screwed itself into memory mold, a face he exaggerated because it so often made her laugh. "Mix," he stated firmly. "Mix with milk. Whip it up, with this," he snatched a fork from the table and presented it to her. "Then we put it all in the floury stuff. Then it's done."

"Pretty good. Wait till you see what happens then. We get even stickier. Where did you put the flour?"

"Here." He dipped one finger into the bag, and placed a white brand on his nose. There was a comic lurking: whoever he might have entertained apart from this select audience, Helen did not know, but he never failed to entertain her. She snatched the flour packet from his hand.

"Now listen, all this goes over your head in a minute. Pay attention: watch, or however are you going to be able to make scones by yourself?"

"I'm being good now," another pulled face. As impossible to reproach him now as it had been on the first meeting, even harder, when she cast corner-of-eye glances in his direction and saw the rapt, creased look he wore whenever he was trying to understand or attempting to commit something to his prodigious memory. The means of making scones might have been the key to the universe and smile as he now did, gesture to please, the boy called Peter took nothing lightly. Not even frivolous things, as if his natural selection program was imperfect. He could not, for instance, treat the scratch he had made on an old table as anything other than a disaster: that was why she had suggested making scones, both to distract him from his tearful grief, and also because food supplies were exhausted, there never being enough to feed Peter, who never asked but always accepted on the second invitation, another of many rituals she had come to understand.

But stung into dramatic apologies by such small things, he was relatively unmoved by serious questions, such as, Peter, you must go home—they'll be so worried; Peter, are you listening, you cannot make people worried, your mother will want to see you. He would only shake his head. "No one will worry," he had said with such great conviction that she believed him, leaving herself without doubt, but with all the guilt in the world to accompany her sheer enjoyment of his company. On the topic of going home, she had given up: let him judge for himself, she found that best. At some point in the five or six evenings of their undemanding companionship, usually about ten-thirty, when his eyelids began to droop, he would jump away from whatever the occupation, grin, wave and leave, all in the space of a breath, forestalling questions with the speed of his departure.

Helen did not know what to do. She did not know how to begin the questions and answers which would lead her to any conclusion. On the topic of being loved and missed, Peter was simply ignorant: the prospect of punishment for this truancy seemed too remote to bother him either, and yet she knew he was acutely sensitive, quick thinking, swift in observation, a child who mopped up experience like a sponge in the same way he absorbed facts.

The cleverness surprised her only in its manifestations, and because she had been so wrong in her initial assumption about his age, gauging him nine years old, ten at the most judging from his size, until he proved her wrong. First, three almost speechless, entirely companionable hours in the garden, all Helen's meager skills copied by the shadowy, earnest little friend, who watched what she did and did it faithfully too. He had been reluctant, she noticed, to throw away weeds, indicating they should merely be confined to a patch of their own, and she had agreed that weeds were not so bad, it was only that some growing things were more beautiful, others more greedy than their neighbors. Simple when seen like that. "These sleep for a long time first," she had told him, pointing to the bulbs they had planted. "You'll be able to see them next year," and saw a solid understanding of the implied promise.

On the next visit rain stopped play, and she had beckoned him into the house via the window. As a means of access, he seemed to prefer it to the door, just as he preferred his normal route to the garden and it did not seem important enough to deserve comment. There was little enough convention in the whole arrangement to justify fussing for any more. On that second evening, Helen worked at her desk and told him to do whatever he pleased, watched him pottering in comforting silence until he asked to try her typewriter, and there began her realization that he was older than she thought, more literate than she could have imagined, and more dexterous even than in the garden. "At school I tried one of these," he had said in answer to an admiring question, proud to show off. "Really?" she had asked, thinking, Yes, how sensible to teach these skills, I wish I had them: but they did not teach you all those words at school.

Hours of Peter only added to the confusion and built a conviction that nothing could be done without his approval since the trust was too profound, too important, and too exclusive for betrayal. Geoffrey was the only person to whom she could have begun to explain, in full anticipation of disbelief, but confident of final understanding. She no longer dreaded the reaction to the telling, only the effort. Wanting to wait until Peter was readier for outside intervention. If ever. He hovered within touching distance, but never touched, while she yearned to hug that skinny little frame and could not: wanted to clothe it, talk to it, plan for it, and all she could do was feed it with food and calm like a stray cat, until one day it might climb into her lap and say, I think you just might do for now.

All of that and more contributed to the eccentric behavior of cooking scones after ten o'clock in the evening. Scones with cheese would be eaten with tummy-ache after; anxious thought which fed them into the oven. Peter kept watch, inches away from the heat despite the advice to go outside and come in again, because you could only tell when they were nearly done by the smell. Her cooking had always been based on such erratic principles, when it's brown it's done, after that sprinkle everything with a different color, it makes it look as if you tried haute cuisine which worked often enough to justify even less effort, but the boy needed to watch, observing the claggy mixture rise like a god creating a universe. Before they were cool enough to handle, half were eaten, and the concave stomach, visible as such beneath too large jeans remained as flat as ever, unswollen by the onslaught as he patted it, grinned with pleasure, waved away offers of more.

"Go on, piglet, eat six: I'm frightened you'll waste away by morning," teasing, eating to keep him company, watching for the eyelids' droop, her anxiety wishing him to go where he could sleep, but not willing on him the prospect of parting. "Time to go home, Peter?"

Nodding, not sleepy yet, knowing he would be soon. Rising from his chair with his usual energetic movement as if he had not eaten for a day, hesitating. Helen who never embarrassed his departures, deliberately casual as always, turned her back at the sink, busy with dishes.

"You off then, Peter? See you soon I hope," ready to turn and smile at the stuttered but unfailing thanks, instead, feeling his arms creeping round her waist, a shy face turned, profile against her spine. Still an uncertain gesture as she wiped her hands, turned slowly while he remained immobile until she hugged him with arms crossed around thin shoulders, his hands locked behind her, head buried just below her chest in one deep, juddering sigh.

"Don't want to go," mumbled into her blouse, fingers locked.

"No, sweetheart, but I know you must," stroking his hair, rocking him as he swayed with the strength of his own embrace.

"Yes," he said, "must, I suppose."

She pulled a face, answering the deliberately exaggerated expression, letting him release himself as slowly as he wished, a quick kiss on his forehead, greeted with that reserve which was half embarrassment, half delight.

"Be very careful going home," she warned. "It's late."

"You be careful too," establishing equality. "G'night."

"Sleep tight: mind the bugs don't bite . . ."

"And if they do, squeeze them tight, then they won't another night . . . I remembered, see, I remembered . . . !"

"You're my favorite boy then."

It was his longest speech ever, this recitation of the rhyme she had told him the second time. "See you soon," the chorus of them both, never specifying when as she waved him goodbye.

It might have been the signal, but she still could not see a direction. Worse than bringing a clandestine affair into the world's unforgiving view, no room for it. Love was what it was: she knew that. It was always love, for man, woman, or child, if it stopped your sleep with the sheer weight of longing to see them happy.

CHAPTER ELEVEN

A blank page, a blank mind, and Helen was angry with Geoffrey, angrier because he did not deserve it: feeling she should savor the fury since she knew it could not last, nor would she be able to afford it again. While before this she had held close to herself the feeling of strength and comfort which follows from being alone in a watertight existence, she had come to need him now, removing herself from all the other helpers because they bore no comparison. Of course she could not tell him anything of the kind, although if she spoke it out loud immediately, no one here would notice. No one in this room paid attention to what Carey was saying; he knew it, but carried on regardless, less sensitive than he would have been before a jury. Helen wanted to tell Geoffrey she didn't know what to do; familiar enough dilemma, but far worse since she had found a waif or stray, couldn't say which, who thought she understood him and believed in her. A burden she longed to share, if only this murder would loose its stranglehold on them all.

Four days to trial after this last conference, and all of them dreaming. Even Bailey, so meticulous with words, stumbled on his own, distracted by the vision of Stanislaus whom he had seen on Carey's instructions. Stocky Jaskowski, coarser, paler, sufficiently accustomed to prison to have learned the vernacular, and so used to the lack of privacy that he greeted Bailey with embraces even in the presence of a jailer, so grateful was he to break the monotony of the day. Time hung on him as heavy as his body; duller, since he still abided by rules in the hope of favors, did not yet entertain himself with plots, and was still anxious to please. "Ask him," Carey had said, "to remember as many details of Mrs. Cartwright's house as he can. Another statement, please. The more he can recall, the more convincing he appears. See how he is; report back." Using him, of course, witnesses are there to be used, but in reporting back, Bailey wondered if Carey could see a quarter of what he had seen himself, Stanislaus, murderer, in the concrete visiting room, remembering instead the overstuffed Cartwright chairs, the antimacassars, the three Victorian dolls, the solid furniture, the gin, not whiskey, the pictures on the walls, three of them, one a Highland cow, remembered well, dictated well for the salvation of his soul, since as Jaskowski explained himself, he had become a repentant sinner, the only one Bailey knew. That apart, he had basked in the glow of approval and a rare sensation of self-importance, but none of that had explained why he had been so reluctant for Bailey to leave, anxious he should stay, even after the surrender of the gift of one half-ounce of tobacco.

"Mr. Bailey, sir?" a long agonized hesitation, one hand on Bailey's arm. The jailer moved restlessly. "Something else . . ."

"What's the matter, Stan?" Gentle, but not gentle enough.

"Nothing, is nothing, you know? Just something."

"Something worrying you?"

"Me? Worry? Too late for all that now," moving away, suddenly dismissive. "But Mr. Bailey, promise me something: look out for my boy, Edward, you know? Just look out for him."

"Why, Stan? Any particular reason?"

"Just do. Goodbye now. Just you do that, I have this worry: he may do something bad, very bad . . ." The eyes were tear-filled.

"Why, do you think?"

Another wave of frustrated defeat.

"You find out: I don't know, but bad . . ."

These last farewells Bailey did not choose to report for the entertainment of the conference, hesitating over his omission, unable to repeat to Carey or anyone else this strange, only possibly significant confirmation of a nagging, undefined caution of his own; unable to describe to them the tingling suspicion which had tensed his muscles on two or three meetings with Ed in the innocent family context, the same doubt which had prompted that fruitless command to Ryan to watch the household. Time had escaped: the imminence of trial had frozen it. Perhaps it was all imagination, but Bailey sitting in conference had ceased to listen to anything more than the father's request, knowing his evening would be spent in fulfilling it. A sergeant to be seen during the night shift, one who knew Ed well according to Bailey's information, which was no more than collators' records and that peculiar, inexact grapevine of police gossip, might know him well enough to give the comfort of sharing impressions, casting some light on that troubled family. He shifted in his spindly seat, angry for wasted time, the frustration of sitting still now that preparations for trial were almost complete, irritated that Carey had only called a last conference to reassure himself, like a prima donna at a rehearsal marshaling all his dressers to ensure that his costume was complete.

Beside him, equally uncomfortable, Ryan listened to the warm, wet world outside, thinking of Annie as he always did during Temple conferences. During the first of them, he had sat planning the next subterfuge: calmer latterly, he simply looked forward to his escape, not daring to recognize how life had improved in the last ten days since he had acquired his own room, half a street from where Miss West lived, scarcely further from Annie, not luxurious unless compared with the frozen wastes of the Essex living room, or the shirtless prospect of Annie's place. A breathing space of his own, where thoughts tumbled into some kind of perspective and sleep was easier. Section House lodgings, difficult to find, organized by Bailey pulling strings of rank on Helen's clear advice, and while Ryan had wondered cynically if this was merely to ensure the revival of his concentration for the important duration of the trial, he knew there had been a genuine kindness in it. He was still in the woods, but he could see the trees. The trial, the bloody trial, preface to uncomfortable decisions, long might it last.

Hope shared by Clive Barrow, inattentive as the rest. Junior counsel for the Crown regretted drinking more than enough with Junior counsel for the defense on several occasions recently, to the extent of making personal promises he was unsure he wished to fulfil: "After the trial, Sissy; you and I, escape somewhere." Good ideas at the time. Barrow raised eyes to heaven, examining the ceiling of his conscience, recalling how definitely he had offered the kind of weekend not remembered for intellectual conversation, the threat of which weighed as heavily on him as the hangover which had followed, loaded with the prospect of deceit as well as the awkwardness of seeing Sissy every day of the trial, wigged and gowned like a suggestive nun. Without the present obligation to fix his eyes on Carey's face with every symptom of rapt attention, he might have yawned, delighted to postpone indefinitely the fate of the defendant, and with it the prospect of Sissy advancing toward him with determined eye across some hired bedroom floor.

Carey's voice, mellifluous and soporific, repeated the obvious for the third time in the last, long hour. Bailey stole a glance at Helen as he often had in this room, guessed she was dreaming from the pristine page in front of her, unmarked even by the doodles which were the usual sign of her restless concentration. She always sensed it, encountered the look with a furtive smile, distant but warm nevertheless, only half guilty in discovery. Thank you, Helen, he told her silently, for the advice on Ryan. You were right, you know, saying there's little I could do, except find him space, and leave the rest to him. But what is it ails you, what secret? No time to see her, no time to explain why he had become so hesitant, so preoccupied, so full of hopeless introverted dialogue which she never heard.

Mrs. Eileen Cartwright had cast a spell on them, watching these lives, all harnessed and postponed by the settling of her own. And at last, the conference was over, aching eyes released into the bright light outside, each indifferent to the burst of sunshine which had followed the downpour and emptied the sky, while the threat of thunder hid behind invisible cloud.

Fickle promise of a clear evening. Instead, a damp, grizzling, bad-tempered heat, encouraging sleep, then denying it. Ryan dozed, more off than on, defeated by the sight of his accounts and bills which were the labor of his evening until he woke from his napping sleep with a mouth as dry as sand, irritatingly awake as he looked for the time on the wall clock in his room. Ten-thirty. Time for one drink in the pub on the corner, and no, he would not go to Annie. He had already told her: Tonight, I have to do paperwork. She had not understood, worrying him with these doubtful reactions of hers to all the tedious necessities of life, promising to sulk in his absence, thinking his time was her own. Strange how they had become so afraid to lose the other, each more demanding, so that for once a solitary drink was preferable, with a walk around the streets for the fresh air in between storms; half-enjoyment of a transient liberty.

Bailey could have wished he was doing the same, cradling a pint, instead of lighting a cigarette offered him by a constable at the front desk, yet another nail in the coffin of CID reputation, taking smokes from uniform, and not even his own station. He had come to see the man who knew Ed, Sergeant Jones, self-important custody officer for the night, form-filler for prisoners, anxious to show how hard he worked and making it his pleasure to keep a Detective Superintendent waiting. Jones had ears like jug handles: from where Bailey leaned against the wall, they increased the dimensions of Jones's over-large head by almost its own size. They were red ears, and they shone; everything in the charge room shone in the dead light of the neon column on the ceiling fixed by a dozen trailing wires through a clumsy hole in the wall of a room painted institutional mustard, glowing grimy, marked browner where leaning heads and bodies had contributed their own impressions on the vicious color. Brighter light spilled from the front office separated by an open door: gloom seeped from the passage which led to the cells, detention room, surgeon's room. In a corner, there were three large, old-fashioned typewriters, all labeled "out of order," other corners adorned with chipped filing cabinets beneath the fraying instructions on notice boards. Most lists of local police numbers for police and prison services bore traces of fingerprints, damp marks drawn down the line seeking hurried help. The notice advertising the services of the Urdu-speaking community relations group for the area was pristine. As many charge rooms, not untidy, not unduly dirty, but never clean: not quite devoid of comfort but almost, stained and worn, battered by humanity. The light inside gave each of them a jaundiced glow, but the air was still clear. Early evening yet, pubs still open, fights only brewing, night shift still fresh, cigarette ends on the floor few.

"Why did you move here from Islington?" Bailey had asked Sergeant Jones, hopefully inviting personal recollections which might inspire confidence.

"I asked for a transfer, sir," no more forthcoming than that.

"Will you excuse me for a minute, sir, I can see a new prisoner; musn't keep him waiting." No, far better keep the Superintendent, he looked far sillier decorating a wall, and Bailey knew he was dealing with a graduate in all the arts of obstruction: the kind of sergeant who was never the subject of complaint for a rudeness which was so wooden, so solidly polite it hit like a blunt instrument, Jones's patent way of making a fool out of a saint. Another version of politeness held him there even after the first minutes with Jones revealed little to provide clues to the working of Edward's fertile mind and why his father should fear for him, not even if Bailey prompted him with every kind of flattery or found the one weak link in Jones's insensitive armor.

"Sergeant, you're the only one who's ever arrested Edward Jaskowski. How did you do it? I hear you managed the impossible; you knew the Hackington Estate better than anyone, I hear. They miss you at Islington."

"Well, sir, so they might."

"So, why did you transfer here?"

"The wife, sir; it's closer to home, well a bit closer. Better area." Each to his own. No middle-class drunks here, only poorer ones. Better than a transfer to Brixton, Bailey guessed; and Jones, a better policeman once, was mellowing slowly.

"Tell me about Ed Jaskowski."

Mollified, as much as he would ever be, more Welsh, more homesick.

"He's a thief, see? A good-class thief, and only a boy. Answer for everything. Worried me sick, that boy. You couldn't pin him down, but I knew he was at it, see. The others told me, I used to . . . well never mind. I knew someone who knew someone who could get signed photos of pop stars, and I used to give them to the kids, for information, see? And they none of them liked Ed, not at all . . ."

"A thief, with a knife? You had him for an offensive weapon. Not his style, was it?"

In desperation Bailey could hear Welsh creeping into his own voice, asking lilting questions, pretending ignorance of facts already well researched.

"Yes. Funny, that. I stopped him. I said, Hallo, Ed, out late aren't we, what you got on you, and he shrugged as if he expected it, as if he'd been waiting for me, pulled out this little knife, handed it to me by the handle, said: Go on then, arrest me. So I did. I said to him, come on, you know better than that, why carry the bloody thing? Do you know what he said?"

"No," said Bailey, "I don't."

Jones leaned forward, conspirational, "He said to me on the way to the nick, 'I have to carry it, see? I've got to learn what it's like, get used to it.' 'Don't be so daft,' I said, 'Do yourself a favor.' 'You don't realize,' he said, 'do you, I'm in training.' 'Give us a break,' I said, 'training for what?' 'Bigger things,' he said. 'Oh yes,' I said, 'Bigger prisons, more like.' Didn't put it in my notes; CID interviewed him later, he said he had it for his own protection. But you know, he didn't, he bloody well set out to be nicked. Wanted the feel of a knife in his jacket and a hand on his collar. Odd little bugger. Not so little now."

Something, not much of anything, leaving Ed still a creature on shifting sands, juvenile psychopath, conspirator with Dad, corrupt child turned corrupt man, only arrested for a laugh, somehow involved with Eileen, he was sure of it, but how, and why, and what, Bailey knew no better.

The back of his shirt was sticky hot: the flies and moths in the charge room were trained by Jones to irritate: he was tired, more than tired, wanting to be almost anywhere else in the world where he could be told he was suffering from superstition, and have someone warn him he was a fool to believe his senses, not his facts, that his imagination needed surgery. But no one said it, and unease festered in the heat. It would not, could not, rain; all this stifling, thundery stillness heavy as he waited for the area car to take him back to his own in Islington, smoking another borrowed cigarette, leaving Jones to dine out on his own superiority, life going on as normal, himself marking time on a strange pavement, wishing he could talk to her, heavy with stray, protective jumbled thoughts: Helen, Stanislaus, Cartwright, Ed, but chiefly Helen and the thunder hiding behind the darkness.

Lust, that was it: perhaps that was all afflicting him, something confusingly new, unlike the more frequent exercise of politeness to which he had reacted in latter years, responses to signals, like Pavlov's dog, with Geoffrey Bailey never doubted for his sexual manners, only for his sincerity in filling a vacuum to cure his own; not like this need, not at all. End of a day where the dawn began tired. Go home, man, go to sleep for the only cure for this: it is not important, any of it, all your imagination. You are beyond reason:

this woman has stopped you thinking straight and no one is worth that, nor should they be.

The driver was apologetic, the car hot. Shirt sleeve order, clip on ties loose, cotton clammy against plastic-covered seats. He considered the word again. Lust—amused by its old-fashioned descriptive power. Lust, the heat of it, the night alive with it, needing a little blood-letting, no wonder it was on his mind. Courts would be busy tomorrow if it did not rain. Nothing mattered. Cruising slowly down the stuffy Holloway Road a traffic light every twenty yards, passengers dozing, wondering if he had remembered to close his windows, persuading himself out of his state of tension, listening to the radio crackle, glad he was officially off duty, relieved, if guilty, to be so close to home, closer, at least than the others with him, six hours more to go. The benefit of age and status. His eyes began to close . . . nothing mattered.

Silly-sounding call signs, "Alpha romeo . . . calling all cars in area . . . Break-in, basement flat, Comus Road, seven nine, ambulance on way . . ."

The car did not alter speed.

"Get there, Fred, will you?" an almost apologetic direction, with his hand clutching the strap. Always so mild when anxiety tore at his throat like the acid vomit of heartburn.

"It's all right, sir, full relief tonight, two other cars on way: we can find your transport first, go back there if they need us." Break-in, only a nightly occurrence after all, look after Sir first, privilege of rank and too much deference, thinking of his convenience.

"No," said Bailey, "we go there first. Faster than this. Now, please."

Nothing mattered. Helen's address: he knew it by heart. White coffin ambulance, omen of harm. Nothing had mattered, nothing but this.

Tired evening, sick with heat, full of a silence far from golden. She had known not to expect Peter that evening, but could not have said why: there was always something in his partings which suggested whether it would be two days, one day, or three days before he reappeared, if only an extra wave, a funnier face poking back over the wall to check she still watched. Sometimes he would say, or she would say, not tomorrow, maybe the next day, both careful to impose no expectations; Peter more cautious than Helen, chattering in short bursts, while she swooped on clues like a magpie toward bright treasures, listening for all he had done at school (which school?), looking at the penknife given him last birthday (by whom?), but never told facts which might fix him in place, or make him less anonymous, so that sometimes she thought he was no more than a hungry ghost.

But no such friendly spirit this thundery evening, exhaustion pouring from the skies instead of rain, spreading lethargy until she slumped into bed at ten o'clock, window open, careless of the night, no sound from the garden, nothing but warm oblivion until morning.

Silence, so complete it was tangible. She breathed out slowly, only a dream. Then the strange sound of restless, hesitant footsteps on the stairs outside the flat's front door. Unlocked, she thought mechanically, always unlocked while I am here, what kind of fool am I? Pausing again, then the click of the latch, softer steps on carpet. The corridor light always burned, a thoughtless attempt to deter burglars and to dispel the frightening visions still before her eyes when she woke from dreams or lay awake listening to the cars and cats of a neighborhood which almost slept. The visitor was not discouraged by light, not ignorant of her presence, was either careless or malevolent, slow feet carrying him into the other rooms, closing on her own, looking for her casually as she lay paralyzed with fear, frozen with instinctive knowledge that he wanted more harm than thieving; her teeth drawing blood on her lip, waiting. The steps, soft, sinister, and unhurried, pulling him nearer until she could see his shadow outside the bedroom door, one hand caressing the handle, pausing, all sound suspended. The door was pushed further: she felt her own eyes reflected and caught like cat's eyes, gazing back into the face of the intruder.

As much face as she could see through a clumsy disguise, scissor holes in a black T-shirt half covering the features above the nose, flapping, macabre, an afterthought to hide him from her and himself from his own fear, which hung on him more rancid than the sweat of the still impending storm glistening on his arms, the scent of scarcely controlled panic. He looked as if he might have retreated, but saw her staring eyes, took a step forward.

"What are you staring at, you silly cow?"

The sound of his voice, high and nervous, broke the paralysis of her limbs: she began to shake visibly, staring, with the sheet clutched in her hands like a rope. The sight of her seemed to give him confidence.

"Go on then, who d'you think you're staring at then?" jeering this time.

"You," she said stupidly. "You, of course. Would you please get out of my flat?"

Helen had often wondered, with no anticipation of ever finding out, what she might have said to a casual burglar, reading in files numerous histories of bizarre, brave, and even flippant conversations between robber and victim, one outfacing another in a war of nerves and wit, frightened children shaming violent thieves into retreat, cooler and more composed in the face of threat than she was now. Trembling, confused by fear of his purpose, she was also ashamed of her immobility, for not moving in all that time since she had heard him first, lying still instead of running at him, screaming the rage which was beginning to take its hold on her, as furious at her cowardice as she was for his invasion.

He brought his stocky, white-skinned bulk further into the room, turned on the lamp by the side of the bed, then twitched the sheet away from her, gazing down at her tensed body, naked against the warm night, and continued staring until the anger in her broke. She grabbed the sheet back, kicking out beneath it, crouching away from him, half kneeling with her face level with his own, and spat vainly, spittle touching the T-shirt mask, not his skin. With a casual move, he raised one pale arm and struck her across the face, jerking her neck until her head hit the wall: then, took her hair in one fist, held it with ease, and slapped her again, one side of her face after the other, sharp, vicious, effortless blows before dropping her back against the pillows like a stunned clown. She was beyond shame now, eyes weeping involuntarily, still angry enough to attempt to choke it back, aware of blood in her nose and throat, but not spitting; not anymore.

Large, ungainly, barrel-chested boy. Why did she know he was a boy, not a man as he ambled round the room, justifiably confident that she would remain still apart from the trembling, stressing his power with half a smile.

"Don't bother moving, will you?"

She shook her head, anxious not to provoke, only remembering to clutch the sheet, watching him through dizzy eyes as he closed the window, strolled from that room into the next. There was the sound of broken glass. With the closing of the window, the smell of him had been pungent. Drawers opening: more breaking glass. Helen shook her head to clear it: blood from her nostrils dropped red on the sheet: she looked into the blackness of the garden with longing. The boy shambled back into sight.

"Not going anywhere?" Again she shook her head, wondering if it would be wise, even if hypocritical, to smile, to speak briskly and sensibly, or to remain as she was, humbly silent, wondering if her throat would give her any choice. "Good." He was holding the clock, Bailey's mended clock. "Nice, this," he remarked. "Does it work?"

"Yes, perfectly."

"Where did you get it?"

"In an auction."

"In . . . an . . . auction," he repeated, a poor mimic of Helen's accentless pronunciation, raising it high above his head, bringing his arms down sharply. She waited for the crash, eyes shut; no sound came. Opened them again, to see the grinning mouth, cruelly teasing, the clock still held. "No," he said, "it's nice, this. I'll have it. I like nice things. It's not what I came for, but I like nice things."

"What did you come for?" She was surprised to find her voice level.

"What? Oh, I was sent. You'll find out." She saw that his hands, gentle enough holding the clock which he had placed on the bed, were clenched. He rubbed one fist into the palm of the other, involuntarily, nervous, as if wanting to postpone the clear message of the gesture, and Helen, aware of the danger from the first, knew now how inescapable it was.

"Why not just concentrate on nice things? Not many here, but you can have what you want. Provided you leave me alone." The voice was still level, almost polite.

"Sod off," angry now. "Don't make no difference. I can have whatever I like, anyway."

"Can you? You're luckier than me, then."

"Sod off." He was by the side of the bed where she curled, shouting at her, willing her to cringe away while she willed herself to refuse.

"No need to shout, you'll waken the neighbors . . ." Her remark was so ridiculous, she began to laugh, an hysterical giggle which gurgled in the throat until she coughed it back, not before he had noticed, and hit again, staccato punches to the ribs, swift and hard, each a stabbing pain, numerous stabbing pains which left her weak, rasping for each breath, ending with a final blow to the abdomen, when even her hands ceased their token resistance. He stood upright, panting, trembling himself, the scent of his excited fear overpowering, choking her more than her lungs. "That's enough from you . . . See . . . who do you fucking think you are . . . ? Me luckier than you! Fuck off, will you . . ." Even in the haze of misery, closing her eyes against what might happen next, knowing how powerless she was, Helen knew that there was worse, and that he, for reasons she had no need to fathom, was postponing it. Her silence calmed him, but he could not for now, stand the sight of her. "Wait," he commanded. She waited.

He had gone. Entirely? There was a moment of hope, quickening of all bruised senses, stretching-out of limbs and opening of eyes into silence, finding the room empty, sitting upright, still clutching the sheet, stifling the cry of pain as she moved, surprised to be able to move, listening on into the death of the hope, hearing him shuffling and exploring yards away, the sound of him determined but nonchalant, not in this room, but certainly in the next, passing now into the one beyond, moving clumsily on small feet, examining as he went, looking for nice things, coming toward her again, head round the door, checking, triumphant, the failing confidence somehow renewed by his discoveries.

"What's this?" Holding up a watercolor sketch, an inexact, lively portrait of an old wrinkled woman, removed, she noticed, from its frame. He held it close to his eyes in the corridor light.

"By W. H. Ford. Is he famous?"

"No."

"I don't like it. Why did he paint her? Wrinkly old thing."

Tearing the old parchment in half and then in half again, scattering pieces on the floor. Helen closed her eyes, pretending complete weariness and the indifference of pain, her voice low and beseeching.

"There's more paintings in the sideboard. Nice things. Perhaps you'll like some of those." Not moving.

"I'll see: I suppose you think you know what I like, but I'll see . . ." Defensive, but distracted, still looking for an excuse to postpone the real purpose, and the room was empty again. It occurred to her she was not the only one who was afraid.

Now. Now the door of the only cupboard in the room furthest away from her would be opened, distracting him. Now was the time, there was no other time, would be no other time, she knew it, could smell the blood on him, he would not stop: he would find something else to enrage him into the courage he needed. Now. Breathe deeply, then move: you are not old, you are not infirm. Move . . . You want to live, don't you? Move then. Bloody well move, you lethargic coward. Move!

She sprang from the mattress, forgetting the nakedness, pushing the whole bed toward the door and across. It was a light, modern thing, comfortable, never enough to keep him at bay for more than a few seconds, surely enough to open the window, get out of it, into the relative freedom of the garden. Where was it Peter found it easiest to climb the wall? Somewhere to the left of it, she would need shoes, or she would go into the next garden, over the steep bricks, another decision to be made in the dark. Fumbling with the catch on the window, she could hear him at the door. Why, oh why had she failed to notice that he had screwed down that catch, always clumsy to undo she had sworn at it in better times than this. Open. Too late. The window was up, curtains flapping in the breeze which was the beginning of the storm, herself entangled in them, the boy's arms embracing her like a lover, dragging her back, hissing unloverlike, away from the freedom of the ground: both of them writhing on the floor of the room, the window so close she could touch the frame, he lifting her back on to the shifted bed like a sacrifice, himself full of the same sickening smell. "Bitch, bitch, bitch . . ." no other words as he leaned on her, hand over her mouth, until she choked to breathe and stopped moving. "Now," he said, a deafening whisper, "now . . ." Her eyes were swollen, blows and tears, but she could see the thick belt in his hand, from where she could not tell, she had not noticed him wearing it, but it was unmistakably his, with buckle glinting, swung at her, once to forehead harmlessly, then again. Its cut was noiseless, the effect a whiplash as she squirmed away over the wrinkled sheets like a squirrel, feeling the sting against ribs, breast, thigh, arms, evading some, catching the most, sobbing and crying rather than screaming, finally subdued with that muscular, fat arm around her neck, pulled to his chest, her head pressed into the pillow face down and retching, no end to it. Fighting, whipping, amazed at the sudden strength of her, the boy was momentarily tired, knew he must not stop, turned her, held her there, elbow across throat, panting, still avoiding the eyes, grinning into the space beyond her head. The grimace receded: she knew it, even seeing nothing but the mouth below the damp, frayed mask as the left side of his jaw began to twitch uncontrollably, making his face so intense she could only stare. He withdrew the hand not pinning her, raised it above her, and it was then she screamed, sad, strangled sound it was from a throat so compressed, thrashing in captivity at the sight of that little, lethal, knife lunging toward her. They were words she formed, nonsense obscenities, reserving the last strength to twist away once and more, half conscious of the blade grazing ribs, twisting back to avert the fist before another thrust, her hand round the knife, watching the blood of her own fingers from a distance. Whose blood was that? Feeling nothing at all like pain. There was a point, one glorious point, when she thought for a moment she had won: the point when she crouched, freed for a moment, picked up the clock and threw it through the window before she knew she was lost, and there they were both, sticky, sweaty, full of the smell of a butcher's shop, all fresh meat, nothing frozen, but losing the sense of touch and all the talents of sight, his black, pale face fading into obscurity. Once in a far off distant state, she remembered; she fastened her teeth into his solid, repulsive arm. Aware, from somewhere, of the longest, loudest scream. Not her own. A sound from the garden, a wail of horror, ending in a shrill and ghostly cadence, No . . . ooo, no, no, no . . . something familiar, half known on the other side of the window. And the sound, at the same time of the relief of pressure on her throat, of her own, insistent doorbell.

I saw him, I saw him; that was my brother. She bit him, on the arm, and I know she is not dead, or Ed would have stopped before. There was nowhere for me to go but out of there, and never home, because he knew it was me, I know he knew it. He will take his little knife to me: I know that too. Ed stopped when I screamed, I saw him, after he was bitten when I saw the knife, it was then I screamed, I couldn't help it, how could he do that? I stopped him, shouting like that. Then I stayed down in the bush while he came out of the window like a cannon ball, looking all round, but not looking at all, straight for the wall, he knew, how did he know? I didn't show him, he knew where to go. Slower than me; I can climb better than him.

Then I watched some more, too scared for anything. She moved, and I could not move, but I cried when I saw her move, not dead, not nearly dead, but hurt, I couldn't bear it, it was Ed did that. So much hurt I hardly knew her face, so strange, the rest of her too, with no clothes, like one of Grandma's skinned rabbits . . . My lady, Ed did that, and I want to kill him for that, but he will find me first.

Lady, I was coming to help you when you tried to get out of the window, couldn't sleep, you see? So I came into the garden just to see if you were there: I wouldn't have woken you, I promise. And then, when Ed ran away, I was coming down to the window, but I heard the shouting, the bell, and it was like the other time, I couldn't let them find me, and besides, I knew they would help you, and I couldn't let them take me home, not with Ed going there, with his little knife, knowing I had seen him.

I hate him. Why did he do that? I am afraid of him, of what he does, so afraid he did that to punish me, and it's all my fault, but why did he have to try and kill her, hurt her like that, just because I fibbed to him; it wasn't so bad, was it, not telling him where I went, fibbing like that? All my fault Lady, I never wanted anything like this to happen to you: you told me you were my friend, and I believe you, and I shall have to come back. To tell you I didn't just leave you. I'll come back very soon, I promise . . . Where else can I go?

Over the wall, struck in the face by great gobs of rain, frozen in light at the top, dropping down, running anywhere through the wet, the hair plastered to forehead, thinking where to find shelter for more, and more crying, he would have to go back. Tomorrow, next day, before Ed found him. Brothers beneath their saturated skins, running from scrutiny, questions, capture, one another. One child, lightfoot with horror, loyalty curdled, aiming nowhere, the other, trudging now, aiming for base, remembering self-taught skills, hiding in doorways: stockily silent, aware of the blood on him, putting the knife into a drain and the T-shirt mask with it, glad of the damp which so masked his progress by blinding stray eyes to his stained chest, washing his arms free of the spatters. It was the bite which ached more than the rest of him ached, weary and sick. She had vomitted: he remembered it, could smell it on the front of his shirt until he too, retched in the street, disgust and relief pouring from him in a thin stream. Ed had not eaten for many hours, stomach clenched beyond digestion or appetite: there was nothing to eject but the poisonous fluid of disappointment, anger and grief.

Not for her. Bitch. Grudging, hate-filled admiration for her; fought like a cat, the bitch, but no regrets for her except not finishing it, but shame for the boy who had seen. Peter's scream, as clear as a siren, the same skinny scream he had heard from the garages when the kids had trapped him in there, arm-twisting, chanting. Dad's in jail, Dad's a con; a helpless shriek, piercing his eardrums like pins, his own first temptation to violence. Poor little bastard, daft little sod, couldn't do it with him wailing like that, knowing he was there, watching. You bastard, Pete . . . Wait till I find you. Stopping me: I told you long ago, don't dare interfere.

The street deserted, warm rain running down gutters, no one stirring, cozy lights in windows, not even a man with a dog. Inside Eileen's maisonette, a careful trembling wash in the dark. She bit me, look at those marks on me, and look at my hands, shaking like Pete's shake. He will not tell. Ed knew him better than that; he had never told for as long as he could form words, which he did so rarely now, too loyal, too frightened, always the same, even in the days when he chattered. And in all the plans for this, every single version of events cast over in his mind, including the prospect of losing courage which he had been honest enough to admit, Ed had never envisaged discovery: to do so would have introduced too huge an element of fear, taken away his legs for the whole enterprise. Besides, what need to consider? In years of escaping, he had always escaped: he was not his father, and even his father had escaped, although he plaited his own noose afterward. Pete spoke so rarely these days, with so much difficulty, he would never confide in strangers, never: Pete could not do that. In the last three weeks' intermittent contact, he had not said a word.

The trembling was slower; Ed willed his hands to stop, no, he would not think of it, and all the same, he would find Pete tomorrow, then think of it. After he had slept with the sound of the scream haunting him more than the face of the woman, waking him from the floor where he lay in a sweating chill. In the morning, he would find Peter.

Why the doorbell? She was not expecting anyone, not even relatives, neighbors, friends, this time of night, but she could hear it, deafened by the sound of her own breathing, peculiar loud sound. Look at the mess of this place, look at it. What shall I do? Who would have believed I could live with this mess, I must be sick to have let it happen: I must get up and tidy it all, what is the matter with me, I must answer the door, but I have no clothes. Answer the door anyway. Press the thing which lets them in upstairs, it doesn't matter who: then tidy up: I'm so ashamed, such squalor here, so dirty, but I feel so weak. Help me please, I hate to ask, but help me, please . . .

Half-way down the corridor, still clutching a sheet, one step, two steps, five steps closer to the Entryphone: trying to press the small red button, unable to make one wavering finger actually touch, mind failing to coordinate with eye, irritating until she was aware she had done it with one gummy palm. Time to sit down. Slowly, legs buckling, back smearing the white wall, knocking aside another picture. I shall just wait here, only for a minute, I would smooth my hair if I could prise my fingers apart.

And thus Ryan found her, hearing such strange sounds on his way back from the pub in the stillness which announced the storm. Found immaculate Helen West, unrecognizable, squinting upward through one huge eye, the other closed by swelling. "Hallo," she said, irrelevantly polite. "Sorry to keep you." Then she had begun to sob, covering her face with sticky red paws, hurting, crying, and even then he had not known her.

"Called the doctor, sir. The ambulance will wait for the doc to finish."

"Forensic?"

"Sir."

"Send the rest away . . . no, wait, leave two, the Sergeant and one more; the rest can look for him."

He was pale, Ryan thought, ashen with worry, frightening in his white skin, older by a hundred years. The mess, perhaps: torn pictures, broken glasses, gunge up the bedroom wall, trailed along the carpet to the door, even red brown footprints, and now the rain obliterating traces in the garden full of wet uniforms. Trainers, she had said; he wore jeans and trainers like a dozen others. He went through the window: his luck he walked into a rainstorm, not a chance, not a cat in hell's chance. And as for her, poor woman, Ryan had always liked her, looking like a boxer at the end of round sixteen, still fighting, but far from pretty.

"Not as bad as it looks," Ryan wanted to hold his arm as he might have done to his son, to any child in need of comfort. "She'll be all right, sir: the doctor said," repeating the common touching faith in the medical man even as he appeared, soft-spoken to patients, loud otherwise, full of staccato phrases, economizing on all his information.

". . . Doesn't want to go to casualty: told her she must. No choice, silly girl. Stitches, fair bit of embroidery. Punctured lung, one or two ribs, nasty, very. She'll live to a ripe old . . . , a few scars. No statements, not now please: I've noted it all. Shock, you see, nasty thing. Brave woman, that. Tries to laugh. Apologizing for all the fuss, I ask you."

Pausing, fussing for breath, adjusting a battered jacket against the still heat.

"Are you called Bailey?"

"Yes."

"That's all right then. It's you she wants. Don't know why. Concussion, I expect."

Helen, he was telling himself: I love you for all the things you are, and all the things you say. Who else would have struggled so hard to keep dignity, trying to refuse the offer of a stretcher, pretending she could walk, a two-step, drunken lurch, but only just? Refused to stay long in hospital, covered in more stitches than he could count, even with all his hands? Broken ribs will heal as well at home, she said. Oh yes? So will multiple, superficial stab wounds, split lip, displaced nose and the blackest eye he had ever seen on a woman. "Is it that bad?" she asked him, shaking all over and joking at the same time, a funny combination which turned his mind sideways, "Will I have to paint the other one to match it?"

Helen, beware of shock, he warned her. Tomorrow, you will feel so low, the earth could swallow you. Stay in hospital.

Then she told him about the boy, the little boy, gabbling she was about the boy Peter although he tried to stop her talking in the ambulance, feeling the pressure of one good hand in his, thought it best to let her tell; she was right, he did not understand, not at first, and not completely, but on the incomplete comprehension spent the next day looking for a small boy named Peter, one of how many in Islington, confused as to why she was more concerned with him than the man who tried to kill her. He was not mistaken in that, knew he was not, but that was what it was. Ryan told Bailey to take no part in finding him, an order, not a request, taken with the wisdom meant, since if the searching succeeded in this present and everlasting mood, it would be a brutal affair.

Someone was deputed to tidy her flat. You cannot stay there alone, he told her, even with patrols outside it, and all the measuring, checking, fiber-picking, photo-taking finished. But he believed her when she insisted, "If I do not," she said, "I shall always be afraid of it, and I cannot live like that: I am already afraid of so many things." News to me, he told her. "Geoffrey, you are sometimes short-sighted," the next humble remark from Helen still breathing shallow in that hospital bed, still holding on to his hand. But he may come back, he warned. "That's why I must go home," she said, drowsy with drugs. "Supposing he comes back and finds Peter? I couldn't bear it." Then he believed in Peter, the real reason for going home: not herself—the child.

"Perhaps you could stay with me? I'd feel safer then." Of course he would, as long as she needed, preferably a very long time. Sleep now, Helen, he ordered her, and she slept, the fingers round his loosening their grip. He kissed one side of her bruised mouth, and in the relief of finding her alive, could not have cared if she were scarred or limbless. Nothing could make her less than, well, his thoughts stumbled on the word, beautiful.

"Clive? It's me. Sissy."

"I know it's you."

The old, familiar lurch. "What's up, Sissy? Must be urgent for you to phone me at home." A rebuke in the words: the woman was moving closer, so close he could hear his wife's voice in the kitchen at the same time as hers, arguing with the children, too close for comfort.

"Sorry. Couldn't find you in Chambers. Don't think I'd do this without reason." His turn to be rebuked, for suspecting Sissy of indiscretion without reason. "Clive, something I must tell you, regarding Cartwright. Now Quinn won't like this, but it worries me to death. I wanted to ask you, better than failing to sleep on it."

"The thunder, Sissy, that's what kept you awake last night."

"Don't be a fool, Clive, listen. Had a con late yesterday with my ghastly instructing solicitor, last minute stuff, you know."

"Yes, I know. So did we."

"And when he went to the loo, or phone, or something, I forget which, I picked up his correspondence file, had a quick squint; he's very selective, that chap, in what he tells us, guards his client's letters like the crown jewels, self-important little bum, but anyway, I found these letters. Mrs. C organizing to pay Jaskowski's seventeen-year-old son—wait for it—five thousand pounds, after the trial. All neat and above board; incredibly sanctimonious, unconvincing reasons, I couldn't believe it. But why Clive, why? It offends the nostrils, more than somewhat."

Silence. Too late in the day to absorb another drama without difficulty.

"Are you there, Clive?"

"Yes. What do you want me to do about it?"

Exasperation oozed from Sissy's tones.

"Do? Well, you idiot, what do you think? For promise of payment, on whatever terms, I read payment for services rendered. God alone knows what services, I don't. But even if we lose this case on the facts, I'll be damned if we lose it because our bloody client's tried to interfere with witnesses: what kind of fools will we look, to say nothing of who might get hurt? Tell the officer. Or tell the solicitor to tell the officer. How do I know what she's doing? At least tell the officer, in confidence, what I've told you. I can't: I'm not prosecuting, but you can. Will you do it?"

Clive shook himself like a dog fresh from a pond.

"Yes. I'll do that now."

"And Clive?"

"Yes?"

"Don't let on how you know. It's not necessary."

Trust Sissy, eyes in the back of her head, more suspicious than he knew how. Postpone supper, back to chambers, look out the papers, find officer's number, or that solicitor, what was her name. Relief in sudden activity, gut reaction to words from Sissy which would always double as orders, not like the softness of Mrs. Barrow, non-ambitious wife and mother. He liked Sissy better now than he ever had. Few had her scruples or her strength.

They would never have that weekend away, not now.

CHAPTER TWELVE

Mary was used to the bullying in her own household. She did not bow to it, she rolled with it like a ship without sail, wallowing in the calm of constant, slight depression. Like her sister-in-law, she clung to her favorite charges, came to ignore the rest. Unlike her sister-in-law, she did not regard the treatment of fate to be sufficiently unkind to justify wholesale abandonment of children she did not like, and Mary's burdens were the product of a duty which Maria, her one time bosom friend, had foisted on her. Said to be temporary, this housing of three extra mouths: by now it had gone on so long she had forgotten when the resentment began, probably the first week. Little Stanislaus, okay, she loved little Stanislaus, and so did his cousin, but Edward, what a pig, a threatening pig; she could have put him out of doors after an hour. He was like his father, worse if anything. Peter had been fine at first, funny thing, but you couldn't get close and there wasn't the time to try, so when Ed waded in on his behalf, adopted responsibility wholesale, she let them get on with it. Enough to do with all the rest, cooking, cleaning, the church, her own mother, and what else? Did Maria think she ever slept at all? As sympathy curdled for Maria, and for Ed, so it soured for Peter, ally of them both, tarred with their brush. She saw he was clean, rigorous in that, fed him his food, and was unnerved by the silence of his presence, irritating little boy, always so nervous, you wanted to shake him. Nothing wrong with him: he went to school didn't he, played and all that? Why should she worry for him, he was spotless. Psychiatrist, that woman from the Social said he needed. Rubbish: it would never be said a child in her house was mad, not even a child like Peter. He was quiet, was all: so let him be quiet. She had her own to care for.

Summer had been a relief. All of them out of her hair, less chance of seeing Edward at all. Why did he stay if he hated them so much, why not shove off and leave them in something like peace. Then maybe Maria would take Peter back, let her keep Stanislaus, and life would be almost normal. Mary hated the meanness of her own thoughts, justified them in confession, did her duty. Peter was easy to ignore; didn't seem to mind whether he was noticed or not, and at least said thank you whenever he spoke at all, better than his brother.

Even so, with the residue of responsibility, she who could ignore his presence could not ignore his absence. Bed used, but no appearance at breakfast, no thin thing in the corner bolting it down with the speed of a hungry dog. Probably out early on a fine day. She shrugged it away. Returning from the Saturday hazard to the shops, dragging the trolley up the single step chipped from many such encounters, wishing she had the kind of husband who deigned to help with the groceries, she found Ed's note. One of them had condescended to come home—that she should be so lucky—written her a note, kind of him, "Pete with me for weekend—Ed." More than that and he wouldn't have been able to spell it. Good of them to let her know, but wasn't Pete a bit young to stay away nights? A weekend where? She knew enough to imagine it wouldn't be luxurious wherever it was, but would it be clean? She didn't like it, didn't like it at all: she must tell his uncle and his mother as soon as possible. Phone everyone, but then what difference if no one knew where they were? Too much, all too much: unfair. They would have to go, worrying her like this, enough was enough after all.

In the middle of unpacking the shopping, four sliced loaves and a dozen eggs slipping to the floor, in came Stanislaus with his cousin, screeching and crying. Down by the canal, fell on a piece of glass, look at my knee: lovely, three-stitch drama, plenty of blood and grime. Blood she didn't mind: grime was more worrying. Mary knew all about grime; gangrene, septic cuts, lockjaw and tetanus: you got it from dirt as well as every other disease known to man. She commenced battle with the grime. Peter was forgotten.

Edward had predicted the lack of panic. Calmer in the morning, he came to look for his brother and recognized the cold aspect of the room. He had sat on Pete's bed, feeling the scarcely used sheets and the same anger he had known in Pete's other absence, a sense of unauthorized betrayal. Another cigarette, the one adult habit Ed had adopted to the manner born, while he thought what to do. Find him, of course, before he was otherwise found. Deflect the half-hearted hunt Uncle Peter might instigate for his nephew, and above all deflect the temptation for either poxy relative to call the police. Ed had embarked that morning prepared for no more than quiet words in Pete's ear since even in his own state of mild shock he had appreciated that the other strong arm tactics had failed. He had money with him, anticipated bribery on a grander scale than ever before, but not this: not this instant frustration, this obdurate refusal to deal. Little bastard, crumby little stinker, wait till I get you, Pete . . . And besides, he had wanted the calm of Pete's presence, wanted a touch of the familiar, a companion for the shops, for buying things, pretending that the night before had been a triumph to convince himself it had; wanted to act normal, a boy with his brother. Ed wanted to kiss and tell: Peter would not play, and Ed hated him for that. Like Michael Bernard with his dead wife, Ed smoking on the bed suddenly discovered his stunning ignorance of his brother's average daily life. Find him? Where the fuck should he start?

Down by the canal, high above the muddy water on the fourth floor of the derelict warehouse, Peter watched his younger brother below fall on the glass from the broken windows from which he gazed. Warm in the shaft of sunlight which he occupied in the way of a cat, he had wanted to move, shout out, but the words strangled in his throat. Not the same scale of blood—look at Stan, hopping around screeching, enjoying the attention—but blood nevertheless, and the sight of it made him sick.

They had found a way in here once, he and his friends from school in the days when they still existed, sworn one another to secrecy until they had grown out of the secret or simply weary of it. Others had found the refuge since judging by the coke cans, crisp packets, smell of unguarded humanity, but not recently. The floor's dust carried no footprints, the litter was old. The place lost appeal in summer, and the guard dog warning sign had done its worst. Stupid. There was no dog. There had been no dog when he had finally scrabbled up the stairs after midnight waiting for torch and bark to drive him back, shivering wet, cold beyond caring. Armed with the memory of how a newspaper could keep you warm, he had found some, but on balance, he did not think it worked: had cried himself to sleep no drier than before, woken colder, and only now, comforted by that kindly shaft of sun, did he believe he was alive. Alive, ravenous rather than hungry, throat constricted from crying, sore with the effect of his screaming, his mind hung out to dry, the rest of him dirty and torn, his hair thick with dust and cobwebs. Unable to view himself, he imagined his own reflection with disgust, and although vanity would not have kept him in hiding, he had inherited some of the meticulousness which was Aunt Mary's obsession and Ed's hallmark, so that conspicuous lack of it added to all the other guilt to make him even less inclined to move, do anything which carried a hint of decision. Peter ached for hope, for a wash, even for the sight of Uncle Peter, longed to be as free as little Stanislaus, longed for an end to it. At one point, when the sun hit the water of the canal, its murky depths had seemed the most comforting prospect of all: and it was that which had woken him, the very temptation of it. He knew he was alive because he knew he did not want to die.

Painful, being alive. So he had slept instead: woke when the sun had moved on, and his bladder was bursting. Through the metal windows, the canal bank was framed in its emptiness like a picture, unreal in its desolation. Early evening: one man and a dog, the rest at their meals. A long time to rest hungry before nightfall: decisions imminent, all of them hateful, his body roaring with hunger, weak with the need for food. Peter paced his way into darkness, drew pictures on the walls with a stone, carving a boy with a knife above the pre-recorded message of "Sadie sucks cock." The inscriptions on the plaster absorbed him for a whole hour before he found the fire escape, whispered down in stocking feet clutching his shoes in search of food, full of the new cunning which made him a scavenger.

When could he go back? Not that night: not to his borrowed home, and not to the garden. Never to his own room, a room he had hated until now when it was barred to him, never there again, or to his mother, before he had made his peace with the Lady. Tonight, the night after all that blood, she could not be there, only others, looking out for Ed. Perhaps the next night he would find her if he survived so long. Before Ed found him. No one else would bother to look.

Lifting dustbin lids at the backs of the dead and silent cafés in closed Chapel market, searching among the debris left by the fruit stalls, Pete made a rich haul. Two stale loaves from behind the bakery, wafers by an ice-cream machine, bruised apples: a huge cardigan from a drain, plastic sheeting abandoned and torn from a stall. Peter had watched winos collecting like this, shuffling in litter for treasures: he had always remembered details.

In comparison with the first, the second night in the warehouse was comfortable. Until the morning, full of new obligations, the same roaring hunger, accompanied now by vomitting sickness. Water from the canal was not suitable drinking for small boys.

Dear God, what had she been saying to Geoffrey when he was holding her hand; what did she say? Too much, but she didn't care; she believed in him, and it made her alive. She didn't care if he thought her a fool, he may as well find out now. She couldn't stop what he thought: she felt as if she loved him, couldn't prevent it. Useless pretending she had anything else to lose.

Expensive flowers from the office made her want to cry again; reminded her of the garden, hemmed her in. She must go home and wait for Peter. Geoffrey must understand as much of this as he could, and, like it or not, help her. She didn't want anyone else.

"Comfortable?"

"I'm Dopey, the dwarf with one eye."

"Sleep then."

It was a triumph to be fetched home by ambulance, settled in her own disfigured bed, with him attending to all the domestic refinements like an efficient butler. Replaced the bedding sent to the laboratory for all its bloodstains might reveal, the rips in the mattress covered with a blanket putting across a mismatched view of normality. The windows were clean, the carpet less so, so that she shuddered at the stains, shame of a sort, noticed it all as she hobbled in, hazy and removed, antennae twitching. More flowers, real flowers, changing her mind from apprehension to the ease of relief, making her weepy. Absent for thirty-six hours, she felt like Rumpelstiltskin returning after a hundred years, but nothing altered beyond repair, Geoffrey so sensitively kind she wondered what she would have done without him and the gratitude weakened her more.

"I can't sleep, but you should. What time is it?"

"Not late."

"Listen to me again, will you? After the trial, tomorrow, isn't it? I'll listen to you for a week. I'm sure Peter will come back tonight. You know that's why I wanted to be sure there would be no strangers in the garden, one of the reasons why I so wanted you to stay . . . I'm sorry, you must think I'm mad."

"No, I don't think that, but was he the only reason you wanted me to stay?"

"Oh, no."

Propped against pillows stiffly, bandaged ribs upright, she was leaning against him, his arm comfortably supportive. "Oh, no," she repeated, leaning her cheek against his shoulder.

Night sounds in another still night. Tires on the greasy road sounding like pain, the rumble of trucks on the North London line. The kitchen light was on, door open, and they were waiting in the bedroom, fighting away sleep. Bruised Helen beneath his shoulder. "It's best you stay on my left," she had said, "it's the only profile I have left." "You'll mend," he said. Sitting like old friends. Playing doctors and patients, he said: Ryan considers it most irregular—it offends his moral code. Rich, isn't it? No one else will like it either. So what, she said.

Weak: kittenish weak, stiff, fingers in bandages, nose askew, stitches protesting, everything protesting, half happy, anxious.

"He'll be here; I know he will."

"Why so sure?"

"Don't know. The way we are. I always know."

Geoffrey felt a tiny stab of jealousy, soon dismissed.

"There's no one," he had told her, "of Peter's description, reported missing: no one on the social services' 'at risk' registers. I tried the football teams, found two out of three coaches who use the playground; no one recognizes him yet."

"He's not a particularly memorable face. You'll see."

"Helen . . . something else . . ."

"What?"

"Edward Jaskowski: I found out something about Ed. Remember Ed?"

But she was painfully upright, motioning him silent. "Shhh. I'm sure I can hear something. Can you go the other side of the door? He might not come in if he sees you."

He could hear nothing, wondered if she was still concussed.

"What if it isn't the boy?"

"I'll scream. No, don't go. I know it's him. Wait."

He was sick, shivering, shaking sick, did not know it was possible to be so sick. Hiding in doorways all the way here. If Ed had found him, he would have asked him to do it quickly while his back was turned. Ed, why did you leave me? Come back, I miss you.

If she was not there, he would lie down in the garden and sleep for ever, but if he had not been so sure of her presence he could not have come so far, and there was still that high wall. He missed his footing at the top, slithered and fell. Waited until the silence resumed, sensed the cat, and a light in the window. Relief swept over him like a wave. He stumbled up, into the camellia bush, and fell. Over the step toward the open door, and fell. Then into the still kitchen, fell against the table, called in a faint voice, fell. Feet regained, on down the lit corridor into her room, and there was the Lady, puffy, bruised, smiling at him, and he knew he was forgiven already: would be safe even with all he had to tell her, all the facts he had been working out, assembling and reassembling, remembered during the longest day, all the things Ed had said, which pieced into some terrible sense. "It wasn't my fault," his first dizzy words. "He didn't hurt you because of me. And you're getting better, aren't you, Lady? Please tell me you're better now. Please?"

He sank into a chair by her bed, eyes fixed on her face, voice gabbling.

"Sshh, sweetheart, stay still a minute; look at the state you're in.

Quiet now. It's all right, I promise, and of course it isn't your fault, why should you think so? And I'm better all the time for seeing you."

Better now, warmer, but still shivering. Coming awake in the chair so close to her bed, he could touch her, and did. She ruffled his hair with one hand, touched his cheek. He tried to control his face, to stop the emotions which twisted it into grimaces where he meant blankness, and he did not see the other disembodied hand which brought him the woolen thing, tucked it around him, spoke from a distance in a voice without shape.

"Peter Jaskowski, I think; we've met before. Hello, young man."

The pale face crumpled with a splintering pain, a look of horror unsoothed by the gentle voice.

"Where is he, Peter? Where's Ed?"

"Don't know . . . please . . . don't know . . ."

"Where is he, Peter?"

"Geoffrey, don't . . . He's not Jaskowski, just a boy. What's the matter with you? Leave him be. The child's sick, leave him."

An edge to his voice which frightened her, a calm, toneless, insistent edge which made her imagine the voice going on for question after question, hour after hour, unhurried, unthreatening, chill in its determination. She was confused. Jaskowski? The name was like a curse, and the child's fate would wait until he had supplied what was required of him. Geoffrey was rationing compassion in the interests of information, and for a moment, she hated him for it.

"Leave him, Geoffrey, please."

"Tell us, Peter, anything Ed's told you." Bailey settled in for long questioning. Regrettable, but the weaker they were, the harder it often was, and Peter began to cry.

He knew when he first turned into the street that something was wrong, knew before he went there. He had been uneasy, but not so much he had failed to hope he would be able to con Aunt Mary into believing Pete was with his mother, and not to worry. He'd be back in a day or two. But the daft cow had already done it, told them, lost her silly head: it was obvious as soon as he went around the back directed by worry, and saw the copper in the road behind, walking up and down the way they did when pretending to be invisible. He went back and checked the front from the corner: another car outside, not one he knew, waiting. Bloody Aunt Mary had reported them missing, an optimistic view, and he refrained from entering the house, preferring not to face the questions: turned tail for Eileen's, but when he reached it, couldn't bring himself to go in there either.

Why had he told Pete? Surely he wouldn't repeat it, he had been so sure of that: Pete would be too frightened. Ed's anger was fading, giving way to anxiety, stupid little bastard. Instead he was angry with himself for never imagining Pete would follow him, if that is what he had done, and since the day before, when all efforts had failed to find him, began to wonder if he was so lucky after all. Ed only wanted to tell him he was not angry anymore, you daft little sod, and please don't run away from me: I can't stand you running away from me like that. I only want to talk to you, and I don't want you scared of me.

He forced himself into Eileen's after a delaying turn of the street. Collect gear, remove traces of presence: find another, safer place, one of the two empty houses he knew, but everywhere felt bad without Pete. Soon after dark Ed sat in a pub, killing time, surrounded by empty seats, as if he smelled, scowling at customers. I don't smell, you bastards. I'm clean at least. I'm always clean.

Told himself not to panic, walk slowly as ever, go on looking as he had been looking for almost two days. Supposing he was dead for lack of food, little sod always needed plenty of that. Ed kept walking, convincing himself it was not he who was pursued, half convinced it was only Peter, unable to remain still any more than he had been able to sleep, body as hot and restless as his thoughts.

Suddenly afflicted with the picture of that garden, the garden behind the woman's house. "Looking at girls," Pete had told him. Was that where he had been, was now? But she was old: she wasn't a girl. He should have guessed Pete was lying: he'd never thought of girls once, never mentioned them. The football playground? Could he be hiding in that? Dangerous instinct: madness to go so close. But he believed the instinct and had tried everywhere else. Peter would starve if he did not find him and would be so hungry he would spill the beans to the first stranger he found. He might die even, unless he was found.

Exhaustion was winning, her own second to Peter's. Geoffrey had been as skillful as a surgeon. Peter had talked, fast, disjointed and furious: Bailey had listened, reacted, busied himself with the telephone, and now watched with Helen as the boy dozed feverishly.

"Please don't take him away, he can hardly walk."

"But Helen, his relatives have to be told. They're not monsters. And he can't stay here."

"Why not?"

"Two of you, walking wounded? Listen, his brother may have been offered large sums of money by Mrs. Cartwright, perhaps for harming you: he tried, he's at large, he's dangerous. Peter's twelve, possibly in danger, needs medical attention. Ryan will come in to stay with you, and someone will take Peter to hospital. I wouldn't be surprised if the boy has food poisoning."

"Why did you make him talk so much then? It's cruel."

"Priorities, Helen."

"I don't understand. Perhaps I shall. Poor Peter; if Ed is the devil, we're the deep blue sea. What will you do?"

"Look for Master Edward."

"Please, Geoffrey, no."

He was waking Peter gently.

"Hush, Helen, go to sleep if you can. Peter my lad, say goodbye for now. I'll bring you back soon, I promise."

The face was so pale it was luminous, sweating in one last pleading. "Can't I stay? I'll look after everything. No? Lady, can I come back then?"

"Soon Peter, I promise."

The last picture of the boy, white calm, cooperating in his own betrayal, half mirroring herself. Helen had lost all sense of time. There was no time, simply a midnight darkness of anxiety for them both, smothered in her own helplessness.

For all the force of the instinct, it was still a vivid shock for him to see them. First, a man going into the house, the way he had entered himself with the clever key when he had gone to kill her. Another waiting outside making it unsafe to go closer. Then suddenly, that tall one, the one who had been twice to their house, coming out with Peter, the bastard. His arm round Peter, walking him toward a car, taking him prisoner. Peter, staggering a bit, pale as death in the street light: what had they done to him? The tall one, who finished it for Dad and for all of them, coming out of the house of that bitch with teeth. What had they done to Peter between them? What did they want with him now, Ed's kid brother, his own?

Bile rose to his throat, in choking fury and screaming rage. "Run, Pete! Get away Pete: these buggers . . . they'll do for you, whether you tell or not, you daft fool, run . . ."

He shouted it out, couldn't stop, screamed at them: Leave him alone, you cunts! Leave him to me . . . and Pete heard it as unmistakably as Ed had heard him scream the other time. Heard him clearly, twisted away and aimed himself for the voice like an arrow. Ed panicked then, ran down the road to get away from them. Bloody fool to have shouted like that, drawing them on him by shouting, not wanting or thinking for Pete to follow, not knowing why it was he shouted, angry beyond his own belief; knowing as he did it how senseless it was, senseless and useless. They didn't need the both of us, nor did he need this white-hot, liquid anger, so he ran. Down to the corner, looked back, and saw Pete following him, running after, screaming, "Ed, Ed, don't go, don't go, wait for me." Funny, jelly-legged run he had: the tall man yelling at him to stop, while he ran, wobbling and shouting for the brother, and for a moment Ed stopped and waved him back.

Then he heard the tires, looked closer, turned forward again, about to run on from the opposite side of the road and leave him to it, no sense otherwise, looked again, couldn't move. Pete was still running, straight for the car. Why so fast, that car on a narrowing road, drunk, maybe: it made no difference now. Straight toward it. Ed wanted not to watch, but did watch, frozen as a frightened rabbit.

He saw the tall man fly into the road after Pete, leap at him, like a kick with his hands, pushing him beyond the bonnet. Pete thwacked into a car parked on the far side, crashed into the door. The tall man was on the bonnet of the car, then rolling off it; he jumped on it as he leaped for Pete, pushed Pete beyond, then rolled off further down the road as the car stopped. All so swift, and so slow. The tall man ended by the curb, rolled in a ball, but moving, the other man, the one waiting in the police car, ran for him. Ed could see Pete, crouched by the door of the car very still, minutely small, an island in the road.

He wasn't hit, Ed knew he wasn't hit. He'd had a big bump was all, but he was so still, such a feeble little sod. Ed stopped running and didn't start again. Pete wasn't dead, they hadn't beaten him; the tall man wouldn't have done that and then almost kill himself to save him, it wouldn't make sense. Pete would have mended, but Ed went back: he ran back, could have kicked himself as he moved, drawn back without a will. Pete would have been all right, daft bastard, he would have been all right, why had they both run like that, Pete to himself, and himself away? But if that tall bloke was ready to lose his legs to save him, Ed couldn't leave him, it was that simple. The little fucker was his own brother; couldn't be left, not just like that. He went back, ready to kill Pete for it, but he went back, streaming back to the hunched shape in the road, careless who saw.

He was sitting in the middle of the road, eyes open but dizzy. "You daft bastard," Ed muttered. "Get up out of the road, or you'll really get killed this time." Peter's eyes were alive with fear and relief: and it was the fear which so arrested Ed. From behind him, he hauled Pete to his feet, half dragged him to the pavement and sat him on it. Pete flopped. Ed crouched beside him. "Daft bastard," he repeated, "Silly sod." He pushed Pete into a sitting position and the boy raised his head. There was a livid bruise on his forehead, instant color on white skin, still swelling. Squatting at his side, Ed was mesmerized by it. The boy grabbed at his arm, leaning toward him helplessly, and Ed heard from beyond his back the dim sound of shouting, footsteps running toward them both. Too late, he should have gone on running: he should not have gone back, never go back. Pete's eyes were full of tears, his eyes designed for them: the mouth working its familiar difficulty with words, his hand tight on Ed's arm. Ed let it rest, did not turn, did not move. "Too late, Pete, ain't it? I hope you know what you've fucking done: you've bloody done for me, Pete, you've screwed it all."

He knew the anger of sheer relief, ready to hit Pete for being alive. Instead he stayed as he was, cursing softly, until the foreign hand fell on his own shoulder. Gently, then, he moved Pete's restraining fingers. "Don't worry you daft git: don't look so worried Pete. What did you tell them, Pete? The lot? Didn't think you'd do that, Pete, really I didn't. Never mind. S'all right, Pete, don't cry, you know I can't stand it, don't cry . . . you all right Pete?" Then turning away, rising stiffly, not looking at the face behind his own, hands in his pockets looking down. "Leave off, Mr. Bailey. I ain't going anywhere. Get off me, will you? Just look after my fucking brother, will you? I'll wait."

"We'll look after him."

"See you bloody do."

"You are paid to look after me, Mr. Quinn, not to postpone the task."

"Madam, so I am; paid to look after you. I have asked the judge to adjourn the case, yet again, until lunchtime today only, all he would grant. My learned friend for the prosecution agreed, so that I can make my best endeavors to look after you. We were ready, madam, this morning, to do our best: I regret to say there have been some developments which complicate matters. Facts I learned very late last night. We have been laboring on your behalf, Miss Malton and I, burning the midnight oil."

Not quite a rebuke for her rude response to the news of delay, this pompous address from Quinn who was by habit more informal than most: a speech redolent of reminders that all respect should be mutual, that he was not simply the hired help, however high his fee. Some of the pomposity was an infection from far too long a conversation with Carey. You have no choice, madam, he was informing her, no choice but to listen to me.

She subsided. Alarm trickled into her strong fingers while her face remained immobile. Aware of Sissy Malton as blank as an effigy behind Quinn, the jailer beyond the door, both impassive in their dislike, she composed herself. Somewhere at the opposite end of the corridor in a cell as secure as this, was Jaskowski, smoldering with hatred, primed to tell all he knew. Eileen felt lonely. She needed the touch of reassurance, any human touch at all.

"Have you read a newspaper this morning, Mrs. Cartwright?"

"No. No opportunity."

She attempted a smile to indicate cooperation, hoping for an answering mellowing of Quinn's handsome features. There was none. Sissy offered her a cigarette which she took with thanks.

"Well, madam, had you had that opportunity, you might have found a small entry, concerning the arrest of Stanislaus Jaskowski's son."

"He has more than one son, I believe."

"Only one was arrested. The eldest. Edward."

Even the knowledge of their combined, shrewd scrutiny, did not control the tiny shudder of large limbs.

"Fancy. What a family." She attempted to laugh. Sissy turned her head away. "Does the father know?"

"Yes. Detective Superintendent Bailey told him this morning. I believe he is incensed, more willing than ever to give evidence. He says he blames it on you, madam. Mr. Bernard is also aware of the facts. He is both angry and upset, I understand. I doubt he will give evidence."

Hope stirred, visibly. Eileen's long sojourn between four walls had decayed the finer edge of self-control.

"But that, madam, makes little difference to the outcome. Now, if I may, I shall present you with the facts as I understand them, and then I'd be obliged for your comments. On Friday evening, Miss West, the solicitor for the Crown, was attacked in her own home by Edward Jaskowski. She was severely injured, presently recovering from those injuries although it will take some time. For reasons I need not explain, even if I could, the attack was witnessed by Edward's younger brother, a disturbed child, I believe, who had come to haunt Miss West's premises. On Sunday night, last night, that is, Edward was arrested."

Quinn paused, wiped from his voice the element of weariness and all suggestion of pity.

"It is doubtful the small boy will give evidence of what he saw on Friday. The prosecution are not inclined to force that issue, and it is equally doubtful if Miss West could make a positive identification of her masked assailant, but the boy has told the police what he knows. Edward Jaskowski says nothing. They could have difficulty proving a case, although there is other evidence. Of course."

"What other evidence? And what has any of this to do with me?"

"The other evidence? Oh, a mere matter of teeth marks. A bite madam, administered by Miss West, I believe, in the course of the attack on her, imprints thereof on Master Jaskowski's left forearm. Mr. Bailey tells me they are hopeful of forensic evidence, but fair as he is, does not rely on it. Bloodstains, I believe he mentioned. Possibility of shards of glass from a broken clock found in the soles of shoes. Persuasive, I think. Obviously, something of a struggle."

Involuntarily, Eileen smiled. Sissy could not repress a shake of the head watching it, a smile like the twist of the mad, reminiscent of a cruel caricature which hung in her chambers. Watching the dark face, she remembered Eileen's other interview: how when told of the struggles of poor, silly, dead Sylvia Bernard, she had smiled. Such a humorous lady.

"Fascinating, Mr. Quinn. Never liked Miss West on our brief meetings, but I didn't even know her. Or Edward Jaskowski. I repeat, what has it to do with me?"

"This, madam," Quinn's hand held the letter, crumpled lined paper, examined by a number of eyes, handled in his elegant fingers with studied distaste. Prison paper, her contents.

"According to this, and according to Edward's words to his brother, in consideration of his injuring an unnamed woman, you arranged to pay the junior Jaskowski the sum of five thousand pounds."

"For the benefit of the family: as stated in the letter. Who gave you the letter? You have no business . . ."

"Madam, I do, with respect, as long as it is my business to defend you. It is regrettable Mr. Lawrence did not see fit . . . but that is a matter for yourselves. Why, madam, why?"

"For the reasons I state in that letter."

"Again with respect to you, Mrs. Cartwright, and with respect to my experience, if you will, and bearing in mind the perceptions of the jury, however limited you may consider these, I shall have difficulty convincing them of that."

The voice was peculiarly flat. Eileen fished in her handbag for the absent cigarette. Sissy wondered if her hands trembled in fury or fear before her sudden explosion of words.

"Edward will say nothing, nothing. He's a good boy, Edward . . ."

Silence fell like a boulder into a deep pool. Punctuated by Sissy's sharp intake of breath. Automatically, she produced her packet of cigarettes which Eileen snatched from her hand.

"So you do know him, Mrs. Cartwright? Know well, I take it?"

Recovery was as swift as collapse. "I know of him, of course . . . His father mentioned him."

"I see."

Silence again. Eileen's an obdurate silence, watching nothing but the smoke curling upward in the stuffy room. Quinn hated cigarette smoke, forbade it in his own home. It was an accepted hazard of his profession to be obliged to tolerate it often at close quarters, but breathing it did nothing for his legendary patience. He sensed Sissy, inches away, the pleasanter smell of her, practical mind already moving on, another case lost, small relief in Lawrence's disgrace and the end of his whining on the phone. Never mind, there was always another brief. The resignation of her hung in the air with the smoke, infecting all three with the scent of defeat, even as Eileen rallied from the dead.

"I don't know Edward Jaskowski. I told you. Why should it affect my case? You've already said the boy says nothing. How can it be relevant?"

"Because the prosecution may make it so, madam, if they can. The letter," he waved it gently, "is privileged, cannot be produced. Should they wish to introduce this new element, and there will be evidential difficulties, I shall resist it, of course; but it is enough, is it not, merely to hint at the existence of another Jaskowski. Stanislaus may do the same. Another Jaskowski, off on a frolic of his own, but nothing to do with you, again? There are means of introducing it. Were I Mr. Carey for the Crown, I should find them." A sharper hint that, were the roles reversed, he would have found them by now. Quinn was beginning to prefer instructions from the Crown.

"One last matter before we leave you to consider. The boy Edward says nothing, promises to say nothing, but Mr. Bailey, a man of scruple, is frank with me, as Mr. Carey has been. Peter, Edward's brother, is injured, an accident. There is a bond there; the child is in care. Should pressure be brought to bear on Edward through that quarter, then this silence of his might not remain . . . as profound. Mr. Bailey is, I repeat, a man of scruple, but I have no doubt that he is not beyond blackmail, no doubt at all. Witnesses are there to be used, madam . . . you understand that."

He rose, height impressive, gown cumbersome, wig in hand.

"May we leave you to digest this? You will know the permutations of it, far better than we, I think. Is there anything else you require? You'll call the jailer when you wish to see us? I beg you, madam, consider carefully. Should you be acquitted here," doubt of the outcome was implicit in his tones, "you are likely to face further charges. You will not be let go."

In a moment of pity, Sissy left her cigarettes on the table. Time she stopped the habit. One day she might look like that, or come to smoke them with such desolation.

* * *

In the hollow distance Stanislaus heard the door slam, retreating footsteps, murmured voices.

"Don't like to be so close to her, Mr. Ryan, you know?"

"She can't get out. Don't fret, Stan. Mr. Bailey has it all in hand. He may look like a punch-bag, but he's got it all under control. Don't cry now, Stan, there's a good lad."

"Why not? My babies . . . I should be crying, you know."

"Look Stan, one of your babies has gone off the rails, but he ain't all bad. He waited for Peter, like I said, didn't he? Mr. Bailey's looking after Peter. He'll do what he can."

Ryan was secretly jubilant, openly reassuring, slightly impatient. Consoling Stanislaus was not likely to be his forte. In a minute, he could stop, leave him to the warder who was kindly; funny how people liked big Stan. Then he could leap upstairs and see what happened in the big wide world.

"She's a wicked woman, Stan: it's all her fault."

"Yes. Very wicked, you know?"

Hope lit his face, hope of exoneration and forgiveness, fading hope, tempered by sudden honesty.

"And my fault too," he mumbled.

"God'll forgive you, Stan. You just give evidence. If you're needed. God'll forgive you." In the earnestness of the moment, and hoping in that brief passage of faith for the same, Ryan believed it.

Eileen had never had recourse to God. Father had murdered God along with Santa Claus and all other minor deities who interfered with his chain of command, leaving her infant mind to create its own plaster saints: clean-shaven heroes of handsome features softened by kindness, gentle ladies. These were the repertoire for her daily prayers. In childhood, these models had been youthfully middle-aged: in her own middle age, she fondly imagined them dead, each shot, with a round red hole between their perfect eyes, laid in rows alongside Papa. Latterly she preferred the images of youth.

Six months of imprisonment had turned the spotlight on Edward, shaky savior. Six months in a shared cell of midnight shufflings, the tauntings of others' nightmares, despite her unspoken authority over them all, had given Edward's image the solidity of a rock, the status of hero, just as years of wanting had given Bernard the status of saint, as well as man to be punished. Of course she had hoped:

hope sprang eternal even in a breast as unloved as her own. She had thought too, that the death of Helen West, the finality requested whatever words she had used, would lend her triumph enough to sustain the worst. Such a good death: a wiping out, ritual sacrifice of symbolic enemy. Eileen had believed in her own salvation as a gambler might believe in luck. Edward might fix the straight flush, Quinn might provide it, Helen might throw away the whole pack of cards with her disappearance. Luck was so infinitely capable of change. Mrs. Cartwright, mature widow, had not inured herself to defeat.

Until Edward's possible treachery unhinged her completely through Edward's hidden weapon, a brother. The substitute son would sacrifice loyalty to her cause for the sake of a brother: for that brother his silence would be, how had Quinn phrased it? "Less profound." She repeated the words out loud, her voice shocking in the silence of the cell.

Puny, lying Edward would be held to ransom for a name he had never mentioned, was only the same as the rest of alien mankind, not marooned on the same island as she had believed. He loved another, this soulmate of hers treasured in memory better than a lover, and Eileen would rather risk life in prison than risk the witnessing of his defection. Anything in the world but that.

Let them sweat: in one last spurt of impotent hatred, let them sweat, all of them. No early recall of legal advisors to relieve the specter of disaster in their eyes. Let them sweat, for as long as she was allowed. They had given up: she had seen it in their faces. They could not wait to be relieved of their duties, Quinn and his woman. Wait for an hour or two until she could wipe the same defeat from her face and her mind. There were all those years afterward to plan revenge. Eileen stood in her cell, nine by seven with bunk, tossed her head, extended her arms, and pirouetted twice. She had seen no mirrors in months: mirrors considered too dangerous for women's prisons. Without mirrors she could admire her own reflection, imagine a strong, girlish profile sparkling with invitation. One day, she would be invited to waltz by a handsome stranger whose lips would tremble with words of passion she had never heard, held in her arms, mesmerized by her dark eyes. Not yet. Not yet. She turned and turned again until she was dizzy, crashed against the wooden bunk and sat still, defying the dizziness to defeat her, bolt upright, staring ahead and counting time. After an hour and a half, she rang the bell.

Bailey had lied, a little, a hint of a lie, closely guarded against retrospective scrutiny. If Quinn believed, or Carey in his current state of suppressed triumph chose to believe, that Edward could have been persuaded to give evidence of Eileen's seduction only to save his brother the same ordeal, then it had been a belief he had merely encouraged, not one he shared. Bailey had no intention of placing such a burden on Peter's shoulders, nor would he have hinted any such possibility to Ed, who was by now in the hands of other skillful interrogators who would handle him with care and achieve nothing. Peter, having babbled once to a small audience was unlikely to repeat those words even if it were justifiable to ask for a repetition of such traumatic confession. The interests of justice would have to wait. Still, it had been an excusable lie, almost an abuse of Peter's confidence, but if Eileen Cartwright could see the light of day, a message from her own gods ordering her to give up the emotional whip of three weeks' trial by simply pleading guilty as charged, then so be it. He moved stiffly. Bruised chin and forehead, raw scraped hands, awkward walk with bandaged knees, all of him painful but clean. Edward would have approved. Sitting and standing were problems equaled by chronic lack of sleep. Geoffrey could almost have wished there had been more fat about him to absorb the impact of his rolling fall and fuel his day, but in comparison with the consequences he had managed to avoid, this was easy.

He hoped Helen would forgive the lie, the manipulation of the truth, this almost-whispered blackmail of Eileen Cartwright. On balance, he knew she would, might even praise such acceptable ingenuity. He waited for the end of tension, the end of tiredness: better places in life than the canteen of the Central Criminal Court, resting tender elbow on a plastic table. Scribbling on the notepaper before him, he made a list of the day's tasks should he be released, the day's tasks against the day's preferences. On the next page, he drafted a letter of resignation, crossed it through. No point: he should simply ask to transfer his expertise into some other direction. He wanted none of these dangers, none of these professional pitfalls, none of these dramas, fewer of the cruelties of persuading a Peter Jaskowski to talk. He wanted freedom of conscience, freedom of evenings, long summers, the sight of children, snug winters, and a woman to make happy. And if she would not have him, he would stay on her doorstep until she did. Suddenly the verdict, trial or no trial, plea or no plea, was less important than it had ever been. Geoffrey had rocked his own foundations, heard them resettling all around him, and for once allowed himself the luxury of hoping.

Today she had declared herself well, not well enough, but well. Life was all compromise, too much in abeyance for anything as profound as happiness, but that would be true three hundred days of the year at least. On some of those future days, the concern for Peter might lift even further than it had lifted today, although the mantle of it had been both lighter and sadder since the morning. He was well, smiling. He would remain in care, a small hostel they had said; he seemed to like it, and his fussy new foster parents seemed to like him. He had been allowed to visit his Lady, and despite his reserve, he reveled in all the new attention. Even his mother had joined the ranks. The boy had pink in his cheeks, spoke of Mam as a man might speak of a sweetheart, she needed looking after, he said. Eileen in prison for ever, after the surprise guilty plea to murder which had frustrated the journalists of three weeks' worth of story. That jump of hers into obscurity had freed them all.

All of them but Edward, the last debtor. Unlikely to be away for more than eighteen months in real terms. Helen shuddered. Hope was the cure, and Peter might be stronger, fitter by then to resist him. For now, she could not read his mind, as if he had removed himself away from her translation. There was a new language to learn before she could swim back to understanding, and only then if he would let her.

Nothing was perfect then, only this October evening. Five weeks away from all those stitches, and the last of them removed. Aches and pains, a sinister yellow eye, a scarred eyebrow, little enough to show above her clothes. Return to work, she supposed; oh no, not yet, not in this mild sun, this Indian summer with garden glistening, warm enough for basking. Untidy Michaelmas daisies, straggly roses, brown-tinged, healthy, dandelion-filled grass. Spring would show where she had put the bulbs. She turned the earth in the tubs with a trowel. Turn the earth in Geoffrey, she thought, and I shall find flint. Pieces of sharp flint in delicate loam, the whole of it rich for growth, unyielding if improperly treated, sensitive to handling. I should like to be this gardener for a long time.

Look at this garden, look at it now: you would not know who had hidden here, what scenes and fantasies had been enacted within its view, secret place, escape route, tranquil and unaffected now, free of the taint of violence. Not so Geoffrey Bailey: the footprints on his life, the marks of anguish, the conscience, brutal scenes from every case and all the episodes of marriage, they would never cover themselves beyond recognition. Good man, fine man: no one had ever advised him of those truths it had taken him so long to learn, that he would never be free of the crippling pity. Others were not afflicted: some never suffered the infection of grief or guilt: she and Geoffrey had drawn a short straw. Life with Geoffrey. A bed of thorn-filled roses.

Life with Geoffrey Bailey, police officer, anathema to mankind. How could she contemplate that, on an acquaintance so flimsy she had not even turned the surface? But there had scarcely been a time in the last three months when she had failed to contemplate it, a slow-burning conclusion, nebulously based, only recently touched by that passion which raised it out of the realms of a friendship. Meeting of minds, she called it; not a collision, but a touching of thinking, now less celibate, and anything but the platonic liaison of two professions allied by cause.

However uncomfortable, the bruises had helped, all those little disfigurements, his and hers, barriers against the awkwardness of nakedness which afflicted both of them, symptom of the dreadful importance of such initiation, sign of a fear of failure even though neither believed there was anything to fear. What was best, and this the agreement of them both, was the hugging which followed, the release of two almost able bodies into the real intimacy of affection. Only for the lucky, this drowsy delight of embraces and talking, nudged out of sleep so softly in the morning with the very relief of his presence.

"Why me?" he had asked. "How can you want me?"

"I could ask the same," she had replied.

"But I asked first," he said. "So you must say first . . ."

"I can't say, but I do."

"Ah, Miss West, evasion; I expected nothing more from a lawyer. Tell me, I need to know."

"If I can. Then you have to tell me; you're being unfair to insist. Do I have to do this? I do? Well then, if this were a love-letter, it would be full of spelling mistakes which would unstring it altogether, and the string, I warn you, is not so confident even without that. Why ask? It's no test of anything to put it into words. I like the little black heart of you, I'll always find it good, even if it isn't mine to know it. Is that enough? There could be more . . . Enough for me. Now you, speak to me."

"I couldn't say why, unless I flattered you until your head grew larger than the pillow."

"Go on then," feeling the hand entwining the fingers between her own, and the soft voice of him, teasing her.

"Oh, no, not here, not now, but I shall, piece by piece. For the moment, it's an act of faith I need. You'll have to bear such simple repetitions; I love you until I'm weak with the thought of it. You must simply believe me . . . Do you believe me?"

"I believe you. If I didn't, I should have to invent it to stay alive."

"Marry me then."

"Now that's foolish. You've run away with words . . ."

All spoken at dawn, before the second waking, soft, passionate trust so strong in its quiet explosion he had wanted to sing out like a happy child, wondered if the hunger would ever die, and God and the Commissioner be damned. If she would not marry or live with him, he would be celibate forever, would dwell in one of those extremes: there was no other choice, no compromise.

"I have known him less than a year," Helen addressed the flowers, "and I know him not at all. For this cliffhanger, give me wings, or leave me marooned. We'd be better like you lot, meeting once a year, plenty of time to adjust the root before each spring. But how would I stand the winters? Marry me? Come home soon, but don't ask me that. Not yet."

Detective Constable Ryan and Mr. Lawrence each tended their gardens flanked by children. Lawrence's eldest was sick among the roses. More fertilizer please, said Lawrence callously, and watched in frustration as she ran away screaming for her mother. Daintrey had been wrong. A month away from the office did not relax the mind or improve the judgment: it clouded every issue with fractious cries, nasty responsibilities and his spouse resented the daily intrusion. Oh to be Michael Bernard, a childless, wifeless nervous breakdown. At least Lawrence's enforced rest was near its end. God knows what would greet his return. Probably a thousand cases of careless driving, and fourteen files on fraud, for what? What had he done wrong?

Ryan had always loathed the garden until he had been deprived of such space, but now he found it restful performing the residual chores of the absent husband and father. She looked so pretty today, his wife, fresh lipstick and a rare unfrozen smile; another man perhaps? Not a thought he enjoyed. The kids had been so pleased to see him, gathering grass with eager hands, rolling around like puppies: Is this right, Daddy? Look at me, Daddy, and look he did. The Essex box, big lawn, nothing special, but when would he ever own the like again?

"Stay for a drink?" the wife had asked cheerfully. He thought of Annie, waiting, impatient these days, couldn't blame her. "Thanks," he said, "I will. Mustn't stay long though. Must get . . ." And there the words tangled. The heart stayed there, in Annie's room, or at least he thought it did: but this, not that, was home.

Peter had found another garden, not an alternative, just another.

"When you grow up, boy, what'll you be?"

"Don't know."

"Come on! No idea at all? You must have some."

This was his new friend, the old man in the park by the hostel: full of stories, grumbles, loved to talk but better at listening, and Peter enjoyed an audience these days.

"Don't know. Anyway, it doesn't matter. I'm running away tomorrow." That would make him listen harder, that would shock him, but the old man was unperturbed.

"Oh yes? Up to you, of course, but I shouldn't if I were you. Come on then, answer the question can't you. What'll you be?"

Peter thought briefly.

"Me and my brother Ed, we're going to have a big garden. Both of us."

"Growing plants, you mean? A nursery? Plenty of work there, plenty work there."

"My brother's very strong, you know." Defensively said.

"I'm sure he is. Plenty to learn though boy, before you can grow things. You'll have to start soon. Tomorrow even. Are you sure about running away?"

Peter adjusted himself on the bench. Six o'clock, almost supper, and still warm, with a hint of winter darkness. A long summer it had been. He would see the Lady soon, but it wasn't the same.

"Perhaps not," he said. "I should ask him first. I'll make up my mind in the morning."